A MIDWINTER MATCH

JANE LOVERING

Boldwood

First published in Great Britain in 2021 by Boldwood Books Ltd.

Copyright © Jane Lovering, 2021

Cover Design by Debbie Clement Design

Cover Photography: Shutterstock

A CIP catalogue record for this book is available from the British Library.

Paperback ISBN 978-1-80048-246-3

Large Print ISBN 978-1-80048-245-6

Hardback ISBN 978-1-80280-208-5

Ebook ISBN 978-1-80048-248-7

Kindle ISBN 978-1-80048-247-0

Audio CD ISBN 978-1-80048-240-1

MP3 CD ISBN 978-1-80048-241-8

Digital audio download ISBN 978-1-80048-243-2

Boldwood Books Ltd
23 Bowerdean Street
London SW6 3TN
www.boldwoodbooks.com

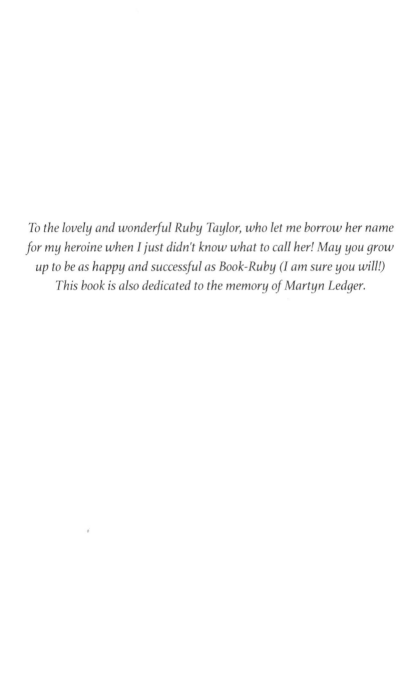

To the lovely and wonderful Ruby Taylor, who let me borrow her name for my heroine when I just didn't know what to call her! May you grow up to be as happy and successful as Book-Ruby (I am sure you will!) This book is also dedicated to the memory of Martyn Ledger.

From the YouIn2Work website:

Our aim is to get you back into the workforce!

With our help you will be able to prepare an up-to-date CV, highlighting your capabilities and expertise, apply for jobs suited to your qualifications, and widen your scope of suitable workplace experiences.

Our Confidence Coach, Ruby Oldbridge, will work with you to make you the best version of yourself that you can be, and will help you boost your self-esteem to enable you to showcase your skills in a marketable way!

Ruby is a qualified therapist, who also offers talking therapies for those who feel that their mental health is holding them back from gaining the workforce experience that they would wish to have.

'Ruby made me feel that I could do anything!' – Mike Williams, out of the workforce for three years, now Deputy Manager at Lo-Cost Stores, Haxby.

'Every time I spoke to Ruby I came out of that room feeling a million dollars. She's just so upbeat that she makes you believe in yourself again.' – Adela Kamal, returning to work after seven years raising a family. Now a Customer Services Manager at Mega-Rail Trains.

1

I was up a ladder painting the front room when Gareth came in.

'Hey, Rubes!' He put down his bag. 'Sorry, but I've been called in. I've got to fly to Belgium this afternoon, sort out a problem with some rotary flanges.'

I had no idea what a rotary flange was, but I didn't think I liked the sound of it. 'But you've only been back a week!' I climbed down the ladder, hands slippery with 'September Morning'. 'What do you think of the colour? Bit blue?'

'It's great.' He kissed my cheek. 'And, yeah, sorry, but it's work.'

'How long will you be away this time?' Gareth fitted big expensive machines all over the world. It meant that he flitted in and out of my life like a crane fly, all long legs and more noise than you could imagine one creature making. Now we'd bought a house I'd fondly imagined he'd want to settle down a bit, but there was no sign of that happening yet.

'No idea, Ruby, love. Now, do you want to give me a proper send-off, or what?'

'But I'm covered in paint!'

'No worries.' He smirked at me. 'We could make a blue movie. Geddit? Blue? Movie?'

Well then, it wasn't his intense wit that had attracted me to Gareth Williams. And to be honest, when he made jokes like that, I found it a bit hard to remember just what it had been.

'Meet you upstairs in five.' He sprang out of the room and I heard the clump as his feet went up the, as yet uncarpeted, stairs. The door to our bedroom slammed open and there was the sound of the bedsprings twanging as he threw himself down on the mattress.

I carefully covered the paint tins, smiling to myself. Gareth was just so – so *enthusiastic*. A bit unreconstructed, sure, but I was working on his rough edges with the sandpaper of my own upbringing. I had no idea how a man born thirty years ago could have all the attributes of someone who'd grown up in the sixties, but he did.

Good job he was so bloody gorgeous.

I noticed his bag, where he'd dumped it in the doorway. He would have made his usual attempt at packing, but I bet he'd forgotten all the clean shirts that were hanging behind the kitchen door and the underwear he'd pulled out of the tumble dryer and left in a pile on the floor in the utility room. I didn't want desperate phone calls at two in the morning again because he couldn't find his Ted Baker shirt or his favourite Tweety Pie boxers, so I unzipped the bag to check he'd put them in.

He'd packed more pairs of jeans than one man with only two legs could ever need. I sifted through, looking for the shirts which, of course, weren't there, and was just about to shout up to him that he needed to repack, when my fingers felt something hard.

A box.

A jeweller's box.

I smiled to myself as I pulled it out. Gareth had never given me a 'goodbye' present before. To be honest, he'd never been big on presents, but his whole family weren't really into gifts of any kind. Christmas in his household had been more about the TV and the food. It was another thing I'd been working on, and with some success by the look of this little leather box.

The thumping of my heart was mirrored by the thumping upstairs, as Gareth strode to the top of the stairs. 'Hurry up, Rubes! It's getting cold!'

Was it a ring? Was he going to propose? How did I feel about that? My mind was going at a million miles a second. Marry? Gareth? For a fraction of a second I had the image: church, white dress, my mum looking cynical, my sister looking relieved – then on to a living room crowded with children, Gareth sitting in the middle in front of the TV while the children played...

Was that what I really wanted?

I pulled the little catch to open the box, wondering how much this had cost. Even the *box* looked expensive, and Gareth usually baulked at buying takeaways. 'Your cooking is much better than any takeaway, Ruby love.' It would have carried more weight if he'd actually helped wash up afterwards.

Inside the box, nestled on a pillow of sumptuous red velvet, was a pair of gold earrings and in the lid of the box was a note in Gareth's slightly childish handwriting.

Remember that pair you wore that night in Brighton? I'll never forget taking them out with my teeth and getting one stuck in that lacy bra of yours! Promised I'd buy you a new pair, didn't I? Can't wait to do that again...

My hands were sweating and my hasty lunch of tuna on toast was threatening the back of my throat. I sat down hard on the bottom rung of the ladder, the box between my fingers and the smell of paint scalding the inside of my nose. Upstairs, the bedsprings twanged again, a tiny orchestra tuning up for sex.

There were three things wrong with this little gift.

One – I wasn't sure any of my bras could have been described as 'lacy'. I favoured the more sturdily constructed variety. Nobody needed their nipples rasped whilst dashing to answer the phone, as I repeatedly told Gareth, who repeatedly treated me to Ann Summers' finest.

Two – I didn't have pierced ears.

And three – I'd never even been to bloody Brighton.

* * *

Eight Months Later

I parked my car in the YouIn2Work car park, which seemed busier than usual. The offices were neatly located behind York Minster, which sat in the winter sunlight, half yellow where the sun struck the stone but with the shaded half dark and sharp with shadows. I wondered if they were holding an event and had, once again, failed to point out that our car park was out of bounds. Religion seemed no protection against dreadful parking, and every space in here was *rammed*.

As I locked my car, I looked around. My usual space was occupied by a Discovery, most of the other cars were high-end brands too; maybe God had seen fit to bestow nice car ownership on His followers. I looked at my ten-year-old Skoda and wondered if it was too late to have a sudden Damascene moment, then looked at where my mirror had scraped along the wall in the tiny space I'd had to squeeze it into. Atheism was still paying off.

Halfway across the car park, I met Priya, who'd obviously

been waiting for me and had bustled her way out to intercept me before I got through the door.

'Ruby! There's a meeting!'

I shifted my car keys from hand to hand, almost as though I expected her to attack me. It was most unlike Priya to come out from behind her desk, which held her computer, her phone and most of the major food groups.

'Okay. In the Minster?' This would be the point where I would be called upon to make tactful phone calls and to use my skills at people management to cheerfully chivvy the enthusiastic (and blessed) worshippers to park elsewhere. I looked back over my shoulder to where my car was quietly rusting. If it had had any sense of occasion, it would have chosen this moment for the bumper to detach and crumble onto the tarmac.

'No! It's *us*!' She was shuffling from foot to foot. 'They're *merging* us!' She set out towards the building. 'They've decided to cut costs by putting us in with the Back To Employment lot.'

I shuddered as though my grave had been stomped on. The Back To Employment group was our rival, our bogeyman. It was what we threatened underachieving employees with. They did the same sort of thing as us – getting the long-term unemployed back into work – but they did it with less finesse and encouragement and more punitive measures. They also looked like the sort of people who went on team-building exercises and called one another 'guys'.

I stopped walking. The full car park suddenly made sense and I felt the clamps around my ribcage start to tighten. 'But I thought... I mean, our success speaks for itself!'

'Yeah, well, apparently theirs also talks and it says "merger".' Priya looked at me. 'Are you okay? You've got that face on.'

I took a deep breath and forced my lungs to expand. 'Fine. No, really, I'm fine.'

Priya lowered her voice. 'Have you taken your tablets today?'

'You make me sound like I'm liable to lay about me with an axe if I'm not sedated.' I took another deep breath. 'Yes, thank you, Pri. I've taken my tablets today.' Ah, those tablets. Another legacy of Gareth's abrupt departure, my anti-anxiety medication.

She didn't respond, just opened the door and we walked through into the corridor, which always smelled of illicit cigarettes and frantic repainting. I automatically turned left, towards our offices, but she shook her head at me. 'Meeting room,' she said sadly.

'Oh God. It *must* be serious.'

'And *that's* why I asked about the tablets.'

The meeting rooms were usually only used for get-togethers: Christmas parties, the occasional visiting dignitary or government minister. It was the kind of room that had photographs of local scenes on the wall, as though we may have forgotten where we worked, because why anyone who actually lives in York needs to see The Shambles By Night in moody black-and-white shots when they could just go out and see The Shambles by night in real life and colour escaped me.

The meeting room was a swirl of people, all milling about on the static-filled carpet like restless wild ponies before the roping started. The YouIn2Work crowd were grouped around the far end, huddled together and whispering. The strangers were also sticking together, close to the door. Presumably so they could make a run for it if we turned out to eat human flesh.

They looked cocky. Self-contained and confident. The men all wore well-cut suits and shiny shoes and the women, of whom there were fewer, looked sleek and professional. I immediately felt crumpled. Beside me, Priya adjusted her collar and yanked at her skirt, clearly as uncomfortable as I was.

I shuffled my way through the newcomers, who moved reluctantly, and over to my workmates who were trying to hide their tattily-trainered feet under tables and were making furtive attempts to tidy their hair.

Priya stuck close behind until we reached the safety of our colleagues and turned. 'It's like a school disco,' she whispered to me. 'If anyone plays MisterMister, I'm off.'

A man stepped apart from the Back to Employment crew and advanced towards us, his immaculately clean trainers raising little sparks from the cheap green nylon flooring, like a special effect. He was tall and long-limbed and, in contrast to his work-mates, was wearing jeans and a jacket over a T-shirt and his hair was tousled. He could only have said 'friendly and approachable' more clearly by having it tattooed on his forehead. I distrusted him immediately. 'You're Ruby Oldbridge?' He held out a hand. 'Zac Drewe.'

Cautiously, as though he may explode on contact, I shook his hand, took a deep breath and assumed my usual, relaxed, friendly work-persona. 'Hello!' I said brightly, without the least idea what was going on. At least he didn't attempt the double-handed handshake, because I would have had to kill him.

'This is all a bit difficult, isn't it?' he asked, almost as brightly as me, but clearly with a *lot* more insight into the circumstances.

'Oh, I don't know,' I said, absolutely truthfully. Priya, who'd been stuck to me like a guide dog, had peeled off and was hiding behind the IT boys. Damn, I'd been relying on her to find a sudden excuse to call me away. 'The worst thing is that someone has parked their Discovery in my parking space!'

'Ah.'

I took the brightness down a notch. 'Oh. It's yours, isn't it.' I didn't even need to make it a question.

'Well, I guess they are going to have to work something out, re the parking, for the time being!' Zac Drewe – a name that sounded perfect for making things out of sticky-backed plastic and PVA glue on children's TV – gave me a slightly cooler look. 'If we're all going to be working together? Until they sort out who's going to have to go?'

The thought that a merger may mean losing my job hadn't even occurred to me. I was the only person in the building who did what I did, who *could* do what I did. I counselled, cajoled and encouraged our clients. I'd personally boosted our success rate from the low twenty per cents up to a near sixty-five per cent job return. And the clients loved me. Most of them *still* sent me Christmas cards and sometimes presents.

Zac Drewe hovered until the management team came in and we all sprang to attention as they started talking. I had to admit that the Back To Employment crew had got the whole 'listening hard, agreeing whilst thinking deeply about what's being said' really down to a fine art. There was a lot of tilting of heads, frowning, slight nodding going on. In contrast, my workmates were all staring at the sickly carpet, shuffling and nudging one another. We looked a bit shambolic in contrast. But then, we'd never done raft building.

The upshot of the address was that we were merging to 'save costs'. Governmental directive. As both teams were partly paid from governmental funding, it made a kind of grudging sense to reduce the overlap. But I was still confident that my job would be safe, despite my sweaty hands and the sick feeling that was creeping up my neck. Our unique selling point was that we counselled; our USP was me and I was good at what I did. So I had slumped into a kind of hubris-laden 'can we all stop talking and just go back to work' fugue, when I noticed that people were walking away.

Our leadership team plus a couple of others who had the well-suited secure smiles of those whose jobs were not in any danger and were, therefore, probably high-ups in Back To Employment, were looming up to me. I'd been looking out of the window at the sun sliding down the buttresses of the Minster, throwing knives of shadow across the stonework when the introductions were done, and not paid attention.

I noticed that Zac Drewe was in tow.

'Ruby!' Our senior leader, Michael, cornered me whilst I was trying to attach myself to Priya and Josh from the front office. 'Have you met Zac?' There was an atmosphere of 'evacuate the building and defuse the bomb' about Michael that I wasn't sure I liked. He was also wearing a smart suit and his grey hair wasn't hanging in one eye. Michael usually looked like a Sociology lecturer on his day off. Today, he looked like he ran the place.

'Yes,' I said.

'I'm parked in her space,' Zac said and Michael nodded.

The other two, a woman with a backcombed beehive hairstyle that looked uncomfortable, and an older man in glasses, smiled beneficently.

'I'm afraid I am going to have to ask you to give up your space, just for the time being, Ruby.' Michael wouldn't meet my eye. This was bad. I wasn't sure what exactly was going on, but it was definitely bad. 'While we all sort ourselves out, what with the others being over from Leeds and not knowing where else to park. But I wanted you to get to know Zac properly.'

Now he looked me right in the eye.

Michael had always left me largely to my own devices. He was happy with our results, he was more than happy with the ecstatic feedback we got from clients and he was positively overjoyed with our increased funding every year. But now he looked like a five-year-old who had been told that someone is Not Happy With Him and can't work out why.

'Any particular reason?' I eyeballed Zac, who was still smiling, and sort of lounging alongside backcomb-woman and glasses man, as though they were his parents.

'Oh, did I not explain?' Another slight nervous look. 'Ah. Well. Yes. Ruby, you and Zac do very similar work for our two institutions. *Very* similar. And, I'm afraid, the new company, which I think we're calling YouBack2Work, aren't we?' Another, nervous smile at the other two. 'It's a wee bit clumsy, but we'll work it out. Yes. Well. The new company only needs one counsellor. We are moving to a rather more *proactive* model, y'see.' He finished, as though he didn't know what a proactive model was and was rather hoping it would turn out to be something that featured very thin people in designer clothing.

Zac was still smiling as though he knew all this already. To be honest, he probably did. There had been meetings and feedback forms and stuff going on with us too, but it had all been eight months ago, when I'd been too busy dealing with the aftermath of being dumped by Gareth; having to sort out the sale of the house, and moving in to a shared house with three other people. It had been like becoming a student again, with the added complication of a mortgage.

Michael was still talking. Something about Zac and I carrying on working, being given a couple of months and then being assessed on results with the 'best fit for the new model' keeping the job and the other being given 'an attractive redundancy package'. I bet that Michael didn't know what either of those things were. At least, he'd know what a redundancy package looked like, but not from the sharp end. I'd been left paying off the house debts, so anything less than Henry Cavill levels of attractive just wasn't going to cut it.

In essence, we were being expected to compete for the job. The very thought made my ribcage ache and worries I couldn't process begin the familiar cascade. And I'd have to compete against this man, who'd already got a Discovery, to my aged Skoda. Plus the bosses from the other company were smiling in a complacent way as though they had already redecorated my office and moved him in with a kiss on the cheek and an increased salary. I'd be out on the street with the surplus confectionary whilst he'd have a cupboard full of colour-coordinated Post-it notes and neat ranks of A4 pads.

To make matters worse, whilst we competed we had to share the office, displacing Priya, who I relied on to be my sounding board, into the tiny office, no bigger than a cupboard, next door.

When Zac and I walked down the corridor in the kind of silence that you could have cracked with a spoon, I found Pri already manhandling her belongings out of the door.

'Don't leave me with him!' I hissed at her, as he swept inside.

'There isn't room for three of us!' she hissed back. Accurately, as it happens.

When Zac and I got into the office together, I feared for the amount of breathable air. Which was odd, because Priya and I had shared for three years without either of us suffocating, but then she was five foot four and Zac topped her by a foot. Quite a bit of which was hair. He had one of those spiked-up haircuts that added to the TV presenter look.

We shuffled around one another for a few moments.

'Is that one your desk?' He eventually pointed at the desk by the window. 'Shall I have this one, then?'

He sat down at the desk which had, until very recently, been Priya's. After a moment he stood up again, removed a magazine and bar of chocolate from the chair, put them on the desk, then sat down again.

Priya duly reappeared, picked up the magazine and chocolate, and left, walking past me with her eyes very, very wide, which was when I noticed that the magazine was a copy of *Your Cat*.

Zac and I sat opposite one another for a few more uncomfortable minutes. When my telephone rang, I seized upon it as though it were a call from God. Although He was, presumably, over the road in the Minster and could just have shouted.

I answered, to hear Michael on the other end, who began telling me that, following consultation, 'they' had decided that it would be a good idea for us to run some getting-to-know-you bonding exercises for both sets of employees. The inverted commas were so implicit in his tone that they flashed in a synasthaesic way every time he uttered another buzz phrase. Buzz phrases weren't like Michael. He usually sat in his office drinking coffee and only interacted with us via his PA, who, come to think of it, hadn't been at the team meeting, which was worrying. Michael didn't usually phone us directly either, which probably accounted for his tone of worry. He sounded as though he wasn't 100% certain how phones worked and wasn't convinced that he was talking to the right person.

'So, I can leave you both to it, then?' he finished, jovially.

'Sorry, Michael, what are you leaving us to?' I wanted to add 'and who is *us*?' but it would be Zac and I. Of course it would. There was an awful inevitability to all this.

'Setting up the exercises? If you run one and young Zac there runs another – well, it will be a chance for the Board to see your different approaches!'

I had no idea why he was trying to make us competing for the job sound like it was going to be fun. Oh, wait, yes I did. It was because his job wasn't in any danger and, besides, he could take early retirement any day on an enormous pension and supported by his much younger wife who earned squillions doing something legal. Legal, as in, she worked in law and wore stylish black suits and knew her way around canapé fillings and the judicial system.

I had a sudden, throbbing image of the amount I still owed the bank, and shuddered. My breath threatened to stop in my throat, but I carefully kept the panic down. *Breathe.*

'Oh yes, that *will* be fun,' I trilled, aware that Zac was watching me over the top of his computer screen. 'I *love* those team-building things.' I had to dig quite deep to find the reserves of sparkle and cheer, but I did it. 'Leave it to me, I'll tell him all about it.'

Using Zac's name would attract his attention, like saying 'Beetlejuice'. And I wanted to steal a march in the organising stakes.

'Oh, Zac's been told,' Michael chirped back. He sounded nearly as bright as me. I wondered if he was putting it on too, and allowed myself a second of imagining Michael in his office with the backcombed lady holding a gun between his shoulder blades as he spoke to me. 'It was his idea, you see. Very good idea, you must admit, excellent way to get us all bonding and working together as a team. Going forward,' he added, as though the gun had been jabbed in his spine to force him to add the obligatory corporate speak.

I raised my eyes from where they'd been scanning the surface of my desk, giving my subconscious a good battering about the mess of receipts, Post-it reminders, sweet wrappers and general office detritus, to see Zac still looking at me. I could only see his hair and his eyes above the screen, but there was a definite tone of smiling complacency about both features. I smiled back. I'd perfected the art of smiling with my whole face and looking as though I really meant it, even when I wanted to crack the object of the smile around the back of the head with a plank.

'It all sounds brilliant.' I injected yet more lightness into my tone. 'I'm really looking forward to thinking up something fun.

Pushing the envelope,' I added, and then hated myself but it seemed that corporate speak was infectious.

'That's the spirit!' Michael hung up, leaving me still grinning like The Joker and trying to beat down the urge to set fire to the curtains.

'Team-building thing?' Zac asked as I put down the phone. 'We talked it through before we came over from Leeds. I wonder why they decided to keep you in the dark?' His brown eyes continued to peer at me over the top of the screen, focused and sharp. He sounded interested and friendly and the tiny part of me that had hidden behind my heart was hating that he was the competition. The rest of me, cynically, wondered *why* he sounded interested and friendly and how much of an effort it was for him to assume that tone. 'Bit unfair.'

I smiled with as much mystery as I could summon. We may actually have been told about it all, but anything that had happened during the last stressful months had got lost in a kind of chute that had poured everything downwards. Feelings of loss, fear of the future, and a financial spiral that had sent me back to my childhood bedroom for a while. My mum had fed me soup and soft-boiled eggs and lectured me lightly, using therapy speak, on equality in relationships, and my dad had threatened to borrow my uncle's shotgun and hunt Gareth down.

So much had passed me by. Including, it would seem, arrangements for my job.

'Oh, it's fine,' I said breezily to Zac. 'I do that sort of thing all the time with my clients, so it's just a matter of extending it across the team.'

A whopper of a fib, of course. My clients didn't need to 'bond'. They mostly needed to get over their fear of the unknown, and whilst building rafts on a muddy pond in November would definitely be an unknown experience, it really wouldn't have helped them much in their attempts to learn to fill in forms and go to interviews.

Zac leaned forward and tilted down his screen, presumably so he could see me more clearly. 'That sounds interesting,' he said, leaning his elbows on the desk and resting his chin on his hands. 'What sort of thing do you do with them?'

'I'm afraid I don't want to answer that question,' I said. 'Confidentiality, you see.' I wondered whether Dad's offer of the shotgun still stood and was transferrable.

'Really?' Zac frowned. 'I wouldn't have thought—' but then his phone rang and I could drop my face down below the level of my screen and let the bright, chirpy smile slide away from my lips and eyes.

Shit. Now I had to think of a team-building exercise. Something original – Zac looked as though he'd learned his team management skills from a textbook. He'd probably resort to the obstacle course or blindfold end of the spectrum. The sort of thing that everyone would complain about because it meant getting cold or wet or being outside, or, in the case of 'leading your blindfolded teammate', having to touch another person.

I peered covertly at my new competitor as he spoke on the phone. He could, at least, have had the decency to be snide, or to have made carefully angled comments about my office; he could, in short, have made more effort to be the enemy. Instead, he was coming over as open, reasonable and decent, which just wasn't fair.

I *needed* to dislike him. I couldn't compete against a man who was happy and friendly and smart, it would be like fighting for my job against a Border Collie. Why couldn't he be sweaty and lecherous and eat pork pies whilst reading emails laboriously with his finger trailing across the screen in a greasy smear?

And now I had to think up something unique, indoors, preferably sitting down, that would bond two groups together. One lot from Leeds, which we regarded as a metropolis only one step away from downtown New York, whilst they, presumably, thought us to be only just moving into running water and not pitchforking one another to death over witchcraft claims.

I had to do it to keep my job.

That gave me a bitter taste in my mouth. I pushed the fear down for now, knowing it would bob to the surface soon enough. There was not enough weight in the world to submerge those feelings deeply enough to stop them coming back up. To keep my mind off them, I switched to listening to Zac.

Zac sounded as though he were talking to a client. Someone he knew well, obviously, from the way he kept calling them 'Bob', and seemingly talking them down from a bad interview situation. Eventually he sighed and said, 'Okay. Okay. Maybe you'd better come in and we can talk about this, before you get sanctioned and your payments cut.' A pause. 'No, we're working out of the York office now, can you get there?' The voice at the other end quacked a few times. Sounded aggrieved. 'Yes, yes, you can get your travel expenses paid.'

Zac looked up and met my eye. For the tiniest second there was communion, as we acknowledged the way our job could pull us in so many different directions; being encouraging whilst wanting to shout. But I soon looked away. I didn't want to have any kind of fellow feeling with Zac. I couldn't afford to like a man who may soon have my office and my job, however pleasant he may appear to be. Besides, I didn't know him. He might turn out to be awful to his mother, or kick kittens when he thought no one was looking or hate *Midsomer Murders*. Nobody could be as alertly agreeable as this, without it being a front for a seething mass of something. Plus, listening to him talking to Bob, he was being a little bit brusque. People who have been out of work for a long time needed more than those who'd never known a moment's unemployment telling them they just had to buck their ideas up and apply for more jobs, and Zac sounded as though he was coming dangerously close to that attitude. Maybe he was going to turn out to be an outrageous bully.

I could only hope.

When he asked his client to come in tomorrow at three, I managed to stop wondering about him and raise a decent amount of indignation at his attitude.

'I've got the interview room tomorrow at three. I have a client,' I said, when he'd put down the phone with a sigh.

Zac blinked. 'Surely there's more than one interview room?'

'Why? There's only me doing this job, I can only see one person at a time, why would we need more than one room?'

He sighed and dropped his head behind the screen. When he raised it again, his hair was less perky, as though he'd had his face in his hands. 'What do you suggest?'

'*I* don't suggest anything. It's my interview room.' I wasn't keen on this problem-solving approach, because it meant me doing all the work. 'The room is free in the morning, why not reschedule?'

'Bob's not a morning person,' Zac said heavily, as though this was an ongoing bone of contention. 'And it isn't just *your* interview room any more. And there isn't just *you* doing the job.'

We sat in a dry, sour silence for a moment.

'I suppose I could take my client to the coffee shop next door,' I said, when he clearly wasn't going to back down. This wasn't *fair*. I did conflict resolution with my clients, I didn't need to start dragging it out in my own office with a man who kept smiling at me, even if that smile had faded a bit in the last few minutes.

Zac stood up now. His hair nearly brushed the beams of the old building. 'Thank you, Ruby.' If I listened hard, I was sure I could convince myself that there was a tone of satisfaction there, as though he'd known all along that I'd be the one to bend.

Another moment of silence. I stared out of the window, to where the winter sun shredded through the bare branches of a lime tree onto damp grass, and took some deep breaths.

'There is a positive to both of us covering the position, of course.' Zac sat on the corner of the desk I was, reluctantly, coming to think of as his. 'You can pass any of your really tough clients on to me.'

The breath I'd started kept going in whilst I thought of something appropriate to say. When nothing had presented itself and my lungs were cracking my ribs, I let it out on a huge sigh. 'I've been doing this job for seven years,' I said, and every year of those seven hung behind the words, keeping them level. 'I can manage even the difficult clients, thank you.'

I swept out of the office, buoyed up by the tiny amount of implied criticism I could take from his words. He *wasn't* perfect! He could carry sexist attitudes, chauvinism and an overinflated opinion of his own abilities, just like everyone else. Thank goodness for that. I'd been beginning to worry that there was nothing going on behind that façade of easy-going, good-humoured openness. Now at least I could start to dislike him with reason.

I slammed the door, to let him know I'd noticed.

2

I sat in my bedroom and stared blankly out of the window. A tiny part of me was comparing the view, over roofs and tiny gardens thickly forested with trampolines, goal nets and swing sets, with the view from the house Gareth and I had bought. It had been in a village on the edge of the city, and looked over fields of grazing cows and newly planted barley. I'd woken every morning to the sound of cockerels crowing and rooks settling in the trees. Here, I woke to next-door's motorbike engine and the shouted greetings of people heading to the paper shop down the road.

The sense of failure swept over me again. Gareth had gone, and his engagement to a slender and beautiful woman had been documented all over Instagram and Facebook, until my friends had forced me to delete him from my social media. The pain of losing him was now more of a dull embarrassed ache. Losing the house hurt more. I'd just found the perfect shade of paint for the stairs.

I stared at my laptop and the files I was trying to sort through. I had seven clients I needed to contact and three who wanted appointments. Normally I would have rung them now and booked them in, but, as Zac seemed to think he had first dibs on the interview room, I didn't want to make any appointments without checking up on the new Booking Page. And I didn't want to do that during the evening as Zac would be able to see, and I wanted him to believe that I partied away the night in a whirl of friends, spontaneous invitations, cocktails and dinners, and Christmas markets and skating on frozen ponds with my millions of attractive and very wealthy boyfriends. Basically, I wanted him to believe that I lived in a Hallmark movie, that allowed me eight hours of restful sleep a night to be the organised and perky person he saw before him. Besides, I had to work out some kind of team-bonding exercise and nothing was springing to mind, unless I could find a large frozen lake and fifty pairs of ice skates in central York.

Well, it was worth a shot.

'Rubes! You coming to watch that Netflix thing!'

Sophie's voice rattled up the stairs to reach me. She was eight years younger than my thirty, and made me feel incredibly old. *Her* life was far more as I wished mine could be, with perpetual changes of boyfriend, lots of cute outfits and an insouciance that bordered on randomness. I shared the house with her, Ed, who was dark and serious and worked for an accountancy firm and was saving like crazy for his own house, so never left the premises to socialise, and Cav whom we rarely saw. Cav had a bike and, when he wasn't working his bicycle courier job, he was mending his bike, cleaning his bike, taking his bike for 'a spin' or reading bike magazines. Cav was the most single-minded man I'd ever known.

'In a sec, Soph!' I shouted back. I was allowed another short moment of wallowing in 'what could have been', surely? I often told my clients not to turn their backs on the past completely. To look at their mistakes and learn from them. Unfortunately, the only thing I could learn from my past was not to trust a boyfriend with a job overseas, and that pale blue was not a good colour for a downstairs toilet. My lungs cramped in a threatening way.

And breathe…

When I went down to the crowded living room where the television had pride of place, Sophie had her legs up on the one sofa, Ed was perched on a beanbag and, to my surprise, Cav was there too, sitting on the floor polishing what looked very much like a wheel.

I squeezed myself into a corner of the ottoman where Cav stored his inner tubes, and we collectively watched four episodes of a drama that had been promised to be 'edge of your seat'. Sophie was utterly absorbed and gave us a running commentary of her thoughts, with highlights such as 'a woman with hair like that has *got* to be guilty', 'urgh, I wouldn't snog him, he could be hiding anything in that coat', and 'didn't she used to be in *Corona tion Street*?' Ed seemed to be watching analytically, he'd nod every now and again as though a line of dialogue was particularly salient, and Cav carried on polishing his wheel.

After we'd finished, we sat and chatted about what we'd watched. Outside the window I could see frost starting to form, creeping its flowery fingers along the edge of the glass. Cars spat grit along the road and the lights lined up the bins and walls of the front gardens, like rulers.

A sudden feeling of almost-contentment swept over me. No, this wasn't my lovely little house in the country and Gareth wasn't upstairs waiting for me. But I was inside on a cold night, with the heating that Sophie insisted on having turned up high crinkling the edges of the wallpaper. Outside was dark and cold. A place of lonely lights and secretive corners. I was here, surrounded by life and warmth and the remnants of the Victoria sponge that we'd all snacked on during the drama. We were all laughing about the ridiculousness of the plot; of overly handsome actors pretending to be down-and-outs and hugely dramatic revelations. Even Cav was joining in.

I could almost forget the breath-snatching terror that descended over me when I wasn't concentrating. The feeling that the worst was about to happen, that I couldn't stop it and my life was millimetres away from sliding down the nearest drain. I felt, for want of a better word, *normal.* Just for this moment I wasn't looking out from the inside of a box labelled 'disaster' onto a world that made sense to everyone else.

And in that moment, I had an idea.

* * *

'Have you sorted your team-bonding exercise?' I asked Zac the next day, as we squeezed ourselves into our collective office.

He looked at me with an expression that indicated he was half-hopeful that my friendliness was a rapprochement after yesterday's door slam and subsequent frostiness and half-suspicious that I was plotting something.

'Er, not really.' It was the first time I'd got the feeling that Zac wasn't in absolute control of every inch of his life, and had a moment of feeling slightly relieved. 'I thought I might go traditional. You know, spaghetti and marshmallows, who can build the highest tower kind of thing. Usually goes down well.'

'Mmmm, marshmallows,' I said, without thinking, and he grinned.

'Yes, I found the cupboard.' He opened the bottom drawer of the largely disused filing cabinet, with his foot. It was rammed full of all the biscuits and chocolate that had previously reposed along the shelves of the big stationary cupboard. 'The bosses were doing a bit of an inspection earlier, so I moved the stuff in here and locked the door. Told them it was confidential.'

There was another one of those moments of communion, when we met one another's eyes and his expression told me that we were in absolute accord with our feelings about the sort of management that does spot inspections of offices.

'Oh, and by the way.' He'd lowered his voice a little now. 'I'm sorry about yesterday.'

'Oh yes?' I tried to look as though I had been waiting for this apology with bated breath and a cool level of acknowledgment of his transgression. Mentally, I was leaping in the air and cheering at the fact he felt he *ought* to apologise.

'I think I implied that you couldn't handle tough clients? It was stupid of me. I really meant that you could pass all those grim jobs that nobody wants to do on to me. I'm not much good at cleaning toilets, but I have fantastic attention to detail when it comes to whitening grout.' He gave me a grin that was so 'open' I could practically see the back of his head. 'So. Yes. Sorry about that. I should have apologised yesterday, but you seemed – busy.'

A polite way of saying that I had avoided him for the rest of the day, unless my presence in the office had been absolutely necessary, when I'd made conspicuously frantic phone calls. Oh bugger. Now he wasn't even the sexist clod I could dislike either. This was awful. Why did he have to be so *nice*?

At that moment, the door flew open, banged off the corner of Zac's desk because he'd moved it a couple of inches to the left for some reason, and Priya stood there.

'I've okayed it,' she said a little bit breathlessly. 'We're good to go next week.'

Zac and I stared at her for a moment. Then I remembered that I'd given her the job of sorting the admin for my team building. 'That's great,' I said.

'You're leaving?' Zac half stood behind his desk. 'But I thought...'

'No, good to go as in good to go on with what we are meant to be going on with,' Priya rattled without making eye contact whilst trying to shuffle back out of the doorway.

'Sorry to disappoint you,' I added.

'Oh, I'm not disappointed.' He gave another one of his presumably patented grins which made him look approachable and sunny-natured. It made me slightly uneasy, mostly because I knew how it was done and did it myself quite often. His phone rang, and, broadening the grin at me over the top of it, he answered.

Priya was slowly retreating, like an outgoing tide, sliding around the wall towards her tiny room, and I got up and followed her into her tiny office.

'What's the matter?' If we closed the door, my knees touched her desk, so I kept it half-open in case of oxygen shortage.

'Did he say anything? Yesterday?' Priya's mouth pulled sideways and she did a kind of 'hunch of shame'.

'What about?' Her entire posture was shouting that she was humiliated. 'Pri? You haven't got history with this guy, have you? He's not going to turn out to be the bloke you shagged one night who now knows all your deepest secrets?' I banged the back of my head gently against the door. 'Because that would probably finish me off here.'

'Always with the sex. *Why* do you always go to the sex?' Luckily the annoyance made Pri stop huddling like a Dickensian miser and straighten up. 'Come on, is there *anyone* in this building less likely to have shagged Zac Drewe, apart from Karen on the switchboard whose tales of the failings of HRT are legendary?'

Well, there's me, I nearly said, but didn't.

'Yes, sorry. No idea why my mind went there.' I stopped banging my head.

Priya gave me a pursed-mouth look. 'You know I'm gay, right?'

'Yes, yes of course I do. I'm sorry, I have no idea why that was the first thing that sprang into my mind.'

She raised an eyebrow. 'You look at him and think of sex. Which is a perfectly normal reaction. If you're straight.'

I moved towards her, so keen to correct her misunderstanding that I bashed both my thighs on the sticky-out bit of the desk. 'No! Oh, God, no, Pri, don't! The only kind of matchmaking I want from you are those ones that are covered in chocolate. I absolutely have no intention of any kind of sex with Zac Drewe. He's the competition for a start and for another thing nobody can be that cheery when they've just been told to relocate and compete for their job – nobody! Unless they are taking industrial-strength drugs,' I added, and then spared a moment to wonder why Michael was so resistant to drug tests for employees.

'He's not ugly, though.'

'Well, no, but attraction doesn't work like that. Otherwise I'd never get out of the house in the morning. Ed and Cav aren't ugly, but I don't want to get into bed with them either!'

Priya shrugged. 'So why are you grinning, then?'

'Sorry. Just imagining Michael spending his evenings smoking spliffs and off his face on cocaine. I got a bit mentally sidetracked.'

She raised her eyebrows at me.

'So,' I tried to divert the conversation. 'Why are you coming over all embarrassed when you see Zac? And what is he supposed to have mentioned?'

She looked at her hands and blushed. 'The magazine.'

'What, the one you left on your chair? Pri, it was *Your Cat*, not *Bondage Weekly*.'

'I know! But, in a way, that's worse. I don't want him to stereo-type me. You know, typical lesbian, who lives with about a million cats.'

I looked at Priya. We'd been friends ever since we'd both started at YouIn2Work within weeks of each other, and our friendship had deepened when budget cuts had meant that coun-selling was forced to share an office with PR and Admin. She was short, curvy and dark, all of which suited her perfectly. I was taller, leaning towards plump and my hair was ash blonde. Well, that was what it said on the box, anyway. I was straight, she was gay. When we'd met, I'd been happily settled with Gareth and she'd been single and dating. Now she was happily settled with Nettie, and I... well, I was as likely to start dating as I was to create team-building exercises featuring rafts, put it that way.

'Pri, for one thing, you are a very long way from the lame cliché of a lesbian and for a second thing, what the hell does it matter what Mr Fly-By-Night thinks of you?'

Priya looked at her hands and muttered something. It sounded very much like 'if you don't keep your job, I have to work with him'. Then she raised her head. 'I can't bear it. Being the "token gay" and everyone smiling tolerantly and sort of patting my head and expecting me to knit for their babies and be all jolly and everything.'

I stared at her. 'Do they? Seriously? Even now?'

She sighed. 'Yes. Give it a try and see. Anyway. I don't want *him*–' she jerked her head towards the next-door office '– to think of me like that. Pity invitations to things because he assumes that Nettie and I spend every evening watching Netflix and baking and talking about our cats.'

It definitely sounded as though Pri wasn't going to form a neutral zone between Zac Drewe and I. She was firmly with me, in the trenches.

'Ruby, you have *got* to keep your job,' Priya hissed, with a meaningful look at the door. 'I couldn't bear it otherwise.'

This was a little further into 'over the top' territory. 'Hang on, Pri. Don't you think you might be a bit oversensitive here? He saw your magazine, and now you are painting him as a heteronormative, pigeon-holing, boor. He might not be like that at all.' I paused. 'He's being surprisingly pleasant so far. In fact, he's *so* pleasant that I've had all kinds of thoughts about what he might really be like underneath.'

Priya began stripping the shiny wrapper off a Twirl bar, almost as though she was doing it subconsciously. 'Aha!' she exclaimed. 'I *knew* you'd be spending time thinking about him. Knew it!' Then she munched a mouthful of chocolate contemplatively. 'Anyway, I don't care if he turns out to be a cross between Mother Teresa and J. K. Rowling,' she said darkly. 'I'll always know how *I* think he sees me.'

'Well, he's not getting my job without a fight. Or, indeed, at all.' I didn't dare think of any other possibility right now. 'Don't worry.'

Pri didn't look massively reassured, unsurprisingly, so I left her to her chocolatey solitude, and went back into what passed for my own office. It was a good job I had, because Zac was just taking receipt of a load of brown boxes, and if I hadn't got back when I did, I wouldn't have got into the room.

'What are these?' I asked, as he signed paperwork and the delivery man backed out, doing a kind of hula move through the boxes.

'Stuff for my team-building morning,' he answered vaguely.

I looked at the piles. 'We're meant to be building a team, not the Forth Road Bridge.'

'You remember that I've got my client coming at three?' He still sounded vague, as though he was thinking of three things at once. 'And you've promised that I can have the interview room?'

'It wasn't a promise, I was railroaded into it,' I answered shortly. 'And only because I can take my client to the coffee shop. I presume that you will cover the costs of our coffees?'

He nodded, still clearly elsewhere, and I made a mental note to include cake. Then I noticed that he was frowning and there were lines around his mouth that hadn't been there before.

'Are you all right?' I asked.

He moved convulsively. A jerk of his shoulders as though something had just landed on them and was settling its weight. Then he smiled, slowly. 'Oh. Yes, sorry. Just had a... phone call. No, everything's good.' Now the grin flashed to its maximum width. 'Fine and dandy. How about you? Have you got your team exercise sorted? Apparently we have to wheel them out next Monday and Tuesday.'

That gave me the whole weekend to really get prepared. I wasn't sure I'd ever be *ready*, but I'd give it my best shot. 'Oh yes,' I put as much brightness into my voice as he had into his. My tone radiated like the sun. 'Looking forward to it. It will be so good to see how everyone responds.'

He carried on grinning. 'Yes, it's going to be fantastic, isn't it?'

If we kept escalating our excitement and anticipation at the current rate, we were going to be ecstatic about it in the next couple of sentences, and greeting the opportunity like winning the lottery by the end of the day. But there was something in his brown eyes above the grin that didn't quite fit. I wondered if the phone call had been from Mrs Backcomb and the Grey Man. Maybe Zac was on a warning? Maybe keeping my job wasn't going to be as hard as I imagined? The thought made me smile.

'Right.' Zac started weaving his way out from behind the desk.

'I'd better get these somewhere more convenient. Is there room next door?' He gave a nod towards Priya's tiny office.

'Oh, I wouldn't go in there,' I said, remembering Priya's words about being stereotyped. 'She's just – on the phone to the rock-climbing club, organising their next climb,' I finished, slightly desperately, hunting for the most esoteric hobby I could come up with.

'Priya climbs?' His eyebrows were in his spiky hairline. Good.

'Oh yes. They're planning on doing the…' Oh God, why hadn't I paid more attention in geography? 'The Matterhorn.' I seized on the only mountain I could think of that could plausibly be climbed by someone who lived in York and only got three weeks' holiday a year.

'Wow. That's quite impressive.' To be fair, he did look impressed.

To change the subject, because we'd exhausted all I knew about the Matterhorn in our ten-second discussion, I picked up one of the boxes. It was very light but a slight bump around the base when I shook it told me it wasn't empty. 'Marshmallows?'

'Yep.' He looked – well, it was hard to describe. As though part of his mind was elsewhere, roaming the possibilities of alternative employment hopefully, but also a touch… defiant? As though he knew how clichéd the 'build the tallest structure possible using only the adhesive power of marshmallows and the rigidity of spaghetti' was but hadn't been able to come up with anything better and was hoping that everyone would assume that this was the only team-building exercise in existence. 'What are you going to do? Not the same…?'

Thanking heavens, possibly for the first time ever, for Sophie, I did my best mysterious smile. 'Ah. You will have to wait to find out. Do you want Tuesday or Monday? Michael said we're only to take less than an hour, so as not to affect productivity.' I gave the boxes another glance. The marshmallow and spaghetti thing tended to degenerate into everyone eating the sweets whilst the spaghetti pooled onto the floor and the cleaners stood in the corner and complained. I wondered, briefly, if he'd ever done it before.

'Oh, I'll go first, if you don't mind.' He smiled at me again. 'Get it over and done with.'

Good, I thought, sitting down to go over my client's file for the afternoon meeting. Going second would give me more of the wow factor, and the cleaners ought to have got the worst of the spaghetti out of the carpets by then.

3

Samantha and I sat in the tiny coffee shop, watching other customers come in and seize gratefully on the warmth in the steamy little room; unbuttoning coats and slipping off scarves. Christmas was starting to loom large in people's calendars as November's gloom was brightened with huge illuminated over-head snowflakes, and shop windows twinkled invitingly. The narrow wooden stalls of the Christmas market crowded the streets and squares, their counters strewn with handmade goods, and the air smelled of roasting chestnuts from the street vendors' carts. York at Christmas was like a Christmas card, pleasingly Dickensian but with proper plumbing and fewer urchins. People had started to shop as though the festive season had caught them by surprise and, in consequence, the respite of the café was being gratefully received.

Samantha sipped at her coffee. 'I've tried, Ruby, honestly I have. But when the only experience you've got to offer is having been a Saturday girl at Woolworths twenty-five years ago – well.' She put her cup back into the saucer and stared at the remaining foam sadly. 'I'm useless,' she said quietly. 'Forty-three and it's all over for me.'

Samantha hadn't worked since she was seventeen. Married and pregnant straight out of school, a stay-at-home mum with, reading between the lines, an obsession with a tidy house and ironed clothes, and a husband who'd left her as soon as the youngest child was away at university, she was struggling with the new need to earn a living.

'And that housekeeping job you put me up for, they told me I'd need to be in charge of the budget.' She rotated her cup as though she was about to try to foretell her future in the dregs. 'Adrian always did the money stuff. I wouldn't know how to do a budget.'

I tried not to let my impatience at her learned helplessness show on my face. This was my job. This was what I was good at. 'You'll know more about it than you think, Samantha. You ran a home. *And* I bet the children were never late for school?'

She gave me a look over her coffee. It was a mixture of pride, horror and a dawning realisation. 'No, of course not. Clean uniform, dinner money paid upfront. I had to be organised.'

'There you go, then.' Inwardly I smiled. She was getting more confident by the second as she became aware that motherhood was a good preparation for quite a lot of jobs. 'Okay. Well, how about I find a course for you? Basic accountancy, financial management, that sort of thing. A qualification in those will help your employment prospects and, in the meantime, you could go back to the agency and see if they've got any cleaning work for you.'

She sighed. 'I suppose.'

'Honestly, Samantha, if you just get your skills up to scratch, I'm sure you'll find something really quickly. You're smart, you're presentable, you've got *loads* of experience at managing a house and children.' I didn't want to overdo the praise, in case she started to wonder why, if she was so great, she couldn't find employment that lasted longer than a week.

'Do you think so? Adrian always told me that I couldn't manage to keep a goldfish alive for more than a weekend,' she said sadly.

'Your children are all fine though, aren't they?'

'Oh yes! Rachel's just gone into her second year at Edinburgh. She wants to be a vet.' Samantha rummaged in her bag. 'Look. This is her before she went back... and this is her brother, he's just graduated. He got a First! He's already got a placement in Liverpool... and this is our Jessie, she's expecting her second baby. Lovely house, isn't it?'

I sat through the photo roll of what felt like Samantha's entire family. I knew she drew her self-esteem from the success of her children so didn't feel that I could stop her without knocking her back and making her feel inferior again. But all the way back to my office after I'd sent her on her way, I cursed the kind of husband who keeps his wife bound to the house and reduces her confidence. Presumably, in the erstwhile Adrian's case, to stop Samantha finding out about his affair. I'd ended up picking up the pieces of too many of these relationships.

I went in through the front door, greeted Karen on reception with a big smile that I didn't really feel but was part of my work character, and then walked through from the smart, tidy part of the building. Past the double doors that led to the main office, where staff helped clients fill in difficult paperwork, past the smaller offices where CVs were drafted and printed and where we accessed help for those who turned out to have left school with only a passing acquaintance with the written word.

The desks were crowded, the YouIn2Work crew doubling up with the Back To Employment staff, until we could all shake down and work out who was going to be doing what. We'd always handled the York and North Yorkshire area, and now, with the merging of the establishments, we were handling Leeds and West Yorkshire too. Some staff had already left and, from the noise level and general fractious atmosphere behind these doors, I gathered that others may also be on their way out.

As could I be, if I didn't pull out all the stops. The tight corset of anxiety, its laces loosened a touch by medication, redoubled its efforts to restrict my breathing.

I gritted my teeth as I walked along the corridor to the unfashionable end of the building where my office – no, my *and Zac Drewe's* office stood. Down the crooked little access way with the shiny lino and the smell of flaky paint, with the huge, old-fashioned metal radiators giving out either enough heat to cook a duck or feeble dust-smelling warmth, depending on the caretaker's mood. Down into the windowless depths, where the building had been extended into three neighbouring plots, back up three flights of stairs which still only took me to street level. It was a long walk, smelling of old lunches for most of it, and, with only the infrequent glimpses of the grey November dusk lighting the way, it was like some kind of fried food-scented labyrinth. I half expected to meet a marching cohort of Roman soldiers or a Minotaur with a taste for McDonald's, but all I actually met, was Michael.

'Ah, hello. Um.' He always behaved as though he couldn't remember my name, but, since he managed to introduce me to people and always came to tell me when we'd had good feedback, I knew that wasn't the case.

'Hello, Michael.' I went to walk past him, but he put out a hand to stop me.

'Er, I know this is a bit of a difficult situation,' he said. 'Never wanted to make you have to justify your existence here, Ruby.'

I smiled a fake smile that I hoped he wouldn't see through. 'Oh, it will be fine.' My cheeks practically creaked with the effort, but that was me. Smiling through it all. I was famous for it.

His face, which always somewhat resembled a bed that had been occupied by a restless sleeper, relaxed. 'Hugely relieved to hear that,' he mumbled. 'Been worrying about you. After that... little incident earlier in the year. Thought you might have left us then. Off to pastures new and all that.'

It hadn't been a 'little incident', it had been a virtual breakdown. Gareth's deception, followed by his leaving to set up a lovely shiny new life with no forwarding address, which meant that all the debts incurred from having to resell the house were mine, had left me temporarily unable to do much more than some light paperwork. I hadn't been able to face clients without wailing for weeks. And 'pastures new'? I couldn't even think about application forms or essays on 'how I deal with conflict' without wanting to hide under a blanket. This job had been my security through it all. The rock I had clung to. The rock *I could not lose.*

'No, that's all over now,' I said briskly. 'Much better. Up and running.' I realised I was copying his speech patterns, and forced myself to stop. 'Honestly, Michael. I've got this. I'm sure Zac is very...' I groped for a word that wasn't prejudicial or outright rude, 'very *efficient*, but I think we have the edge in emotional support.'

'Right. Right.' He smoothed back his hair. 'That's the ticket. Just wanted to... yes.' He looked quickly over his shoulder in the direction of my – of *our* – office. 'He's quite bright and breezy, though, isn't he?'

'I'm sure he's good at what he does.' I could hear the edge in my voice, subtly implying that he may not do quite enough to hang on around here. We dealt with more than the practicalities of talking clients back into work. We counselled them. They left feeling worth something, as though they could be a vital cog in an, as yet undiscovered, machine. Despite his 'I am a refreshing, honest and sincere man' persona, I still couldn't quite believe that this was the real Zac, and was slightly worried that there was an air of 'machete and deep wells' in him somewhere.

'Always had a soft spot for you.' Michael gave me a distracted smile. 'Wouldn't want to see you...' He paused. 'Good reference of course. If necessary.'

There was nothing I could say to that. I left him wandering his way back towards the more familiar territory of his own office, and wondered, had he been coming down here to warn me? Did Zac have a track record I didn't know about?

I could hear his voice as I passed the interview room. 'It's no good, Bob! You have *got* to apply for more jobs or they will take away your benefits!'

Mumble mumble, presumably the chastened Bob.

'That's as may be, but it won't cut any ice with those who make the payments. If you can't show that you are actively looking for work—' There was a sudden slam, as though Zac had dropped a pile of filing onto a table. 'Can you not just have singing lessons in your spare time, if you want to work in music?'

Another moment of mumbling, the sound of a chair dragging on lino and footsteps.

I didn't want to be caught eavesdropping and dashed the few metres along to the office, where I hurtled in, sending boxes flying. I'd forgotten about the Great Marshmallow Delivery stacked randomly all over the floor. It looked like one of those detective shows, where the cops drive through a mass of obstacles during their chase of the bad guys, only with less car and more cardboard.

'Ow.' I wasn't really hurt, just startled.

'Are you all right?' Zac came in behind me.

'Yes, I...' I was about to explain that I'd just been taken by surprise by the Great Wall of Cardboard, but the concern in his voice disarmed me for that second and I found, to my horror, that there were tears in my eyes that I couldn't even begin to find a reason for.

Before I knew what was happening, Zac was bending over me, and he smelled of something nice. Nicer than the Lynx body spray that Gareth had poured all over himself, convinced that it made him irresistible in bed. I realised that this was the first time I'd been this close to a man since Gareth, and I was tired and had had a shock, so I sniffed hard and forced the brightness in my eyes to be enthusiasm rather than upset.

'Only you looked a bit...' His eyes were tracing the lines of my face. I could see them moving, up and down, to my hairline, to my mouth and then back to my eyes again. 'You seem a bit upset?'

A deep breath and I centred myself. It was fine. *I* was fine. Nothing to see here. 'I caught my ankle on the edge of your desk.' I refused to let even the tiniest wobble into my voice. This was me, Ruby Oldbridge, and I couldn't show weakness. Not to a man who could use it to take my job, that's for sure. 'Why the hell did you move it?'

The concern was gone from his voice and his posture. 'Oh, right. I moved it a few centimetres, just so I could actually get to see out of the window rather than having it there as decoration.' He gave me a quick look, not sympathetic any more, but not totally pragmatic either, and it disturbed me that I couldn't read him. 'It seemed a bit unfair, with that wonderful view out there and all I was getting was the shadow of pigeons as they came down from the roof. Seriously, there's a *lot* of pigeons in York.'

Unwilling but drawn as though he'd commanded it, my eyes went to the window, where the dark poked in around the ancient panes, interrupted by the bulk of the Minster, illuminated by the streaks of floodlighting. A pigeon flew past, on cue. I'd forgotten about the view.

'It's a bit like having a postcard nailed up across the window,' I said, swallowing hard again. 'In spring, there are peregrine falcons nesting up there.' I nodded toward the huge craggy façade, like a man-made cliff.

'I bet that's amazing.' Zac sat back onto the corner of my desk.

'Well, it's noisy.' I was just about to add that he would never know because he'd be gone by spring, and I'd be watching the sun edging its way across the buttresses over Priya's shoulder, with the falcons sweeping and diving and the pigeons in desperate confusion, like I had for the past three years of us occupying this office. But it seemed – what? Unkind? Too pointed?

My email blipped, a reminder that I was supposed to be sending Samantha the details of some evening classes, so I gave Zac a bright, completely composed smile and went to sit behind my computer and do some work. I saw him shrug, a small, almost defeated movement that made me half-ashamed of myself, and then he sat behind *his* computer and began rattling at the keyboard, typing furiously.

I hoped he couldn't hear me carefully managing my breathing as I sent the email and arranged some more appointments, getting them in the diary before Zac could fill all the slots for the interview room and force me to reserve a permanent table in the coffee shop. Whilst it was warm and steamy in there, it wasn't the most private place for clients to discuss their personal details, so it was his turn to conduct a session in hissed whispers and crumbs.

But all this was desperate displacement activity so I didn't have to sit and think about the forthcoming team building event. Zac's boxes were heaped hugger-mugger where I could see them out of the corner of my eye. He knew what he was doing, he'd got *ideas*. All I had was some half-thoughts, which had made me giggle at the time but now, faced with the tried-and-tested potential of the marshmallow and spaghetti tower, seemed weak and self-indulgent. *What if nobody else thinks it's funny? What if they all walk out?*

My breathing stuttered and I gave a little half-gasp, which made Zac pause in his telephone conversation and look at me. I turned it into a cough – *breathe* – and made my face assume an expression that indicated I was having the time of my life filling in these spreadsheets and forms. I pushed the thoughts of failure as far to the back of my head as I could, where they ground and rotated and polished themselves into perfection.

I needed distraction and the sending of emails and follow-up paperwork wasn't providing it. My typing became irregular, my brain and eyes weren't working together and my mind kept sending my stomach messages about the advisability of this morning's breakfast bacon. In the end, I stopped typing all together and let my eyes wander to the window as though I'd never noticed it before.

To the side of the Minster, there was a small strip of street visible, cobbles shining in the illuminated dusk, Christmas lights throwing swinging shadows and sudden bursts of light into darkened corners. The jumble of buildings from all eras gave the roofline the uneven look of a badly trimmed hedge and shoppers hurried along, shoulders hunched under the weight of bags, or hesitated, peering into bay windows heaped with books or toys or knitwear. It looked a bit Lowry for my liking. I preferred the peregrines and the panicked pigeons and the spring.

'Is there a Christmas party?'

The question startled me and my fingers typed a line of

qwoeuw, which I didn't think I could possibly pass off as my Application for Funding.

'Party?'

'Mmm.' The pineapple-spiked hair was back, peering at me over the screen, although the new desk angle meant that I could see more of his face. 'Party. Awful music, dancing with your boss, trying not to get drunk enough to photocopy your bum – I'm pretty sure you know what a party is, Ruby.' The bit of his face I could see was grinning again. 'And, as it's Christmas, there's mistletoe everywhere and desperate attempts to lure unfortunates into a seasonal snog.'

I averted my eyes from his smile. 'I'm fairly sure that comes under the heading of Inappropriate Office Behaviour,' I said distantly. Did he think that I looked like the sort of person who'd try to get kissed by coercion? Did I really look *that* desperate?

'Yes, I know.' A pause. 'But is there? A party? Do we get summoned up to the meeting room for warm orange squash and a mince pie and all the bosses pretending to mingle, whilst we all do our best to avoid the IT boys telling us why our machines are running at reduced capacity? Which is, I have to say, not at all seasonal.'

I tried to look at him without catching the edges of that smile. He looked like the kind of person who would be out every night in the run-up to Christmas. I could just imagine him, bar-hopping with his similarly trendy-haircutted friends, leaning on one another's shoulders, laughing uproariously at nothing and slapping one another's backs. He'd have friends called Caz and Dex, who'd have similarly singularly monikered girlfriends with shiny hair and tight dresses and they'd go to posh wine bars and... He was talking to me and I realised I'd missed most of the sentence.

'...exercise, yes?'

I looked down at my keyboard and widened my eyes in panic. If I said 'yes', what was I agreeing to? Exercise could mean anything from a trial run at putting up the Christmas tree in Reception, to agreeing to run a marathon. 'I... oh, sorry, I've just got to...' And I got up and fled from the office. Even the corridor, which smelled of fish pie, was better than sitting in there with his relentless cheerful attempts to get me to talk. Now I knew how budgies must feel.

My mobile rang and I bustled further along the corridor to answer it. I didn't want Zac to think I was hanging about outside the office desperately trying to think up an excuse for dashing out, even if I was, and I silently thanked the caller for the excuse.

It was Taylor. He'd just received a call asking him to attend an interview and he needed me to tell him what to say. He didn't put it like that, of course, but it was what he meant. He'd been out of work for three years, his anxiety had been keeping him from getting jobs he was well suited for, and he sounded terrified.

'Can I come in now? They want to see me at ten tomorrow and I don't know what they're going to ask me!' The panic was audible. I could almost feel the waves of fear coming down the phone at me.

It was late. The office would be closing soon. But, if we could get Taylor into work it would help our statistics and it might make me feel better. I balanced heading back for an evening listening to Sophie singing Christmas carols off-key in the kitchen whilst pretending to watch TV with Ed's silent presence on the ottoman in the background, like The Ghost of Christmas Spreadsheets, and Cav outside the back door oiling his gears.

I'd been hoping to use the time to try to come up with some extra WOW factor for my team building, although I felt so lacking in any wow of any description that I may even have been driven to asking Ed for advice. Which would have led to my pension looking a lot healthier, but not really much of an improvement in the company bonding stakes. Accountancy, apparently, was not big on wow.

A brief memory pang hit me, of last Christmas, when Gareth and I had just moved and I'd spent every evening with pots of paint and fairy lights, trying to make the place festively ours. All that time I'd wasted. But right now, wasting time could lose me my job, and Taylor needed me.

'Of course. Come straight through the back door to the interview room.'

I rang Karen to tell her that I'd set the alarms and lock up after my late session, and went back into the office to read through Taylor's notes and remind myself of his background.

I put the coffee machine on in the interview room and found the emergency biscuits.

Priya passed me in the corridor. 'Got a late one? Want me to stay?'

'No, it's fine.'

'Okay.' She wafted past me on a scent of *Daisy* mixed with Cadburys, and Taylor arrived shortly afterwards; terror and anticipation as much a part of him as his motorbike leathers and tattoos.

He sat with his helmet on his knee for the next hour, while I talked him down from the state of raging panic that the invitation to interview had caused, wished him luck and sent him back on his way, sloshing with coffee and with his nerves practically jangling. Maybe I should switch to something more calming in the room? Camomile tea perhaps.

The building exhaled quietly around me as I locked the back door behind Taylor's screaming exhaust. I liked being alone in here, despite the fact it was rumoured to be haunted, but then, so was practically every other building in the middle of York, and I'd never seen anything scarier in here than Priya with a hangover. There was something comforting about the history, about the uneven floors and randomly placed windows. We were six weeks from Christmas but that hadn't stopped some extra-festive person from winding tinsel along the bars on the ground-floor windows and sprigs of plastic holly were taped on top of the security cameras. It did make it look a bit like 'Christmas on D Wing', but the effect was, overall, cheerful.

Boards creaked and roof joists settled as the heating clicked into night-time mode. The place even smelled different now, as closed doors locked each section down into its own olfactory aura – the lunches of the main office stopped blending with the hot electricity of the photocopying room and the overused plastic and people-under-stress scent of everywhere else. Now the corridor smelled of ancient dust and Victorian floor polish.

I headed back to the office to collect my bags and keys and was totally astonished to find Zac still there, pacing round the room and talking on his mobile.

'No, of course I'm not leaving you. No, honestly, look, I'll be over soon. Please, just eat your dinner and I'll see you soon. Yes, honestly. No, I won't be much later.'

There was a gentle exasperation in his tone that was unlike anything I'd heard from him so far. Almost a tenderness. So, Zac had someone waiting for him at home, did he? Well, of course he did, Priya had been right, he wasn't offensive-looking. And he was good at his job, damn it. It had been too much to hope that he spent his evening alone in a solitary basement building models out of matchsticks and eating microwave meals for one. In the dark. And damp. Wearing big fluffy slippers and a onesie.

I snorted to myself at the mental image of the trendily clad Zac living like a rejected hermit, and he heard me and turned round, hanging up the call as he did so.

'Ah.' An almost furtive look shaded his eyes for a second.

'Why are you still here?' I pretended I hadn't heard anything.

'Saw you had a client. Thought I ought to stay, for security.'

I stared at him. 'I've got keys.'

'Yes, but—' he spread his arms wide to indicate the whole building. 'Anything could happen. You shouldn't really be alone here after hours.' He slid the phone into the back pocket of his trendy trousers, as though he was using the words to distract me from the call.

'I do hope you aren't going to turn out to be one of those people who characterises all long-term unemployed as only one waved fiver away from a bag snatch,' I said sternly. 'I wouldn't be alone on the premises with anyone I didn't know.'

He jerked as though I'd slapped him. 'No! I didn't mean that at all.'

I felt a tiny little tickle of triumph. I'd managed to score a point, get past his defences. Maybe he was protesting too much? Maybe he really did have a well-buried notion that our clients were all potential muggers and rapists? 'Well then, why did you stay?'

He dropped his gaze from me to the floor. 'It's an old building.' Now he looked up, there was challenge, defiance in his eyes when they met mine. 'And you can get attacked by someone you know well too, you know.'

'Zac, there are security cameras everywhere, and panic alarms in all the rooms.'

He raised his eyes again and held my gaze, almost as though he was trying to will me to read something in his look. That he thought I'd been stupid? Well, maybe, but I was confident in my knowledge of the building, and in Taylor. Then it dawned on me that perhaps Zac was trying to unsettle me. If I started to get even the slightest bit concerned about seeing clients alone, after hours or in unknown places – wouldn't that make me far less suitable for the job?

'There are measures in place. I feel perfectly secure.' I added a little more force to my tone now.

'That doesn't mean it can't happen,' he began, but now I'd got wise to his reasoning, I wasn't having it.

'Right. I'm locking the place up now. If you don't want to be here all night, you'd better come with me.'

We grabbed bags and coats and he followed me through the building, watched without speaking as I set the alarms and padded behind as I went out into the cold, and locked the doors.

It seemed churlish to stride away into the night without another word, so I said, 'Thank you for waiting for me anyway.'

He was wrestling his way into a big coat, juggling his laptop bag and keys. 'No worries. I'll know, in future.' His face emerged from the collar of the coat, bright-eyed and sunny again. 'That you are immortal and immune to all known forms of danger.'

'Just bear that in mind.' I found I was smiling back and then cursed myself. I *knew* smiles were infectious, I could resist, so why was I doing it?

'Would you, er, like to grab a coffee? Before we head out?' Zac looked around the deserted, frost-shiny streets. 'It feels a bit like a horror movie set here and I feel I should be somewhere warm and well-lit, armed with a coconut latte, in case of an apocalypse.'

I looked around too. 'This is York. No zombies, except very well-behaved and domesticated ones.' Was he insulting my lovely city? 'And thank you, but I ought to get home.' Besides, my car was parked in the riverside car park, half a mile's hike away under the swinging snowflake lights, because *someone* had taken my parking space. I thought about saying this, but didn't. So, instead, I used a different form of attack. 'Isn't there someone waiting for you?'

'Someone…?' He looked genuinely puzzled for a moment and my opinion of him plummeted a little further. A girlfriend – wife maybe – had been on the phone to him only a few minutes ago, expecting him. He surely couldn't have forgotten her already. 'Oh, the phone call. No. No, that was something else.' He dropped his head. Looked away. As clear an avoidance technique as I had ever seen, and I wasn't falling for it at all.

I stifled another laugh at his obviousness. 'Well, goodnight then, Zac.'

I walked off in the direction of my car, leaving him standing outside the darkened windows of our building. When I furtively looked back over my shoulder, whilst pretending to glance in a shop window, he was still standing there, with the floodlights of the Minster grazing one shoulder and the rest of him in shadow.

I snorted again and began the trek through the winding medieval streets to my car, whilst managing not to be attacked by any zombies whatsoever.

4

Monday, and Zac's team exercise was going well, bugger it.

He'd set up the groups so that two from YouIn2Work were paired with two from Back To Employment, to build not, as I'd assumed, the tallest tower possible with marshmallow joints and spaghetti infrastructure, but the most imaginative. And I, apparently, had agreed to judge the results, which meant that at least ninety per cent of each company was going to hate me.

Neatly done, Zac, neatly done.

I wasn't allowed to be near where he was carrying out his 'team building' – which I thought was distinctly unfair. Was I not part of the 'team'? I gritted my teeth and finished all my paperwork from the latest interviews, sent some emails, did some research, and then stalked the corridors like a vengeance-filled ghost, while the sounds of laughing and conversation drifted through the building, making me feel as excluded as, presumably, any spirits still hanging around the place might feel. Then I stood in the frosty car park for a while, with the feeble warmth of the sun trying to crack through the ice on the puddles and wondering about letting down Zac's tyres.

His Discovery looked smug. It fatly filled my space and bulged slightly over the lines, so Priya's Micra and Ian-from-accounts' MG which occupied the spaces to either side were drawn as far as possible to their further extents, like ladies pulling their skirts back from an undesirable contact. This had caused a knock-on effect all down the line, so that late arrivals had had to squeeze themselves in to spaces *slightly* too small for their actual cars.

I stared out at the snaggle-parking. Only the Discovery and the battered old Audi of the caretaker were properly parked, which meant that Zac and Sam had been first in. Either Priya or Ian must have been next, with others arriving pretty much simultaneously, as usually happened, and that's what had caused the disarranged parking.

The Discovery's windscreen was thick with frost. Even Priya's car was only sheeted with the lightest coating and I knew she'd got here early because she'd texted me while I'd been on my way in, to say that the meeting room had been set up for the exercise and she wasn't looking forward to it. So Zac had been here *really* early. Not necessary, surely, to set out a few marshmallows and packs of spaghetti and to put a few inspirational quotes and 'amusing' memes up on the screen? On a *Monday*? What kind of weirdo got in early on a Monday?

Well, the kind of weirdo who'd managed to make it look perfectly acceptable that I wasn't part of the team bonding, for a start. Also the weirdo who was running out of the building calling my name.

'Hey, Ruby! Think we've got as far as we can – it's judging time!'

We walked together back through the building.

'Why were you in the car park? Not trying to make a run for it were you?' Again that grin, totally trustworthy. He just *had* to have corpses in the attic or an addiction to peculiar practices in body-tight nylon.

'Just wondering how early you must have got in, to get absolutely everyone else to park like dicks. Don't you *have* a life?'

Yes, it was sharp. Yes, it was mean. But I was feeling isolated. As though he'd single-handedly cut me off from the rest of the workforce and was running me out of town.

The grin died. It was replaced by a shadowing behind the eyes. An unconscious hunching of the shoulders. 'Not really.' It was said on a dying tone, ending almost in a whisper.

'But you have to be home for someone, I heard you on the phone the other night.' Guilt at the wiping of the smile made me press my point, as though I were trying to explain myself.

'It's... complicated.' He stopped walking. He'd been slightly ahead of me in the narrow corridor, and I walked into his shoulder before I stopped too. His whole body was tense, I felt the rigidity of bone and muscle, a smell of something nice and 'outdoorsy', wood and leather and fresh air. Whether it was a cologne or just the smell of him I wasn't sure. 'Ruby. That call...' He looked down at the floor.

I looked down too. There was nothing remarkable about that bit of floor, where generations of paint had been laid over boards and then worn off by feet, leaving a wafer-edge of border. 'What?'

'Can you not... I mean, please don't mention that phone call to anyone. It was personal.'

He looked so dejected, his body so stiff and his gaze on the floor. Like a little boy who's been reprimanded for stealing sweets. I knew I had the upper hand here, but couldn't bring myself to use it.

'No, I won't. Of course I won't if you don't want me to.'

'Thank you.' That *was* a whisper.

Then he started walking again and, within a stride, the

bounce was back in his step and the grin back on his face, as though that moment of pain had never happened.

'Right. So, there's some good efforts in here–' he wheeled around in the door to the meeting room '– but I mustn't influence you. So...'

He flung the door open to a scene that most closely resembled an explosion in a food development kitchen. The air smelled of half-melted marshmallows and the sweat of creativity and my feet crunched over discarded spaghetti sticks, scattered like a really ambitious game of Spillikins. Well, at least the cleaners would hate him.

They would be the only ones, by the look of it. The place had descended into hilarity. Several creations had fallen apart in the time it had taken Zac to fetch me, and were holey blobs of marshmallow surrounded by snapped spaghetti, like odd alien creatures. Others had held together better, and several were impressive. Two teams had built giant willies, but frankly I was surprised it was only two. The team at the back, which consisted of Priya and Karen and two of the Back To Employment crew, were leaning on one another practically crying with laughter as their structure fell apart slowly, piece by piece as we all watched. As the weight of my gaze fell upon it, it gradually leaned further and further to one side, finally resting its top half on the model next door like a sleeping drunk on the Tube. I wasn't at all sure what it had been meant to represent, but there was a certain 'Peppa Pig' vibe about it. Karen had grandchildren, so maybe it was intentional.

I picked the winner from the edifices that had managed to retain structural integrity. I wasn't sure what it was, but it was sturdy enough to be lifted from the table, and that was good enough for me. Everyone cheered, a tin of sweets was awarded and promptly handed round.

From everyone's faces it looked as though the bonding exercise had been a success. Bugger. I felt my stomach prickle. My event couldn't live up to this. Everyone, even Pri, was laughing, sharing sweets and shoulder-slapping, it looked more like the aftermath of a successful takeover bid than an exercise in Being Ridiculous With Food. And Zac was in the middle of it all, being congratulated, laughing with the rest. Being accepted. Being popular.

My idea, which had been looking thinner and thinner every time I'd caught sight of Zac's cardboard boxes, finally waved a gossamer goodbye, but I grabbed its tattered edges and held on. It was too late to come up with anything else, too late to book an assault course or source proper blindfolds. In my desperation I had even asked Cav for ideas. He had suggested getting people to strip down and reassemble a Festka One Road. I didn't even know what that was until I looked it up, and just imagining the faces of my workmates if presented with building a road bike as a bonding exercise had forced me to take an extra couple of my anti-anxiety tablets. Even my idea was better than that.

But I'd been so certain that Zac's exercise would fall flat. I mean, *nobody* liked marshmallows *that* much, did they? Oh God, I was going to fail. My attempts at getting natural competitors to work together was going to make nuclear disarmament talks look like a primary school's colouring competition. They were all going to hate me.

* * *

Two client interviews, a run-in with IT about my computer, lunch with Pri who wanted to do some Christmas shopping and needed my help, mostly to carry bags, and an afternoon listening to Zac in the interview room with a lady who came out clutching tissues and in a clear state of shock, didn't give me any additional thinking time, and then the day was over.

Zac swept back into the office, distracted and with his hair slightly flopped on top of his head, like Tintin, if Tintin had been six foot four and less preppy and more designer-casual. He collapsed into his chair and put his head in his hands. 'I cannot imagine,' he said slowly, 'why some people seem to think that they are just going to get money handed to them without even having to fill in any forms. How do they think we are meant to know who they are?'

'Last client?' I had a certain amount of sympathy. Sometimes people could be – not stupid, but naïve, to the point of exasperation.

'She's been unemployed for six months. She thought – God only knows how – that the agencies would somehow "know" and send her money. She's been sitting at home spending money she doesn't have, and waiting for benefits to come in, without even applying.'

I'd come across similar cases before so it didn't startle me as much as it might otherwise have done. 'Poor woman. She must be horribly in debt.'

Zac closed his eyes slowly and tipped his head to rest against the back of his chair. 'Yeah. I've done what I can, she's got all the addresses now, but...' A big sigh. 'I'm still not sure it went in.'

He looked so utterly defeated that a warm wash of pity rose up inside me. 'Your team-bonding exercise was great, by the way. Priya is still giggling. And she's even going out for a drink with your guys that were on the team with her tomorrow night.' I hoped that the hurt and betrayal I felt at Priya's apparent defection from my cause didn't come over in my voice. She couldn't help it. She'd been wooed with confectionary.

Zac opened his eyes. 'Wow, result.' He nodded, his hair scuffing the back of the chair. 'Great stuff.'

There were dabs of blue tiredness under his eyes, I noticed. Faint lines he was too young for alongside his mouth.

'Have you got yours all ready for tomorrow?' He was looking at me very steadily, as though he knew that I was analysing his face, and didn't mind.

'I am not going to answer that.' The words were unfriendly but my tone wasn't. There was something about that steady gaze that made me not want to look away and I found my eyes were catching on those lines and shadows and wondering.

'No, of course. You want to surprise us all.'

It was quiet. No sound at all from the other offices, not even anything filtering in from the street outside. Just the faint whirring of our computer fans and the buzz of the overhead light, I could hear the rasp of his breathing, the tension in it. I wanted to ask about the new tiredness under his eyes and the fresh worry lines across his forehead, but I needed a tactful way to raise it, without it sounding accusatory.

'Zac, are you all right?' I asked gently.

'It—'

The door burst open and Priya stood there, decorated with bags like a small and annoyed Christmas tree. 'Rubes, you said you'd give me a hand to the car with all this stuff.' Then she stared at both of us. 'Am I interrupting something?'

'I'll be with you in sec.' I gave her a wide-eyed stare, trying to indicate a mixture of 'bugger off' combined with 'it's getting tricky', adding just a soupçon of 'could be important' spiced with a warm dash of 'anyway, you traitor, you're getting to actually *like* the Back To Employment lot and had better plie me with much cake, or you are dead to me'.

'Okay. I'll wait by the doors.' She did the wide-eyed thing back

and shuffled her retreat, carefully closing the door behind her
with a hand that also swung two Thornton's bags and something
from Browns.

'Zac?' I made my voice soft. The tiniest part of me was
rejoicing in the fact that I'd been right, he wasn't as carefree and
easy-going as he appeared on the surface. As though, if I was
really honest, it may be something I could use to my advantage,
as long as it wasn't anything to do with machetes. But the rest of
me was squashing this feeling down hard in favour of talking to
someone who clearly *needed* to talk.

But the moment had gone, shattered into high tension fragments by Priya's arrival, like the dropping of a Pyrex bowl.

'No, nothing, it's all good.' There was a gleam of artificiality
about the grin, now I knew. 'Honestly, everything's fine.' He was
packing up his gear, not looking at me, smiling a general smile
that relaxed his face. 'See you tomorrow. Looking forward to your
exercise!'

He swept past me, briefcase almost as shiny as the smile. I
stared after him for a few seconds, still torn. He wasn't as perfect
as he appeared. There were cracks. He wasn't invincible. I needn't
lose this job. I could blow him open, keep my job, keep paying the
bank.

But that thought came teamed with awful sympathy. I knew
how it felt to have to keep up the bravado; pretending that everything in the garden was rosy whilst feeling underneath like a
glacier about to shear off into deep water. To have the knowledge
that everything could be snatched away, everything you'd worked
for and competed for and hung on to. That, where currently there
was certainty and a pay cheque, there could just be a big black
hole.

Being in our profession meant that we, of all people, knew
how hard it could be to get another job. There were always open-

ings in the supermarkets, but even stacking shelves twenty-four/seven wouldn't cover the bills.

I had another burst of fury at Gareth, swanning off into his new life and love without a backward glance or any warning. Landing me with all the concomitant bills of getting out of a very, very short-lived mortgage arrangement and selling the house. Plus all those things I'd committed to, thinking there would be two salaries to cover them. Severance of those had also been expensive.

That invisible corset gave another tweak and I could feel the panic rise into my throat.

And... breathe...

I gathered up my belongings, slipped on my coat and scarf and went out to help Pri.

* * *

I didn't sleep much. Instead, I sat up all night smoothing the seams to make my team-building appear less cobbled together out of disparate elements. I got in early the next morning, set up the screen and arranged the chairs, then turned on the machine I'd borrowed from Sophie. Then I rearranged the chairs again. By the time people started to arrive in dribs and drabs, unloading their gear into their offices and then making their way through to the meeting room, I'd reorganised the room three times, drunk an unwise amount of coffee, and the air smelled of vanilla syrup and toffee. I greeted everyone, feeling horribly like an unslept usherette, although without the protection of a nice tray of ice creams. There was a lot of awkward shuffling.

Fortunately the sound of the popcorn machine broke a lot of the ice for me. Sophie had said that it could be a bit temperamental, and by the third time it had fired its lid across the room and people had fished popcorn out of one another's hair, everyone was, at least, talking. They helped themselves to drinks to the occasional ricochet of kernels hitting the light fittings; it was like a gunfight in a teetotal speakeasy, but at least it made them laugh.

Then I dimmed the lights, started up the computer, and heard the recognition flood the room as the titles came up on screen.

Some people sighed and complained. Some were grudgingly accepting and others were happily anticipatory. I was showing them an old episode of *Blackadder*. It was the episode 'Chains', where Edmund Blackadder is tortured but, since neither he nor his inquisitor speak the same language, they have to mime the various insults and implications to one another. I thought it nicely reflected on how two cultures have to come together to work, despite their differences, but I suspect this nuance was missed by most of the viewers.

It was also as far from marshmallow and spaghetti penises as I'd been able to get, watching TV as a bonding exercise. It had worked for my housemates and me, why should it not work here?

By the end, it wasn't a totally unqualified success, but everyone was talking, some were laughing, and most of the weaponised popcorn had gone. A tight little knot of Haters were discussing *Monty Python* – I couldn't tell whether the discussion was for or against – one group were trying to decide whether Baldrick's pencil case disguise was anachronistic and there was a subset of 'how fanciable is Queenie' discussion breaking out.

When the room had emptied to let everyone get back to work and I'd started scraping the popcorn off the curtains and worrying about the stuff embedded in the ceiling, Priya came to join me.

'Are you coming out for a drink tonight?' she asked, desultorily sweeping rubbish into a black sack. 'Please come. I agreed yesterday on a high from the marshmallows and now I don't know what we're going to talk about.'

I gave her an exasperated look. 'Pri, it's a drink, not an arranged marriage. Two gins and you'll talk about anything to anyone anyway.'

'I know and I need you there to stop me. You *know* what I'm like, Rubes.'

Priya had a way of getting herself into trouble through a combination of being too nice for her own good and hating to stand up and say 'no'. She'd once got talked into going fishing with a bunch of anglers from the local club after a session on Prosecco, and the trauma had never left her.

'Please come. Why not invite some of the new guys along as well? You could extend your team bonding as far as the pub,' she added slyly. 'You might even be able to get it on expenses.'

Thinking back to Zac's success with *his* team bonding, and my effort which seemed to lack a certain something, this wasn't a bad idea. I might just get extra points. So when I got back to my office, I circulated an email to the entire staff, arranging a meet-up in the local pub straight after work. I had a take-up rate of about one in ten, but that was good enough to make me feel I was getting somewhere. Quite a few of the Back To Employment crew still headed home to Leeds every night, but some were staying in hotels and B&Bs, and a lot of the usual suspects from our workforce were looking for excuses to party. It would be a nice mix and, as Priya had said, could count towards 'team building'.

There was no reply from Zac.

I sat with a client in the interview room, listening to him unspooling a scroll of reasons why he hadn't had a job for four years and wondering why Zac hadn't replied. That phone call, he'd had to reassure someone that he wasn't going to leave – was that a worried spouse or partner? And why were the reassurances necessary? Was he planning a separation; were they the last to know? And the way he'd been cajoling them to eat – could it be a *child*? He'd said it was complicated, which meant not a straightforward amicable arrangement with divided-up property and childcare. And tension that sometimes seemed to descend upon him—

'...and then the wife left and took the kids. And the doctor said I was depressed, well, not kidding, but when you're left with all the shit and she's taken herself off to Cardiff and I can't afford to get to see the kids more than a couple of times a year—'

But Zac seemed generally to be a happy person, not letting any assumed 'complicated' life affect his work. I wondered how he did it.

'...so now they're saying I've got to take any job I'm offered or they'll cut my benefits and I'm hanging on by my fingernails as it is!' wailed my client.

'Could you relocate to Cardiff?' I glanced down at his notes, feeling rather guilty that I'd tuned out so much of his backstory. 'You're experienced in machinery, do you have any other family keeping you here?'

'Er.' My client, small, balding, in his forties and with a defeated slump to his whole body which seemed to extend to his mindset, frowned at me. 'Well, it's in Wales, innit?'

'You don't need a passport.' I smiled to soften my words and also because some people really did think Wales was foreign and, in some cases, overseas. 'Is there any reason you couldn't move closer to your children?'

I'd seen pictures of his family, it had been the first thing he'd done after he'd sat down, showed me photos on his phone of his children. I had no idea why all my clients seemed to want me to be able to pick their family members out of a line-up.

'I mean, would they accept my qualifications there? Don't you have to speak Welsh?'

I gently reassured him and we looked up some of the jobs available in his quite specialised field, around the Cardiff area. By the time he left, he was perkier and more optimistic and the beaten-down air had been replaced by something more positive. He seemed taller, too. *This* was why I loved my job – helping people to see that there was a way forward, however hopeless the present looked. I just sometimes wished I could work that magic on myself.

When I came out of the interview room, Zac was leaning against the wall in the corridor.

'You're very kind to them, aren't you?' he observed, falling into step with me as we headed back to the office. 'I mean, you didn't seem to get annoyed that, in four years of unemployment, nobody has suggested he just move closer to his kids?'

I looked sideways at him. 'Maybe they did in the beginning, but it was too much for him to take in back then. Depression is a bugger, he may not have been able to process the idea of moving when just getting out of bed felt like a huge thing.'

Zac pulled a face. 'I think I'd have been a bit more direct with him. Half an hour listening to his woes just to suggest moving to Wales?'

We'd reached the office and bundled in through the narrow doorway. The room really *was* too small when one of us was over six feet tall, but at least the boxes were gone. 'I like to treat my clients holistically. What stops people getting a job isn't always lack of qualifications. Sometimes they have lives that get–' I looked pointedly at him '– complicated,' I finished.

'Back To Employment have a sixty-seven per cent rate of success. Our methods don't seem to hold people back you know.'

He sounded a little bit prickly. Maybe it had been my choice of words, maybe he felt defensive.

'Our success rate is sixty-five per cent and rising,' I replied. 'So my methods clearly work too.'

Zac sat behind his computer. 'Sometimes you need to be straightforward. Break it down a bit, sure, but sometimes the truth is just unavoidable. No amount of sugar-coating can make… some things acceptable.'

He sounded as though he was talking about getting people into work but thinking about something else at the same time. As though there was a topic in the back of his mind that was seeping through his conversations.

'That's one way, but it doesn't work for everyone. That's why we do what we do.' I sat behind my computer now. The screens felt like battle lines, as though our chairs were the trenches and we were digging in. 'There's all the rest of YouBack2Work, or whatever we're called now, to do the straightforward helping with the other stuff. Our team's unique selling point is that we give clients the opportunity to work out what's keeping them out of work. I think you are too hard on your clients. From what I've heard when I've been passing,' I qualified, as I'd never sat in on one of his sessions. But then, he'd not sat in on one of mine either – he was getting his opinion from as brief an exposure to my methods as I was from his.

To think I'd been gradually warming to him. Huh. I'd even been going to ask if he was coming to the pub tonight, well, now I definitely wouldn't bother. If he didn't have the manners to reply to my email and he was calling my methods of counselling my clients back into work into question, he could die of loneliness and dehydration back in Leeds with his 'complicated' life situation for all I cared. Maybe it was a vengeful ex who was, even now, cutting the crotches out of all his trousers and throwing his pop art collection into damp bushes.

I hadn't liked his subliminal suggestion that depression could be overcome with a forceful approach either. There were tablets in my handbag that proved him wrong. But what could I do? If I dragged up my past to prove my case, then I'd give him ammunition against me. I *needed* this job. He, presumably, already knew about my short-term hiatus from others, and that was as much of a mark against me as I could take. If he found out that I'd not quite shaken the knock-on effects of the crash of my relationship, I didn't yet put it past him to bring it up in any private conversations about the role, 'going forward', as Michael would no doubt have put it.

I ignored Zac for the rest of the day. He didn't seem to mind, he was in and out of the office or clicking away at his keyboard in an unconcerned way, which annoyed me even more. Had he criticised my approach to upset me? Because he was worried that my efforts at bonding the teams together may be seen as better than his? Or because he genuinely was concerned that his method of counselling might be a little less effective in the long term?

I narrowed my eyes at the top of his head, which was all that was currently visible over the computer, and muttered 'sixty-five percent'.

I was sure that, among the clatter of keys I heard 'sixty-seven' come back, almost inaudibly and smiled to myself. He was rattled. Good.

5

The pub was noisy and warm. We'd got in early and managed to occupy almost an entire room, alcohol was loosening tongues and inhibitions, and Priya and I were trying out a new flavour of gin, when Zac walked in. I didn't know if I was happy to see him or not, but the gin certainly helped me be less annoyed at his presence.

'I've just spent twenty minutes looking for you,' he said. 'I thought you were still in the building.'

I indicated, with the hand not holding gin, the pub. 'No,' I said. 'I'm here. Why did you think I was still at work?'

'Your car is still in the car park.' His mouth was tight, as though his lips were pursed around an invisible cigarette. 'I thought, maybe, you'd got another late client.'

Priya made a bug-eyed face at me and sloped away, clasping her gin to her chest.

'I'm getting an Uber home.' I didn't know why I felt the need to explain myself. 'Otherwise I couldn't have a drink.'

'Oh.'

'And I did tell you that I'm perfectly happy being alone with clients after hours.' I sipped at my drink so that the glass formed a barrier between him and my expression, which I suspected may have been a wee bit gloaty.

'Even so.' He looked, I was glad to see, a bit awkward.

'So there's no need for the white knight to wait around all chivalrously.' 'Chivalrously' took a bit of getting out, because of the gin. I turned around in search of the bowl of chips that Priya had ordered and left on the bar. 'I'm fine.'

'Well, I can see that.'

Michael, who was bonhomie-ing his way through the crowd, caught up with us. 'Glad to see you two bonding!' He slapped Zac on the back. 'Another one in there, Ruby? Zac, what are you having?'

'Oh, I'm not... I mean, I just popped in to check...' Zac tried, but Michael was being his traditional unstoppable force. I think he was trying to make an impression seeing as the Grey Man and Beehive Woman were sitting together at a nearby table like a couple of aliens planted on Earth to observe our customs.

'Well, just a swift half then,' Michael carried on, overriding Zac's attempts to get out of having a drink. 'Lager?'

Before we knew it, Zac had a half pint of lager in front of him, and my previously unoccupied hand now held another gin. Michael slouched off to buy drinks for the IT boys, which was being a lot better received than his attempts to jolly us into partying.

Christmas music came through the sound system over our heads. Zac's hair practically touched the speakers that were warbling 'I Wish It Could Be Christmas Every Day' and I sipped at my gin and regretted the flashing Christmas earrings I'd put on especially. The noise level was rising.

'You didn't reply to the email,' I said for want of something else to kick off the conversation. The stretching silence between

Zac and I was beginning to be obvious in the midst of all the chat.

'I wasn't coming.' He took a sip of the lager, made a face and put it down on the bar behind him. 'I didn't think a negative warranted a reply.'

Accounts were holding a raucous discussion about something and occasional loud laughs broke out. It was only a matter of time before peanuts got flicked. They were like that in Accounts.

'Why not? Team building.' I finished the current gin and started on Michael's round. Priya had taken possession of the chips and whirled them away to take part in her conversation with some of the newcomers, which was disappointing. I was hungry.

Zac looked pointedly around the bar. It was hot and crowded and noisy, filled with the smell of beer, hot fat and wood polish. 'It's not really my kind of thing.'

No, it wasn't my kind of thing either. Alcohol was turning up the volume of the voices so people could hear themselves talk over the music, it was almost impossible to turn around without getting an elbow in the ribs, there was nowhere to sit that wasn't already occupied and I'd passed 'drinking as a hobby' nearly ten years ago. But it would have made my jaw creak to have to agree with Zac, so I just raised my ongoing gin glass to him and smiled.

'Didn't think it was yours either,' he observed. 'That's why I was surprised by the email. I didn't have you down as spending your spare time pubbing.'

He was standing so close to me that I could hear him quite clearly, despite the fact that the IT department were singing along to 'Do They Know It's Christmas?', with some quite obviously made-up lyrics straight out of the schoolroom.

'Oh? What did you imagine I'd spend my spare time doing then?' I asked pointedly. I really hoped that he wasn't going to guess that I spent it sitting in my room staring out of the window, or watching entire Netflix series squeezed onto a couch between Sophie and a disassembled road bike.

'I dunno. Country walks. Sitting by the sea, reading, that sort of thing.'

'That's not a list of hobbies, Zac, that's a dating profile.' I realised I'd used his name and took a big mouthful of gin to try to cover it up. In my jacket pocket, my phone rang. 'Sorry, got to take this.'

I grabbed my phone and moved away into the entryway to try to answer without the caller being drowned out by cheesy Christmas novelty hits, as sung by the combined choirs of a rapidly tipsy IT and Accounts departments.

It was my dad.

'Hi, Dad.' My father sometimes rang to check up on me. My semi-breakdown in the spring had hit him hardest; seeing me have to return home to my childhood bedroom after having been, as he saw it, successfully launched as an adult with partner and own home, had caused him near physical pain. 'I'm fine. I'm out on the town tonight.'

I held up the phone so he could hear the lively background.

'It's your mum, Ruby,' he said slowly, when I returned the handset to my ear. 'She's had a bit of an accident. She's up in the hospital now. Thought you ought to know.'

'Mum? What...?' The walls I had so carefully constructed between me and the rawness of emotion trembled.

'Oh, she had a bit of a tussle. Out running with the dogs. There was an incident, she got pulled into traffic and hit by a car. She's all right, but very knocked about.'

'I'm coming now.' I put my gin down on the nearest surface and began searching for my coat, keeping the phone under my chin.

'There's no need, darling, she's all right.' But the faltering note in his voice told me he was glad of my reaction.

I hesitated. I couldn't drive, I'd be over the limit. A taxi or Uber all the way from York to Scarborough would be too expensive. I'd have to get the train and then the bus up to the hospital, I could run to the station from here. 'It might take me a while,' I said. 'Are the trains to Scarborough still every hour?'

Suddenly Zac was beside me. 'I'll drive you. I've barely touched this stuff. If you need a lift somewhere…'

I wanted to turn him down. But what was the alternative? Priya was on the gin, so in the same condition as me and almost everyone in here. I could ring Ed and ask him to drive over, but he may still be at work, or out partying… No, Ed didn't party, it cost money. But I needed to go now.

'Thank you,' I said, distractedly. 'Scarborough hospital. My mum…'

'I gathered,' he said dryly. 'But it will save me from having to keep face by drinking whatever the hell this is.' He glanced at the lager. 'I'm not totally convinced it's not something they keep for wiping down the bar. My car's just round the back.'

We hustled swiftly through the packed bodies. Some noticed us leaving together and whooped and nudged but I was too stressed to take it on board.

The Discovery was still warm inside. Zac span out of the car park and then said, 'Which way's Scarborough?' which told me he was also distracted, because it was written on the road, in quite large letters, and there was a sign on a post ten metres away too, for good measure.

We buzzed out of York and along the main road that covered the thirty or so miles between my hometown and the city. An early frost was already breaking the dark into fragments along the windows and I felt almost as sharp myself. Tension was sitting along all my edges and I had to keep it there. I couldn't risk thinking about my mum.

'Your mum...' Zac said, eventually, almost as though he knew I was trying not to think about her. 'Is she often ill?'

'Oh, she's not ill.' I seized on the distraction of words. 'She's had an accident. She's almost never ill, my mum.' *Keep the tension reined in tight. Don't let it run away with you.* 'She's a runner. She used to be a fell and trail runner when she was young and now she's retired she likes to keep her hand in, so she runs along the beaches and over the hills with the dogs. From what Dad said, I think she's been hit by a car.' The bluntness of having to say it made my voice cut off. The walls were still there though, just about staying up. I breathed deeply.

'She sounds super-fit.' There was a bit of a tone to Zac's voice. Almost a resentment?

'Oh she is. She runs marathons and things.'

'Is she quite young?'

'Fifty-five.' And admitting only to fifty, although the fact that my sister was thirty-three was beginning to make that increasingly unlikely. 'She retired quite early, she had her own psychotherapy practice, Dad's sixty, but he doesn't run any more, since he had his knee replaced.'

We crunched down the salted and gritted hill into Scarborough, where the sea widened the view into a patch of cold grey movement. I directed Zac towards the hospital on the far side of town, and we drove through the mostly silent streets, where the cold wind funnelled down through closed shops towards the harbour. Lights shone from clifftop windows, bright and hard against the absolute dark of the bay, and then we turned inland towards the bigger houses, cushioned from the worst of the weather.

Zac parked outside the hospital and I ran through the cold night to find my father.

He was standing drinking coffee next to my mother, who looked bruised and annoyed in a hospital gown.

'I'm perfectly all right,' she said, waspishly. 'I have no idea why I'm even here.'

'Which is precisely *why* you're here, dear.' Dad sighed. 'You were knocked out cold and they need to make sure you don't have any damage to your brain. How they will be able to tell is quite another matter,' he added in an undertone.

It turned out that Mum had been running over the top of the cliffs along a small road with the spaniels. Another dog coming the other way had caused the dogs, who were on running leads, to pull my mother over across the road in front of an oncoming car. Luckily there had been no great speed involved and her injuries were mostly gravel rash and bruising and the bang on the head. My mother was more concerned about the dogs, who had apparently been taken home by a neighbour and were currently under house arrest in the utility room.

Zac joined us. I had no idea how to introduce him to my parents, who were bickering lightly over the arrangements for the spaniels when he turned up, so I settled for telling them that he'd kindly driven me over from a work party. They didn't need to know he was my nemesis. And anyway, nemeses don't drive a Discovery and refuse lager, not in my head anyway.

'Do you want to stay over tonight?' Dad said. 'Mum's being let out tomorrow. Eva is coming down with the children on Thursday, for the weekend.'

'Eva is my sister,' I told Zac.

'Or you could both come up for the weekend?' Dad ploughed on, having grasped the wrong end of the stick as firmly as one of the spaniels. 'Zac could meet your sister, have Sunday lunch, that sort of thing.' He glanced again at my annoyed mother, who had a huge blue bruise forming along the side of her face. 'Everyone's going to think I beat you,' he said glumly.

'Oh, I think Mum will be dining out on this for months,' I said cheerily. 'I don't think you need worry about that. And Zac and I ought to get back.' I looked at him where he was standing a little away from our family group, arms folded and pretending not to listen. 'Work, and all that.'

'So, you'll both come for lunch on Sunday?' Mum sounded uncharacteristically eager. And a little frail. Maybe she wanted me to give all the gossip on my 'new relationship' which, as it wasn't any kind of relationship, she'd not heard a word about. Maybe she just wanted us there to mitigate the effect of my sister, who could be rather forceful and would, no doubt, spend the weekend telling Mum that she should be giving up running at her advanced age and take to crochet and Agatha Christie, like a decently elderly grandmother.

'I... We... errr... I can't,' I said, at exactly the same time as Zac said, 'That sounds lovely, thank you.' I tried to eyeball him sternly, but he refused to make eye contact, so I had to finish with, 'I'll let you know.'

'Your mother will make her special trifle,' Dad said hopefully. 'Er, if she's up to it,' he added, when Mum glared at him.

Zac and I left them to it and went back out to the car. The relief of having seen that my mother was really all right, and not my father's version of all right, which would have had her making her 'special trifle' with two broken legs and her neck in a brace, made me giddy and talkative.

'Thank you so much for driving all this way,' I trilled, as we climbed out of the town, leaving its lights swinging behind us as the sea heaved. 'You really didn't have to.'

'I did,' he oversteered slightly. 'It could have been bad. You weren't to know.' He flashed me a sideways look which I saw reflected in the windscreen. 'You needed to see her.'

'Yes.' My brain ran away with visions of what could have been, my mother critically injured, operated on, dying there in that hospital bed whilst I carried on partying with my workmates. 'Yes, now I know she's all right, it's not so...' Then I stopped. I'd been *going* to say that it wasn't so bad, that the anxiety was manageable when I knew everyone was okay. That the awful fear that rose around me in the middle of the night, threatening to suffocate me, could be stilled for a while. But it was Zac. So I couldn't. 'Not so worrying,' I finished, which made no sense really, but 'worry' was what I actually felt, downgraded to something socially acceptable. Something non-prejudicial.

'I like your parents.' Zac swung the car up over the hill and the wheels found grip amid the gravel. 'They've certainly got bickering down to an art form.'

'They've weathered thirty-three years of marriage, there must be some kind of affection there. You didn't have to agree to Sunday lunch, though. Now I've got to think of a way to get you out of it.'

'I don't mind coming to Sunday lunch.' He gave a brief grin. 'Your mother's making her special trifle, after all.'

I sighed. 'Stop it. I know, I know, you were just being polite, but I really can't bear them all grilling us about our non-existent relationship and having one of those awkward conversations where we have to pretend to be in love whilst hating one another. I've read those books. I think I have to have a secret baby at some point too.' I watched the road flash past. The relief was still there, burning through my veins, making me talk to Zac as though he were a friend.

'I'm sure we can leave the baby out of it. And we can just say we're workmates. They aren't going to force us to have sex in front of them to prove we're in a relationship, are they?' He frowned. 'They seem fairly normal and not given to that sort of thing.'

'You haven't met my sister,' I said darkly.

'And what's your objection to Sunday lunch with your family?'

I wanted to say 'you coming along,' but didn't. He *had* just driven me on a round trip of sixty miles, waited in a boring hospital room without complaining or chatting up nurses and been polite and pleasant to my family. 'I don't have one. I go over about once a month anyway.'

'There you go, then.'

'But you can't seriously want to go for a meal with people you hardly know!'

There was a moment in which the only sound was the thrum of the car engine and the crack of the grit under the wheels. A moment in which I realised that I didn't know much about Zac at all. 'I know you,' he said at last. 'And, let's face it, Sunday lunch is always a winner. Plus, trifle.'

I was smiling. I couldn't help it. I *knew* it was partly because of his cheery tone and the talking up of the trifle, but the way my spirits rose as I fought to stop the grin spreading made me not care. 'As long as we don't have to do the pretend relationship. I'll ring them tomorrow to check on Mum and tell them we just work together.'

'Damn. No secret baby, then.'

'No. I think it's for the best.'

We both laughed then, a more relaxed kind of laugh, something that sounded as though we both meant it, and finally something inside me let a little tension unspool into the night.

6

The rest of the week was busy.

More clients than usual wanted to come in. Normally we offered counselling to anyone who wanted it after the initial consultation, and the take-up was around one in five. Now, with Christmas on the horizon and short-term jobs available in shops and Post Offices, more people were faced with the possibility of returning to work and the resultant anxiety, doubt and interview fear that came with it.

Zac and I alternated possession of the interview room, and I found an empty office which had been occupied by two members of YouIn2Work whose jobs had been rationalised out of existence with the merger. We turned the empty office into Interview Room Two, which enabled both of us to help clients at the same time, but the reason the room was empty hung over me. I could feel the weight of redundancy whenever I sat in there.

So it came as no real surprise to me that I woke in the small hours of Sunday morning and lay in the darkness feeling panic binding my ribcage and stopping my breathing.

Redundancy is real. It's not just Michael trying to get us to work harder. I could be out of a job, and then what? Stay here and try to find something else after Christmas? But what? And in the meantime the debts still need paying.

I could go home. Back to Scarborough, to the old house on the cliff, to my old bedroom, but the debts STILL need paying and there won't be the money... and can I really face it, am I really up to applying for something and starting something new? Learning new stuff? When I can barely concentrate on the stuff I already know?

I got out of bed and went to the window where at least the air was breathable. Cold, scything into my lungs.

Mum could have been killed by that car. Dad would have to sell the house, what would he do? Move up to Durham, nearer to Eva? Then I'd have nowhere to go back to if all this falls apart.

I can't lose this job. I CAN'T. But Zac seems so professional, such a safe pair of hands, can they all tell that I'm really just making it up as I go along? That so many of my clients getting work is just a fluke?

I felt sick, but being sick wasn't an option because I couldn't breathe if I was vomiting. The band around my ribcage got tighter and tighter and my heart was splitting itself against the bones of my chest as I tried to force in air which was suddenly as thick as treacle.

No money. Nowhere to go. No job. On the streets, sleeping in the park. Begging outside the station.

And then all the Instagram pictures that I'd seen before my friends had made me block Gareth came flashing in a montage sequence into my mind. All those images of the Greek islands, the iridescent blue water, the sun, his shiny new life with his beautiful girlfriend, while I starved and caught TB and died, ignored, on a trolley in an A&E department of some big city hospital.

The walls, those carefully constructed walls that I imagined as sturdy Yorkshire stone surrounding my terror and my inadequacy began to crumble. I felt each crack coming, dreaded its appearance but was powerless to stop it, and ended up back on my bed, curled into a foetal ball and sobbing.

The light of the slow-dawning morning brought some relief and about five minutes' sleep. Before I knew it, Sophie was knocking on my door to tell me that Zac was downstairs and had I forgotten that we were going to lunch with my parents? And, oh dear God, did I want to borrow her Touche Éclat because I was going to need some serious help if I was going out with my face like that...

I uncoiled myself from the tangle that my duvet and I were in and sat up. Sophie threw her make-up bag at me and headed back downstairs. I looked at myself in her tiny handbag mirror. I hadn't forgotten about lunch, but half of me had hoped that Zac wouldn't turn up and the other half had been too busy trying to keep breathing. Clearly I should ring my parents and cancel. Tell Zac I'd got norovirus or something. Take my tablets and go back to bed for the day, deep-breathe my way through Sunday and hope that I looked less like a corpse in time for work tomorrow.

But that would be to admit weakness. That would let the panic win. If I let the fear and doubt and horror have its way this time, then next time it would be so much harder to fight off. And, besides, I couldn't, *daren't*, let any failing show in front of Zac. I'd even have staggered out with noro, just so that Zac couldn't win this point.

When I got downstairs, ten minutes frantic make-up application later, I found him in the hallway, with Cav. They were looking at Cav's bike, which was upside down, wheels off again, outside the understairs cupboard.

'...and then I upgraded to the carbon fibre frame,' Cav was saying.

'Ah, Ruby, there you are.' Zac moved slowly back towards the door as though he was worried that Cav might go for him with a bag of spanners. 'Ready?'

There was a note in his voice that said *please be ready, please don't disappear back upstairs and make me listen to more about bikes through the ages.* But his face was friendly, open, engaged, as though Cav and he had been having a simply fascinating discussion and my arrival had meant that it, sadly, had to come to an end. He could have listened to bike talk all day.

I just grunted. Now, with the grey light of the short day coming in, the panic of the night seemed stupid. Overblown. Of course, the effects of the tablets helped with the assumed calm, but even so. It was easier to see in the light, in all ways.

'Fine then. We don't want to be late. Nice to meet you.' Zac reversed even faster away, when it looked as though Cav may want to continue talking about his bike. 'But we ought to hurry.'

The Discovery was parked at the end of the short driveway, blocking my Skoda. I frowned at it, and then him. 'What is the deal with you and my car?'

'Sorry, there was nowhere else to park. It's fine, I'll drive.'

I frowned again. 'But I...'

'...Have control issues. I know. But it makes more sense, otherwise we're going to have to play Car Shuffle and we're already a little bit late.'

Behind us, the front door opened and Cav appeared, pushing the bike. He was lycra'd up for a long ride but didn't look beyond engaging Zac in more in-depth discussion, and we scrambled into the Discovery with almost indecent haste.

Once we'd got in, Zac blew out a long sigh. 'Seriously? You

share a house with him? It's like *What We Do In The Shadows*, only with bikes.'

'They're my friends,' I said stiffly. I didn't add 'and it's cheap', because I really did not want questions about why I didn't have a lovely little flat of my own.

Cav cycled past and I gave him a little wave. I got 'serious racing face' in return.

It crossed my mind then to wonder again about Zac's 'complicated' living arrangements. Arrangements that let him drive randomly to Scarborough one evening, or spend a Sunday out for lunch without having to check in with phone calls. Maybe he *was* married and just had really good alibis. 'Do you have your own place?'

'Er.' Zac raised his eyebrows at his own reflection. 'Like I said, it's...'

'Complicated. Yes.' Well, if he didn't want to talk about it, that was fine. It meant that I could pull the same stunt on him.

'You look tired. Were you out last night?'

I looked at Zac's reflection in the window as we drove. 'Yes,' I said, seizing on the explanation. 'A late one, with Priya. She wanted a hand with some organising.'

'The Matterhorn?' he asked and for a second I was totally confused.

'The *what?*' Then I remembered that I'd told him she was a secret climber. 'Oh. Um, yes. We were... looking at flights.'

'She's not going in the winter though, surely?' There was a light in his eye, a slight curve to his mouth, and I turned and looked at him accusingly. 'I can keep this up all day,' he said, cheerfully. 'I know perfectly well Priya is to rock climbing what I am to all-in wrestling, but I just want to see how far you'll go to keep your story intact.'

'You bastard,' I said, without any real rancour.

'Yeah, sorry.' He was properly smiling now and I was almost winded by the sudden realisation that Priya was right, Zac was actually quite good-looking if you ignored the daft hairstyle and the unstructured clothes that made him look as though he'd been dressed by a personal shopper who thought he worked in TV.

This was an uncomfortable thought. And also an unaccustomed one. My libido had fallen off the same cliff I'd imagined pushing Gareth off and I hadn't really 'noticed' men since we had split up. Frankly, if my sex drive did have to come back, I'd rather it didn't choose to come roaring in batting its eyelashes at Zac, of all people. The competition. The man who could see me out of a job. I breathed carefully.

The secret is to breathe.

In, out. Don't give the panic headspace.

I shuffled in the seat and did what I usually did when my anxiety began to rise, I stuck on a smile and brightened my voice. 'Anyway, I ought to brief you about my family before you get the full effect. You've met Mum and Dad, and my sister, Eva, will be there with her two children. Her husband is a doctor who, I suspect, chooses to volunteer for on-call at weekends to get out of gatherings like this.'

'Okay. I think I can cope with that. Dysfunctional?'

'No, not in the slightest. Well, Eva is a bossy cow, but that's older sisters. Her children are a bit wild, but she calls it "spirited" and my mother calls it "badly managed" and that's about the limit of our dysfunction.'

I opened my mouth to ask him about his family, but then closed it again. I'd only get 'complicated' again, I was sure. I'd given him all he was getting about my lot and I'd briefed Mum on the phone not to mention anything about my recent past. Gareth, the breakdown, none of that was anything to do with Zac, except as a nice little opening for an interview that began 'Ruby can't cope with the stress of the job and I can do better'.

* * *

Sunday lunch was fine. Better than fine, actually. I'd never realised before how much stuff got fired at me over the table and having Zac there formed a kind of barrier against the personal questions. I'd explained we were workmates until I was hyperventilating with desperation, but they'd all done the soft smile and knowing looks until I resorted to sulky silence and picking the pine nuts off my carrots. Mum knew I hated pine nuts. I had no idea why she persisted in putting them in.

Eva spent the meal 'performance parenting', as she always did in front of strangers. It made a nice change from her usual 'sitting on her phone and letting Mum and Dad manage Albie and Xavier'. The boys seemed slightly intimidated by Zac and his height and therefore didn't riot quite as much as usual and we didn't get gravy up the curtains. The special trifle was well received, especially by Dad, and Mum seemed, apart from the bruises, to have made an excellent recovery from her accident. The spaniels were still in disgrace and in the utility room.

After lunch, we walked down the cliff to the beach, with Dad explaining how there used to be a caravan park and a corner shop between our house and the cliff edge, and now there was just a road, a small wood and then a severe plunge down towards the ocean, and a beach which contained some incongruous shelving units. It was a somewhat sobering conversation, especially since Dad did a lot of sound effects of the storm of 2013. Fortunately, though, today the tide was out and we could all distract ourselves from the seemingly inevitable journey towards entropy and decay by watching the two small boys poking seaweed with a stick.

All in all, Zac and I drove back to York in a state of well-fed contentment.

'They're nice. I like them,' Zac said, breaking the several-mile silence.

'They have their moments, but they're not bad.' I rolled my head against the back of the seat. 'Xav can be a bit much. I've suggested ADHD to Eva, but she won't hear of it. I'm sure when he starts school he's going to be flagged up.'

'People don't always want to hear their fears confirmed,' Zac said, almost as though he wasn't thinking about it. 'Ignorance is bliss and all that.'

I thought back to when I'd got together with Gareth. I'd introduced him to Priya and sat back to wait for her excited gushing praise, so when she'd looked at me directly for a minute and then said carefully, 'He's a bit of a player, don't you think, Rubes?' I'd ignored it. Rationalised it away as Gareth trying over-hard to make an impression. Being flirty was what he *did*. It was who he was.

And when that turned out to be literally true, Priya had been kind enough not to point out that 'she told me so'. She also skated over the fact that she'd repeatedly tried to alert me to the fact that Gareth probably wasn't telling me the whole truth about what happened when he was working away, and I'd brushed it all aside. Underneath, I'd known exactly what Gareth was really like, but I'd tried so hard to turn him into the perfect boyfriend that I couldn't acknowledge it, even to myself. That ignorance hadn't led to bliss, though, had it?

'I'll see you tomorrow then.' Zac pulled up at the kerb outside the house. I was startled that we were back already, I must have been so lost in thought and conversation I'd missed most of the journey. Cav had the bike upside down again and was doing something to the chain in the entryway. All the downstairs lights were on, streaming through the windows so the house stood in a pool of brightness, and we could hear Sophie singing, even from the car.

'Don't remind me. I've got a new client coming in, which is a bit annoying. I was hoping to cruise downhill to Christmas with everyone too busy to need me.' I scrabbled under my seat for my bag.

Zac looked ahead, without saying anything, while I gathered up my coat and put it on. Just before I opened the door to slither out into the cold of the evening, he put a hand on my arm. 'The new client,' he said. 'It's a lady called Miriam?'

I stared at him. 'How do you know that?'

Zac sighed. 'I don't know what it is with this place, Ruby. Or whether they are trying to play games with us, divide and conquer or something?'

I felt a kind of fear prickle up my back. 'Why?'

'Because they aren't playing fair with either of us. I know they want us to kind of compete for the job, but they should realise that we don't work the same way and they shouldn't be trying to compare our working methods.'

'Is that what they're doing? I thought they were just seeing which of us was most successful at getting people back into work.' I knew there was a slight smugness in my tone. I'd got Taylor into work, Samantha onto a training course, these both counted as successes. As far as I'd heard, Zac hadn't managed to place any of his clients yet, and Bob was bombarding us with emails saying he'd been unfairly treated.

Zac looked at me, almost sadly. 'It's never that simple,' he said, and I wasn't sure if he was speaking from insider knowledge or whether he was trying to unsettle my complacency. 'It's all about whose face fits. Who's going to work best with the new model for the company.'

'Going forward,' I put in, because I was still fairly sure that I came out ahead, however they were judging us.

He smiled. 'Moving in any direction.' Another sigh. 'Only, Miriam used to be my client. I worked with her for nearly a year in the old place.'

'And you're not taking her up again?'

He shook his head. 'Miriam is... difficult. I just hope they haven't decided to pass her on to you to...' he tailed off.

'To, what? What sort of difficult?' I felt the anxiety give a tug, but then my pride cut in. 'I am trained, Zac. I didn't just wander into this job after a previous work experience stint in Boots.'

Zac looked straight ahead. A small black cat was creeping along the pavement on a mission of its own among the ice-shiny slabs and overhanging frost-stiffened foliage. 'I don't know. I'm just a bit worried that they've already made their decision about who goes and who stays and they may be playing games with us.'

I thought of benign Michael, who'd always kept a hand of jelly on the tiller of YouIn2Work. Playing games, apart from mannered hands of Bridge, didn't really seem his thing. But then I remembered the Grey Man and Beehive Woman, who could, presumably, talk him into anything, including using jargon like 'going forward'. Before they'd arrived, he would just have said 'in the future'. Like a normal person.

'Like giving me a difficult client to show up that I'm not all that?' I didn't know whether to feel insulted, afraid or slightly exhilarated. Whether Those Above thought that I'd be so easily defeated, or that they were giving me a challenge to live up to. 'What sort of difficult is Miriam?'

He shrugged. 'It's hard to say. She was difficult about appointments, wouldn't turn up for weeks and then came in every day for a fortnight and when I pulled her up about it, she stropped off and made complaining phone calls for about a year. She's confrontational, loud, stroppy, won't listen to suggestions – all of that, and, yes, I realise that, among our clients, that hardly makes her a standout, but... Well. Just be careful.' Then he smiled. 'I really did enjoy lunch today.'

He clearly felt he'd said everything he wanted to on the subject of work. Well, that was fair enough, even though I did suspect that he was trying, ever so slightly, to scare me. I'd dealt with difficult clients before. I opened the door. The sound of Sophie's murdering of 'Oh Little Town of Bethlehem' grew louder. 'Thank you.'

I meant it. After all, by giving me a heads-up, Zac may have just ruined his chance of having the upper hand in the competition for our position.

'Goodbye, Ruby.'

The Discovery slid slightly as it pulled away. The roads were icy again this evening. It wasn't just the cold cutting through me, though, as I shivered on the pavement; the thought that YouBack2Work had already made its decision about who would stay and who would go left me with a feeling as empty as the bleak dark that arched overhead.

Plus Sophie's voice was slicing the night like cheese wire.

* * *

As I'd been forewarned, I got into work early the next day. Early meant I'd been able to get the car into the car park, so I pulled with abandon into one of the spaces usually occupied by Payroll. To hell with it. I could be assertive too. There was no sign of Zac's Discovery yet.

Priya was just tucking her little car into its usual space as I got out, and she waved to me. 'Blimey, you're early. Good weekend? I hear you and Zac went for Sunday lunch?'

I sighed. Gossip ran faster through our offices than the smell of tuna sandwiches. I was used to it and knew it would be dead before the day was out. 'The rumour mill has got its wheels in a twist. He came for lunch with my family.'

Priya bounced. 'Did your mum do her special trifle? I love her special trifle. I must get the recipe. Anything to wean Nettie away from the spinach whirl.'

'Yes.' I sighed. 'Mum did her special trifle. And Eva and the boys were there.'

Priya made a face. 'And Zac's still speaking to you?'

'They were restrained.'

'What by, industrial-strength duct tape?' The boys were, as Priya said, another nail in the coffin of her reproductive drive. 'Anyway, you'll be pleased to know that you're practically married to him now, by the office staff anyway, and they may throw you together into a mistletoe-lined room, if you aren't careful.'

I couldn't help but grin. Priya was so desperate for me to settle down and come round for drinks and dinners with her and Nettie in a couple. She said me coming on my own made the house look untidy.

We walked in together through the front door. Karen wasn't even on Reception yet, although there were noises from the office of coats being hung up and computers switched on. It was still almost dark outside, a sulky sun slowly painting the Minster a gloomy grey as it rose.

Priya's office was snug and warm. She gave me two squares of slightly moist chocolate and I perched on her desk while she fired up her machine and sorted through the endless series of Post-it notes that she'd left herself on Friday, stuck all over the surface of her desk like a very easy jigsaw.

'Zac thinks they aren't playing fair with our... with *my* job.' I nibbled at a corner of the chocolate.

'Well, they do seem to be taking their time, don't they?' Priya was bustling about in the cupboard, sorting out biros. 'Presumably they must know how both of you work by now.' She turned around to face me, her hair swinging. 'Although office gossip has it that Zac is fancied by over half the female staff, and his going may cause a backwash of oestrogen and eyeliner that carries us to the brink of destruction.'

'So, he's going?' I felt suddenly cold. 'Really?'

'I dunno. I'd have thought they'd do the deed pretty fast, once they decide. Save a salary, and all that. So maybe it's not a done deal?'

'But that's the word on the grapevine – that it's him, not me, to leave?'

Priya patted my arm gently. 'That's what you want, isn't it?'

I suddenly couldn't eat the rest of the chocolate and slipped it into my pocket. Priya would only ask awkward questions if she thought the potential of Zac leaving made me go off my confectionary. I left her sorting out her work for the day and went next door into the shared office. Zac's computer screen was surrounded by tinsel and there was a photograph I'd never seen before in a frame on his desk. A wedding picture, of a very pretty woman in a very overblown dress on the arm of a man who must be Zac, although it was hard to tell without the startled hair and jeans and jacket look. He had the sideways smile and the square chin, the dark eyes and the lanky height, but, I realised now, I hardly ever looked at Zac's actual face.

I picked up the photograph in its wooden frame. The woman really was very pretty, in an understated way that spoke of hours in the make-up chair. The man, Zac, was smiling down at her with a look of mischief and incipient recklessness, as though they were both about to shout 'FOOLED YOU!' and tear off the wedding finery to reveal ordinary clothes, then fall about laughing. There was also a tenderness in the way the couple looked at one another.

I put the picture down, carefully squaring it up exactly where it had been. Had Gareth and I ever looked at one another like that? Probably not. Whenever I'd looked at him, he'd seemed to be doing something daft, pulling a face or trying to see if he was growing hairs out of his nose like his dad. There had, I reflected, usually been much more exasperation than affection in any exchanged glances.

And, just like that, I realised I no longer missed Gareth, as if the gentle smiles in that photograph wiped out the image of him that I'd built in my mind. He wouldn't have held my arm like that, for a picture. He'd have had one hand on my bum and been trying to look down my cleavage, or been making stupid jokes that wouldn't even have made the 'cracker selection'. What did I *really* miss about him? A presence, someone to share the bills with, someone to cook for – and had he ever cooked for me? No, what I really missed was having a boyfriend. Not the man himself, just the role filled.

I sat down at my desk, fished in my pocket, and finished off the chocolate.

Yes. When I probed my memory, it didn't throw up wonderful instances of communion between Gareth and I. No long walks in summer silence, hand in hand. No unspoken jokes that could crease us up without a word being said. Nothing that would have made us into the couple in that picture on Zac's desk. Just lots of sweaty sex, arguments over meals, a good-natured falling into a relationship that suited us both but never had any real loving passion, unless it was his, for football. And, evidently, my gorgeous blonde replacement. I silently wished her well and hoped she was ready to mother a grown-up.

Zac was a little bit late. He arrived on a gust of cold air, his hair tipped with frost and several scarves wrapped round his neck.

'Bloody cold out there,' he said, unparcelling himself. 'Snow for Christmas, you reckon?'

I forced my eyes to look at his face. Not to take in the general outline, the 'tall, upswept hair, shoulders, legs' that said 'this is Zac', but his actual face. Brown eyes, straight nose, dark eyelashes that gave him a slight appearance of wearing mascara. Square chin and cheekbones that gave his face definition.

'Why are you looking at me like that?' Zac squinted down his nose. 'Is there something stuck to me? I had to run the gauntlet of Accounts coming in, they've already got the party poppers out, so I wouldn't put it past them to have reached the "kick me" sign stage.' He glanced at his back view. 'And it's still a month to Christmas. They are going to be *unbearable*.' Another suspicious look at me. 'You're still staring.'

'Sorry.' I pointed my eyes at my screen. 'I just realised that I don't really know what you look like. If I ever had to give your description to the police, I'd struggle.'

'That does not allay my fears. Is Michael threatening to have me killed and dumped in the river or something?'

'Well, it would be one way to get rid of you,' I said, without thinking and then realised how harsh it sounded. 'I didn't mean...'

But he was grinning again. 'Ah, he's old, I reckon I could fight him off.' There was a complacency to his words, as though he knew he was never going to be 'got rid of' in any context. The tiny worm of doubt crept back into my brain again. 'Coffee?'

He didn't wait for my answer, but disappeared through to the interview room, from where I could hear him wrestling with the coffee machine and he came back bearing two mugs whilst I was still trying to get my computer to acknowledge my presence.

'Here. Watch out for your keyboard.' He handed me a mug slopping full and went back to his side of the office with his, sitting on the corner of his desk and staring out of the window in an unfocused sort of way. 'What time is Miriam due in?'

'Half past nine.'

He sipped and then made a face at his coffee. 'Right. I'm going to be a long way away when that happens.'

I wondered if this was a power play. Make me nervous, unsettle me. 'I'm sure she will be fine.'

Eyebrows raised over the mug. 'Okay. You just keep on believing that. I'm going through to the office to check over some CVs they were sorting out for me. Scream when you're finished, I've got someone coming in and I need the room after you.'

'Scream?'

'Or bang your head against the wall. Honestly, it will be mild compared to what I've done after a visit from Miriam.' He swung himself off the desk and over to the door. 'I'll remove all the breakables.'

Yep, he was definitely trying to scare me.

I checked my emails and there was one from the bank, mentioning – just *mentioning* in the lightest possible tones – the bank loan and encouraging me to make increased payments to clear it off faster. My throat threatened to swell and I had to breathe slowly and carefully to prevent the panic from rising. I *knew* I owed them. I was paying it back at the only speed possible to me, did they think I was keeping secret millions from them and only paying the loan at the minimum rate for fun?

Grounding myself was usually the best way to ward off these feelings. I looked around the office. Noticed anew the off-centre window, the uneven flooring and the walls which met and joined at odd angles in unexpected places. The smell of hot electronics, and paper, old dinners, paint upon paint and the cleaners' spray.

It was as familiar to me as the inside of my car, and I usually paid about as much attention to it, but now it was taking on a new aspect, tinged with the fear of loss. No, forget that fear. Look at the details, derail the brain from its cycle of worry with minutiae, force it to pay attention to the tiny things and use them to blot the bigger things out.

Tiny things. The scatter of staples across Zac's desk. The sun just creeping through the corner of the window, uncertain as to whether it was going to stay. The photograph, which Zac had moved slightly so I now couldn't see the picture from where I sat.

And breathe.

I couldn't lose this job. I *couldn't*. Apart from the fact that it was my job and I loved it, I knew that prejudice and narrow-mindedness would make another job like this hard to find. My three weeks' off with 'stress' would count against me in another appointment. They might not be allowed to ask about my mental health at the interview, but you could bet there would be a 'health questionnaire' as part of the process and the merest sniff of anti-anxiety medication or extended time off would flag me up as unstable. Unreliable. Unable to cope with sudden crises. I could explain to them until I was purple in the face that the 'crisis' that had precipitated my need for antidepressant medication was a one-off, never-to-be-repeated love-life disaster, but it would be too late. I'd be labelled 'flaky'. Probably in a handwritten note attached to my file, destined to be destroyed should I ever challenge it.

Plus, those bank loans were not going to be manageable on National Minimum Wage.

My hands shook a little as I sipped coffee from the overfull mug and, when my phone rang and made me jump, I spilled a tiny bit on my keyboard.

Zac must never know.

It was only Reception, to tell me that my appointment was here. Over Karen's voice, I could hear another woman speaking, a loud rattle of complaint in a tone like gravel in a tin can. That must be Miriam and it sounded as though Zac hadn't exaggerated at all, damn him.

I made my way down to the interview room to meet her, holding my coffee in front of me like a shield, and slightly glad of the distraction from my circling thoughts.

She was there before me. Sitting, uninvited, in the best chair, smoking, despite all the signs thanking her for not smoking; mid-fifties, thin in a way that made her tendons stick out, as though she smoked all three meals a day. Hair bleached so often it was fragile. Wearing an expensive coat and trainers, cheap scarf knotted around her neck. She didn't bother to look up as I came in.

'You're not allowed to smoke in here,' I said mildly.

She gave me a look that was both shrewd and challenging. 'I,' she announced, 'can do what I fuckin' like, right?'

I didn't bother to reply, I just sat down opposite her and watched her smoke for a moment. She smoked with long in-breaths, then taking the cigarette out to blow the smoke from the corner of her mouth, like a docker on a furtive tea break.

After a few puffs, she rested the still-lit cigarette on the edge of the box of tissues on the small table next to the chairs and looked at me, sucking her teeth. 'Well, you're an improvement on the last dickhead they told me I had to talk to. At least you know when to shut up.'

In an instant I reached out and stubbed her half-smoked roll-up out on the glass tabletop. The sad scribble of smoke trailed away into nothing and Miriam narrowed her blue-shadowed eyes at me.

''Ere! That's my fag! You can't do that!'

'I,' I enunciated carefully, 'can do what I fucking like, right?'

A pause and I half-braced myself in case the leopard-print bag that squatted under the chair made a swing for my head. But instead, after a few seconds of adrenaline-fuelled silence, Miriam laughed a rattled staccato laugh.

'You've got balls, girl, I like that.' Then she started to unbutton the coat and unwind the scarf. 'Right then. Looks like I'm stoppin'.'

I checked her notes. Miriam had made a job of resisting all attempts to place her in work. She managed financially on what looked like cash-in-hand jobs here and there, badgering the local benefits agency into paying her dribs and drabs, and sharing a council house with her two daughters and their children. She was here because several tethers had reached straining point, and she was about to be denied all payments unless she showed that she was seriously applying for actual, real jobs.

But, oddly enough, I liked her.

Because the first interview was more of a 'getting to know you' chat – not all counsellors were a good fit for all clients, and some clients subsequently decided that 'work counselling' wasn't going to be quite what they thought – we drank coffee and I let Miriam talk. She *liked* talking. I heard how she was enjoying the fact that the offices had moved from Leeds to York, because she now got her travel expenses paid to come to a lovely city and do her Christmas shopping. She told me about her two daughters, their feckless partners and the resulting children, although I didn't quite get to the bottom of how many there were and which belonged to whom, but they made Albie and Xavier sound like models of decorum.

I could see why Zac hadn't got on with her. I could see why people might find her difficult and brittle and confrontational, because she was. But she was also funny, self-deprecatory and sharp with lived wisdom. There were no family photos from Miriam, just wicked little observations and vignettes from what sounded like a tough life, and by the end I didn't just like her, I admired her. But quietly, because any hint of patronisation would, I suspected, have ended in complaints. And – I eyed her handbag with suspicion – possible knuckledusters.

Once her hour was up, and she'd been told to make another appointment and left winding herself back into scarves and her coat, I went back through to the office, where Zac was hiding in a corner, trying to look as though he was doing something important.

'Well, she didn't disembowel you with her teeth,' he said, looking at me over his shoulder. 'So that's a plus.'

'I quite like her.' I sat behind my computer, ready to type up my notes. 'She's sparky.'

'So is an electrical storm.' Zac made a twisted-mouth face at me. 'She's lulling you into a false sense of security, I tell you. Next time, she'll be shouting about her rights and threatening us with the ombudsman. I don't know if she actually knows what that is, mind.'

I felt suddenly defensive on Miriam's part. 'She's brighter than you think.' I remembered that thin face, slightly out-of-date make-up and the lines around her mouth that said she'd probably been smoking since she was twelve. 'I think she's had a hard life.'

'Maybe, but the fact remains, she has to look for work or get her money cut.' Zac came to stand in front of his desk, blocking the light.

'Yes, but do you have to be so... so *reductionist* about it? There's obviously something going on there that's stopping her from working. She seems desperate to get out of the house, her grand-children sound as though they are only one step up from being fed out of saucers on the doorstep. They make Eva's pair sound like cherubs. Although,' I added hastily, 'not the sort of cherubs with bows and arrows because that would be a very dangerous idea.'

He shook his head slowly. 'You always see the best in people, don't you?'

'I have to try. Otherwise what's the point of this job? We could just sanction them until they're starved into job seeking.' I knew I sounded sharp, but this was an argument I'd had before. With Gareth. Who couldn't understand why everyone didn't walk into jobs with the ease that he did.

'Ruby, it's all right. We're on the same side here.'

But we're not, are we? I wanted to say. We're fighting for the same job. And I don't know who's winning, and I don't know what your real game is. *And I need this job.*

I went back to typing up my notes and he, seeming to feel that he'd said enough, sloped off to see his next client.

7

Priya and I sat in the little café by the river. We'd spent the Saturday Christmas shopping together, mainly because, as usual, she needed someone to help her carry her bags. But she'd promised me coffee and cake as a reward for struggling through the crowds, getting rained on and standing outside shops whilst she picked up and put down their entire selection of stock, so I went along. She brought the coffees over to our table, which was right by the window, looking out over the swollen brown waters that swirled and plunged under the nearby bridge.

She sipped at her coffee and regarded the big gooey bun on the plate beside it with almost indecent anticipation. 'Are you getting Zac anything for Christmas?'

'What?' I nearly choked on my cappuccino. 'No! Of course I'm not. Why?'

'He asked me what you might like for Christmas, so...' Her eyes were mischievous over the foam.

'Oh bugger. You could have told me this whilst we were in the middle of Fenwicks, rather than now, Pri.'

'I forgot.' Priya stared over my shoulder at the crowds we'd just extricated ourselves from, massing across Skeldergate Bridge in both directions. There were shoppers everywhere, shouldering their way through the sleety drizzle with their heads down, adorned with bags, like herds of buffalo had been driven through M&S. 'Sorry.'

'But he's the enemy! We agreed, he's the opposition! What kind of person buys Christmas presents for their nemesis?'

Priya lowered her cup.

I took a deep breath. 'Do you like him, Pri? I mean, I don't know what to make of him. He seems just so... *nice.* Mostly, I mean. I don't like the way he is with some of his clients, like he thinks they just need a good scolding to get out there and get a job as a brain surgeon, but apart from that...' I trailed off. Surely I should be working up a case against Zac? Amazingly it wasn't just my tablets stopping me from being righteously indignant about the way he'd been foisted on me; about the whole job situation. He was good at what he did and he didn't even have the decency to be a shitty human being.

She jerked her head in an awkward sort of movement.

'He's got a bit of a "holier than thou" attitude though.' I picked on the only part of Zac's character that could really stand up to a bit of assassination. 'All this "my life is complicated" stuff, like it's designed to make my life look like it's straightforward, and therefore anything I say about, well, about the depression or the anxiety, it's just going to make me look a bit...'

Priya kicked me under the table.

'What? That hurt. You'd better not have broken that ornament I got for Mum...'

The kicking got harder and more metronomic. She'd dropped her head and was whispering into her coat collar like a spy communicating with HQ, but I couldn't hear above the background hubbub of the café.

'Maybe I could get him something like a whoopee cushion?'

'Hello, Ruby. Priya.'

The voice came from behind my right shoulder and I jumped with surprise and stiffened with embarrassed annoyance. 'Oh God.' Terror about how much of the previous conversation he may have heard made my brain go suddenly cold.

'Hi, Zac.' Priya stopped kicking me but kept her head down. 'Fancy seeing you here,' she said in the flat note that told me she'd arranged the meeting.

'I thought you lived in Leeds?' I spoke to him without turning round. 'Why are you here?'

'Christmas shopping.' He swung himself into the seat next to me, with an evident lack of shopping about his person. He didn't *seem* annoyed. My mind started to loosen with relief, he couldn't be this insouciant if he'd heard me assassinating his work character, could he? So maybe he hadn't heard any of it. It *was* noisy in here, after all.

'There are shops in Leeds. I've been there. Big shops. Nice shops. Why do you need to come to York to shop?'

'You sound as though you aren't pleased to see me.'

I looked accusingly across at Priya. She'd practically tortoised her way inside her coat so that only the top of her forehead was sticking up from the velvet collar, and she'd slithered down low in her chair. 'Zacsaidsomethingaboutshoppingbeingboring,' she muttered indistinctly into thick red velvet.

'Priya was trying to tell me that Christmas shopping is the epitome of an experience in York,' Zac said cheerfully, and my relief increased. 'He *couldn't* have heard me and still be this sunnily disposed. 'But then, she also promised to buy me a coffee, which hasn't happened yet, so I'm beginning to doubt her opinions all round.'

Priya got up with such speed that the word 'alacrity' was

insufficient. She practically left skid marks across the floor. 'Coffee,' she said and disappeared down the stairs.

'Is she setting us up or something?' I stared suspiciously after her retreating red wool back.

'Or something, I think.' Zac settled his elbows on the table, which rocked. 'I don't think either of us want to be set up, do we?'

I thought about his 'it's complicated'. The wedding photograph on his desk. 'No I don't.'

'Good. Neither do I. I actually think she just wants someone to help carry the shopping.'

Despite myself, I laughed. 'That's usually my job.'

'I am sure you will bear the disappointment manfully.'

We lapsed into silence. I remembered what I'd been saying when Priya started kicking me and had the dreadful, creeping feeling that maybe Zac was just covering up having overheard. I'd mentioned the anxiety and depression. *Had* he picked that up? Had I just handed Zac the weapon he needed to defeat me?

To cover up any trace that he may be searching for, I became ultra-bright. 'I love Christmas, don't you? Best time of the year, and Pri is right, York is such a wonderful city in December. Have you seen the decorations all lit up yet?'

'Er, yes.' Zac stared over my head, out at the darkening sky beyond. 'I work here, remember?'

'Well yes, but other parts of the city, I mean. Not just outside the office. Down on Parliament Street, where they've got lights in the trees that flash so it looks like snow falling.' I thought for a second. 'Purple snow, which does seem odd, now I come to think of it. And down Fossgate, where all the shops have lights in the windows and the market...'

'Yes, all right, you can stop talking like the tourist brochure.' He smiled at me. It was a bland smile, innocent even. No sign that he knew I was talking to try to distract him. To baffle him with the mass of words so that he'd forget any mention of depression. I didn't know why I thought this, because the torrent of talk actually made me sound more as though I'd overdone my medication. 'I haven't seen all the lights, but there's plenty of time for that.'

Plenty of time. Did he mean this year? Or was he anticipating taking over the job and having many future years to stroll around the streets, relishing the illuminations?

Priya came back with his coffee and he wrapped his hands around the mug as though he were cold, which seemed strange in this overheated and tiny space. People bustled in and out constantly, packages and parcels swinging and clonking against other customers, amid good-humoured commiserations about the grey weather, the early darkness, the expense of the season. The smell of wet coats rose and fell above the pungent coffee aroma and the scent of baking from the kitchen downstairs, and there was a concentrated cosiness about being in here whilst everyone went about their business.

Zac was looking around now. He'd stopped staring out at the river, which was being enveloped by the night, and was glancing at the other customers. His eyes flickered from face to face and I wondered what he was looking for.

I watched him cautiously out of the side of my eye. He was wearing a big grey duffel coat, unbuttoned to show a bright yellow distinctly hand-knitted jumper which seemed to sit halfway up his torso as though it were much too small, and he'd taken off a red knitted hat when he came in, so his hair was flatter than usual. There was a scattering of melting sleet still on his shoulders, soaking into the grey wool of the coat and the warmth of the café after the cold outside had made his cheeks flush.

He looked wholesome and scrubbed, and open-hearted. Exactly like a counsellor should look. I was wearing knee-length flat boots, jeans and a hoodie with the slogan 'I'm sorry I'm late; I didn't want to come'. I looked like a student who's got lost on their way to Freshers' Week. The contrast between my uneasy and too-young clothes and his professional look made me feel 'wrong' here. As though Zac was laughing at me. As though I wasn't quite good enough.

'Look, Pri, I'm going to go.' I drained my coffee.

A look of concern crossed her face. 'But you...'

'You've got Zac to carry your stuff for you. I've just remembered I've got to...' I struggled to think of a plausible excuse. 'I promised to bake some mince pies for Sophie's cake day at her work on Monday.'

Zac and Priya were both looking at me. She could clearly see the panic rising in me and had a sympathetic expression. He just looked baffled by my sudden desire to bake.

'Okay. I'll see you on Monday.' Priya toasted me with her cup. 'Thanks for coming.'

I grabbed my bags and coat and began weaving my way through the crowd coming in. The café was suddenly too small, the air too thick and unbreathable. The dark outside didn't help, it concealed too much, made all the familiar landmarks into patches of shadow. I elbowed my way through the narrow door and out onto the flat riverside, where the water had risen far enough to be lapping threateningly over the concrete embankment, turning the grass into slippery mud. I stared down the river towards the centre of town, where the elegantly arched bridges suspended lights that reflected in the water and the medieval towers on Lendal Bridge sent narrow beams through their arrow-slit windows. *Breathe.*

A hand grabbed my shoulder, but my adrenaline levels were already so high that I couldn't even jump. 'Are you all right?' Zac had followed me, his coat still undone and flapping open to show flashes of the almost fluorescent yellow jumper, like an emergency signal. 'Did I say something?'

Part of me wanted to explain. It wasn't him, it was the crowd, the sudden feeling of inadequacy, that I was failing at adulting. But because it was Zac, because I didn't *quite* trust him not to tell tales to our bosses of my defectiveness and my inability to manage under pressure, I couldn't. I just *couldn't*. Even though to just confess to sudden panic attacks and generalised anxiety would make my behaviour more explicable. It was a catch-22 situation.

'No, it's not you.' I was scanning the street, looking for an escape. 'I've just remembered...'

'Mince pies, yes, you said.' He let go of my shoulder. 'If you're sure. Would you like me to walk you to your car?'

His offer was such an old-fashioned courtesy, and rather kind. But I wanted and needed to be alone, to be in a space I could control. 'No. Thank you.' I took a deep breath. 'Priya needs help, carrying.' Then I turned and half walked, half stumbled my way up the slope, away from the river towards where my car was parked on the top of the hill.

I chanced a quick look back when I reached the pavement, and Zac was still standing there, jumper strobing, watching my retreat. I couldn't see his expression, it was too dark, but he'd got both hands in the pockets of his coat and his shoulders hunched against the cold, as though he was going to watch me all the way.

I hurried my way up towards the bulk of Clifford's Tower. Usually it sat on its hill, a friendly landmark at this end of town, like a rather austere cherry on a bun. Tonight its illuminated walls seemed to shine with menace and its gateway looked sunken between the shoulders of stone, like a defeated shrug.

Breathe. I told myself. It's an old castle, not a dragon on its hoard. But I kept my head down and tried not to look. Even the

Christmas lights that swung above Castlegate and Tower Street looked sinister; sharp points and weird shadows that patterned the skin of passers-by with bilious colours and leprous shapes.

Once inside the car, the panic started to abate. I was in a closed space and alone, which always helped, except in the middle of the night, when I craved the opposite. I sat and gently bumped my head on the steering wheel, berating myself. The panic attacks had become far less frequent lately, and there was every sign that I was managing better. They were gradually being subsumed under the general business of life, and only arose now when I felt overwhelmed.

But *had* I felt overwhelmed? What had triggered it this time, apart from Priya's relentless pursuit of the perfect stationery set for Nettie? There had been nothing particularly unusual about anything – did this mean that the panic and depression were making a reappearance, after having been reasonably well controlled? The doctors were happy with my dosage, these drugs seemed to suit me well, everything had been moving in a positive direction. And then Zac had arrived.

It had been Zac. His quiet confidence. His seeming assured-ness in his role, his general easy-going adaptation to the new location and the situation we found ourselves in. The way he was taking this 'making us compete for our job' nonsense in his stride. The calmer and more confident he was, the more discon-certed and insecure I was becoming.

'Oh, stop it!'

I leaned my head back against the seat and noticed a passing group of young girls, easy in their tight jeans and Puffa coats, catch me talking to myself and start giggling as they moved on through the car park. I saw them nudging one another, glancing back over their shoulders. Laughing about the crazy woman, talking to herself in her car, no doubt. But I had to remember that this paranoia was just another symptom. Of *course* they weren't laughing at me. They had a million and one more pressing demands on their gossip time.

I also had to remember that of *course* Zac wasn't responsible for my patchy mental health. Nobody was. But that didn't stop me blaming him, ever so slightly. Well, maybe not *him*, but this whole damn situation – if we hadn't been competing for the job, I'd have been able to admit I was struggling now and then.

I closed my eyes and then opened them slowly. Here, insulated in my car, I was starting to feel better. Better, and slightly stupid about the way I'd run away and dumped Priya and Zac, to dash off through the night like a curfewed Cinderella. The thought of Sophie, Ed and Cav as the Ugly Sisters made me smile, and the smile raised my spirits enough for me to be able to start the engine and head for home, before the roads filled up with shoppers heading home too.

8

Things ticked on into the next week. The weather improved slightly, lifting from the grey blanket which was guaranteed to depress even the sparkiest Christmas lover into bright crisp days. The sun did wonders for my mood, even if it did only appear briefly, flaunting itself as it stood proud over the top of the Minster in a couple of hours of flashing overdone brightness, like a five-year-old's school recital.

I trudged into work on Thursday morning, through acres of leaves which had fallen into soggy drifts and were now crisping in the frosts again. I'd had to park my car further away today. Now Christmas was approaching in all its inevitability, even those who put off their shopping until just before the day itself, were being forced onto the streets, and all the free parking got jammed up very early. The shops squeezed into the narrow ginnels and lanes had windows so heaped with seasonal offerings that they almost seemed to burst out onto the pavements and the market stalls set out along the main shopping streets were already humming with activity. The smell of hot chocolate trailed promisingly like a Pied Piper, weaving in and out of the shops and trees and lamp posts, making my stomach rumble with forgotten breakfast as I headed into the back entrance to work, through the car park.

Zac's car was there, frosted over again. Did he ever *go* home? I wondered what the pretty girl in the photos thought of his early starts and late returns. Or did the 'complication' of his home life mean that she was never there? Maybe she wanted to break up but he didn't? Maybe they couldn't afford to sell the house – I knew all about how expensive it could be to have to quit a mortgage after a very short while. Maybe he still loved her, was using the opportunity of them being forced to live together to try to win her around again?

In that case, he had some work to do – I scratched a finger through the ice on his windscreen. It was so thick, the car had to have been here for several hours. I knew he hadn't left it overnight, I'd seen him drive away yesterday evening – why the hell was he spending so much time in the office? He'd never get her back that way, unless she was devoted to workaholics who leave before dawn and don't get home until midnight.

The building wrapped itself around me in familiar comfort. Karen, on the phone, raised a hand in greeting as I went in. I had a Christmas card pressed into my hand as I walked past the main office, and the smell of fresh baked mince pies being unpackaged drifted up to meet me before I went through the double doors that airlocked our part of the building off from the rest of the place.

Some sad tinsel hung around the lampshades, making the light throw shredded shapes onto the floor, in a slightly threatening way all down the corridor, and someone with more enthusiasm than artistic ability, had pinned a home-made MERRY CHRISTMAS banner to the wall, decorated with shakily drawn snowmen and oversized robins. At least, I thought that's what they were, there was something vaguely penile about the snowmen and the birds that had been drawn without any recourse to scale or nods to realism.

The door to our office was open and Zac was standing drinking coffee in the middle of the room. He was wearing a well-cut suit and jumped when I walked in.

'Don't you ever go home?' I asked testily, dragging my scarf off over my head.

'Went once, didn't like it, came back,' he replied perkily. 'Oh.'

'Oh?' I paused, coat half-unbuttoned. 'What?'

'Well, I thought you'd be wearing... um, not that there's anything wrong with... but something, formal?'

I stared at him. 'Did we just institute Dress Up Thursday or something?' I looked down. I was wearing my normal office gear, black trousers, a long-sleeved black T-shirt under a red cotton top. It wasn't exactly formal, but equally it wasn't a sequinned thong and tasselled bra combo. 'Why?'

He looked awkward, then his eyes widened. 'Oh God. You *did* get the email, didn't you? Yesterday?'

The uncertainty started. I could feel those walls forming the faintest cracks. 'From whom?' I tried to distract him with grammar.

'From our esteemed bosses? Well, mine, now I come to think of it?'

'I mean, no. I checked before I left last night.' *Email? What email?* The cracks started to widen and I felt my breath catch.

'Shit.' Zac went to run a hand through his hair, encountered its evidently product-filled texture and stopped. 'Maybe you'd better check now.'

Keeping one eye on him, as there was a tension about him that I wasn't sure I liked, although the suit made him very easy on the eyes, I fired up my computer and went into our intranet. There, virtually throbbing in its unopenedness, was an email from the Management Team. My hand was shaking as I pressed the button to open it and, as it flickered onto the screen, my mouth was flooded with a sour taste as though I'd been licking metal.

Miss Oldbridge,
We would be very grateful if you and Mr Drewe would give a presentation of your work and what it entails to an external group tomorrow morning at nine. It need only last half an hour, so will not impact on your workday.

It was signed by Michael and two unfamiliar names. Presumably the aliens.

'Shit.' I echoed him. Then I squinted at the mail. 'It only came in at half past seven last night. I left at six, so there was no way I could have read it.'

'Unless you picked it up at home.' He sound half-apologetic, as though he were ashamed to have known about it. Maybe *he* had picked it up at home?

'Well maybe, but it shouldn't be assumed that we access work mail when we're not here. And besides, I do have a life.' I thought about yesterday evening, when I'd helped Ed put up the tree that Sophie insisted on and then had eaten half a tin of Quality Street watching a *Gogglebox Celebrity Special* and Cav fiddling with a rear derailleur on his bike all over the carpet. 'Sort of, anyway.'

Zac stared at me. 'They want us both there at the same time too. So a team presentation. Are you up for it?'

The walls trembled, but just about held and the bitter taste was receding. 'Well, I know what the job entails pretty well, so I can do that. Are they interviewing us, do you think?'

'Looks likely.' Zac gave me another once-over. 'If you take the red thing off and put a jacket on, you may get away with it.'

I instantly felt insecure again. 'I haven't got a jacket. Just my coat.'

There was a bustle in the doorway and Priya poked her head in. 'I brought Christmas cake,' she said. 'We made a trial batch and this is the failure. I hope you like nuts, Nettie went a bit bonkers with the almonds. She's been forbidden from touching the marzipan this time round, she's rather heavy-handed with the essence and it tastes a bit like cyanide.' She looked at us, staring at her. 'It's fine, it hasn't *really* got cyanide in.' She gave a quick glance at the heavy, foil-wrapped parcel in her hand. 'I don't think.'

'Pri, can I borrow your jacket?' I asked quickly and slightly breathlessly. 'And your shirt.'

Priya was wearing her usual office wear, a black blazer and white shirt with a cord skirt that *definitely* wouldn't fit me. The tops would be touch-and-go, I was taller, plumper and more booby than her, but it was worth a shot.

'What?' She crossed her arms defensively. 'Why?'

'Sartorial emergency,' Zac said.

'Well, I need to wear *something*.' She kept her arms folded.

'We can swap. It's only for half an hour or so.' I had Miriam coming in at half-past nine and I definitely didn't want to keep her waiting, she might dig her way out of the interview room with a spoon through force of habit. 'We have to do a presentation.'

'What?' Pri's eyes widened. 'Seriously? Now?'

'Yep.'

She looked me up and down. 'I see. Okay. Clothing swap. Just, you know, try not to move too much. This jacket's snug on me, sale bargain and all that, but the seams might not take the stress if you have to run.'

We went into Priya's office, while Zac paced up and down outside, periodically saying things like 'ten minutes and we ought to be in there,' which didn't help my anxiety. But doing something did help. Instead of giving rise to panic over not knowing what the hell we were going to face, the adrenaline kicked me into action, and over it all was a tinge of anger. How dare they not give me warning in good time? Were they trying to wrong-foot me? Put me at a disadvantage?

And then I found myself anchored to the pragmatic by the tightness of Priya's shirt under my armpits.

'I'd keep the jacket done up if I were you.' She stood away and looked critically at me. 'You look a bit Late Night Channel Five otherwise.'

'I don't think it *will* do up.' I stretched the buttons over my chest. 'I feel like I've been through a hot wash.'

Zac tapped on the door. 'We'd better get in there,' he said indistinctly. 'It's five to.'

I burst out of the room and he stepped backwards, then stared.

'Wow,' he said. 'That's... errr... distracting.'

Priya waved us off, my red top making her look as though she'd got her mum's clothes on as Zac led us, at speed, down the corridor.

'Don't hurry,' I said, 'it's like wearing a corset. I can't breathe if I rush, especially up those stairs.'

'I guess if we're *both* late, there's not much they can do.' Zac slowed down. 'I'd... er... I'd keep your jacket done up if I were you.'

'That's not an option.' I demonstrated.

'Oh.' He seemed to lose the power of speech for a moment, then cleared his throat. 'Okay. Right. Just don't breathe too heavily then. I'm definitely not looking but those buttons don't seem that secure.'

'You aren't making this any better.' I took little shallow breaths as we reached the upstairs corridor. 'Where are we going?'

'Michael's office, apparently.' Zac went even slower. 'Look, Ruby—'

'It's fine. I can talk about my job all day.' I matched his pace.

'It's the way they've gone about this. Do you think they deliberately held off emailing you? To put you on the wrong foot?' He stopped walking and grabbed my arm. 'I don't like any of this. I think they're playing games with us.'

I looked at him sharply. 'Us? I don't see you being left at a disadvantage here.'

'No, but, it's like Saturday. When they called me in at the weekend to do something that I'm pretty positive could have waited.'

'Ah, *that's* why you were in York.'

'Priya knew I was in so she asked me to meet up, otherwise I'd have been at a loose end until I went back to Leeds.' He lowered his voice and his grasp on my arm intensified. '*They* know that weekends can be... difficult for me. Yet they sprang it on me without giving me much time to... to make alternative arrangements. Almost like...' his voice went down to a whisper. 'Like they're testing us.'

'Isn't that unethical?'

'Obviously it is.'

I looked down at his hand on my arm. 'Well, we'd better get in there before my circulation is compromised any more.'

'Oh. Sorry. I just... I don't like any of this, Ruby.'

I took as deep a breath as the over-tight shirt would allow. 'Well, I need this job. So I guess we just do our best for now, and worry about it later.'

'I need the job too.' He spoke quietly, almost as though I wasn't meant to hear, but I did. And those five words kept repeating in the back of my brain, even when I stood, in the too-tight shirt and jacket, in front of the 'panel' – a group of people I'd never seen before. Michael was there, looking uncomfortable as though he was sitting on a hairbrush, with Grey Man and Beehive Woman, whose names I really *must* find out, and three other people who all had a sort of stunned look about them. I wondered if they really were the people behind YouBack2Work or whether they'd been dragged in off the street, like witnesses at a particularly unfortunate wedding. They all had expressions of people who'd rather be somewhere else. I knew how they felt.

Michael introduced us, and then waved at me to speak first, which made me feel even more at a disadvantage. No preparation time, no warning and an unrehearsed talk about my job? *Was* it deliberate? None of the watching faces gave anything away as I launched into a brief rundown of my role. 'Some people aren't in work, not through laziness or unemployability, but because something is holding them back. Fear, past trauma, an undiagnosed condition – these are often missed in the conventional jobseeker interviews. We give clients the opportunity to receive counselling to get to the bottom of their inability to find employment.' I added a few pointed remarks about our success levels and sat down to let Zac do his thing.

As I sat, one of the buttons of the front of the shirt popped off and rolled to the floor. My lilac bra with the butterfly embroidery was suddenly front and centre for everyone to see. I could *feel* the four men on the panel trying not to stare.

'As Ruby explained, we believe that long-term unemployment isn't usually a life choice.' Zac flicked me a quick glance, just in time for button two to part company with the shirt, and quickly looked back at the panel. 'Clients... err... clients can have many reasons for not... ummm... seeking employment even in fields they seem well qualified in.' He coughed and turned a little so that I wasn't in his field of vision.

I could feel my face getting hotter and hotter, the blush extending from the roots of my hair sweatily down my throat, to where it began to clash with the bra. Everyone determinedly kept their eyes on Zac. I wriggled about a bit to try to pull the jacket over the flapping edges of the shirt, but it wouldn't stretch, not when I was sitting and the third button, the one that had been maintaining my decency, suddenly gave up the ghost and pinged, to quite dramatic effect, from Priya's shirt, landing at the feet of the Grey Man, who studiously ignored it.

Oddly enough, this didn't spiral me into panic. In fact, it made me want to laugh, despite the horror of the situation. The tiny voice that usually whispered to me through the fractures in my mind-walls was practically shouting 'Serves them right! If they'd given proper notice, you could have worn your own clothes and not had to perform some weird kind of burlesque show!'

And at least the bra was a nice one, offering a decent amount of coverage, good support and some rather pretty embroidery. Not that I would have worn a plunge push-up bra to the office anyway, but I did own several mixed-wash-accident ones that lent a certain greyness to my chestal area and made me look as though I was wrapped in net curtain left over from an industrial workshop. So things could have been worse. Not much, admittedly, but I would take the small mercies.

The blush gradually subsided. I tried not to breathe too heavily and just listened to Zac finishing his explanation, looking confident and calm in his wonderfully cut black suit and polished shoes. My boots were slightly muddy from my recent trek through the streets of York and I tucked them under the chair, not that anyone was looking in the direction of my feet right now.

'Well then.' Michael stood up. 'Does anyone have any questions?'

All the eyes travelled to my chest and then away again like a flight of panicked birds. All the heads shook, and I had never been so relieved to be dismissed without being able to go into more detail about my work.

Michael went and held the door open for us to go, smiling benignly as we passed him and without looking at me at all, although I could almost hear his eyeballs creaking. The door closed behind us and we heard a burst of voices, followed by a couple of laughs.

Zac took his suit jacket off and handed it to me. 'I don't know whether that was a catastrophe or dirty tricks,' he said. 'But I have to admit you carried it off.'

Gratefully I clutched the jacket around me as we passed a few of the office staff on the stairs. 'Definitely not intentional,' I said. 'And what else could I do but sit there? Run out in tears?'

'I wouldn't run anywhere, if I were you,' Zac said darkly, then started to laugh. 'Their faces though. I don't think anyone listened to a single word I was saying.'

Two of the girls from the main office, who produced CVs and application letters for clients, gave us a strange look as we walked past. To be fair, we must have looked slightly peculiar, Zac in his suit and shirt and me wearing his jacket pulled around me as though he'd just saved me from drowning in a frozen pond. I suspected that the remnants of the intense blush had hung around on my cheeks too, my face still felt hot and uncomfortably tight.

'You carried it off very well too, I thought,' I reassured him. 'Bearing in mind that I was sitting there popping buttons like a cartoon.'

He caught at the jacket and whirled me around, pulling at the same time, until we stood in an alcove off the main corridor, tucked into shadow. 'Ruby,' he said, his voice low and slightly hoarse. 'I meant it, before. I think they're doing all this deliberately.'

We were squeezed together in a space that had once been a built-in cupboard. Behind us, the wall was still covered in wallpaper that looked as though it were Victorian. Spiky pink flowers coiled in a menacing way out of a dark background.

'But why would they?' I hissed back, my eyes unconsciously tracing the mind-bending floral patterns. 'What would be the point?'

Zac looked down at me, slightly pityingly. 'Well, there wouldn't be a decision to have to make about who stays and who goes, if one of us resigns. There'd be no redundancy to pay. I think they have some twisted idea that only the strong survive, so if they make it difficult enough, the one who stays must be the "best". And that's just what I've come up with for starters. There is also the thought that making us compete means they are getting us both to work twice as hard for the same amount of money.' He stuck his head out of the alcove and scanned the corridor. We didn't want to emerge into a crowd of IT people, the rumour mill would already be on overtime about our appearance on the stairs. By lunchtime it would be all round the company that we'd been caught shagging in the toilets. 'They are trying to put pressure on. I reckon that's why they didn't let you know about this morning. You *could* have picked the mail up at home, which would have shown you were working unpaid hours, or you could miss it, like you did, thus pressurising you to perform.'

I stared at him. 'Michael wouldn't do that! He's all soft and wibbly and he forgets my name half the time.'

Zac sighed. 'I'm pretty sure Michael didn't get where he is in business without cutting a few throats.'

I shivered. 'Please. That is not a great image. And what if you're right? What can we do about it, really? If we raise this, they could always sack the pair of us – I'm sure they could find a reason. And I need this, Zac.'

I hadn't wanted to sound as though I were pleading with him. After all, he was still the enemy, of sorts. But my voice, even in a hissed whisper, sounded desperate, and I could hear that edge of anxiety, the one that kept itself sharp on midnight wakings and bank statements, running underneath my words like a flensing knife under skin.

'Yeah. Me too.' His face looked shaded suddenly, hollowed and older. 'And therein lies the problem, doesn't it? Only one of us can stay.'

I need this job too, he'd said. And it looked as though he meant it.

I heard a voice raised in complaint and hardly muffled at all by the big doors that led through into the main building. 'Well, you'd better fuckin' find her then, hadn't you? I've come in on the bus and I'm not wanderin' around here like little Miss Fuckin' Muffet while you prise her arse out of bed!'

A sudden moment of horror made me clutch Zac's jacket around my throat. 'Miriam! She's my half past nine! How long were we in the presentation?'

'Long enough.' Zac gave me a little push. 'Go, Before she blows up.'

I dashed the back way to the interview room, down musty passageways and in and out of offices, like a one-woman French farce, eventually erupting through a pair of seldom-used swing doors into the hall outside, just in time to meet Miriam sauntering in the more conventional way.

She looked me up and down, slowly. 'Havin' a shag round the back, were you?' She eyed Zac's jacket, which at least matched my trousers by being black, but was several sizes too large to be called a suit. 'What the hell have you come as, Madonna Nineteen Eighty?'

I ignored her and opened up the interview room. At least Miriam wasn't smoking today.

Someone had put Miriam's file on the table in there and switched on the coffee machine. Probably Priya, flapping around inside my cotton top. I picked up the file and sat down, vowing to buy Pri the biggest box of chocolates I could afford and to sew all her buttons back on by the weekend.

Miriam helped herself to coffee and wandered about while I flipped through the file. Most things were computerised, but forms filled in by clients were often in paper format, and we also included any other relevant information printed out. We'd had too many power cuts to rely totally on the computers.

There were several application forms in there. We took copies before we sent them off, so we could go over them with clients if they wanted, at a later date. Miriam had filled in a *lot* of forms.

'So. How's life?' Miriam said as I laid down her file. Her hand kept twitching towards her bag. 'I'm not hangin' round here too long, mind. Yankee Candle are havin' a pre-Christmas sale.' She walked some more small circles.

'Life is fine, thank you.' I buttoned up the jacket. I didn't need Miriam's acerbic views on my underwear. 'How are the applications going?'

Over the next half an hour, Miriam drank three cups of coffee and complained about the lack of suitable work, the threat of sanctions which still hung over her, and the computer games that her grandchildren played and which gave her a headache. There was absolutely no reason for her to be here at all, as far as I could tell, apart from the expenses-paid shopping trip, which, I suspected, was all the reason she needed.

At last, she put down her coffee cup decisively. 'Right. I've been, I've seen you, you can put that in the files.' She nodded towards the paper file on the desk, her blonde updo bobbed, taut with hairspray. 'And you can tell 'em I'm tryin', right?'

'Right. As long as you are trying.' I gave her a look, but she just grinned cheerily at me, winding her scarf around her neck and putting her coat back on.

It occurred to me that getting Miriam into work would be such an enormous plus on my side that even the management team couldn't ignore it. Maybe I'd take her file home and read through it. I might just get some ideas about the ideal placement for her. Even training would count, I would have to see what I could come up with.

'What's your dream job, Miriam?' I asked, walking her through to the back door.

She already had her cigarettes out of her bag. 'I dunno.' Before we reached the door, the cigarette was between her lips, and it was lit the second the door opened. 'Yours?' She gave me a grin. 'Or Prime Minister. Reckon I'd do a better job than most of the tosspots in government. But yours looks like a proper doss too.'

Then she gave me a cheerful wave and walked off into the sharp sunshine, leaving a smoke trail behind her like a vanishing demon.

Oh, if only she knew.

9

That evening I sat with Miriam's file on my lap, half under my duvet. The central heating was playing up again and our landlord was not as prompt as he could be with repairs – one of the reasons this house was cheap. Another reason my rent was cheap was that I slept in the room that would have been the nursery, had the house had more conventional occupants, and a single bed plus my small chest of drawers occupied all the floor space. I had to get out of bed off the end.

Ed was thumping, mysteriously, in his room next door. Packing, probably, to head home to his parents in Glasgow for Christmas. I certainly hoped that was what the noise was. Sophie was downstairs on the phone and Cav was out on the bike, despite it being several degrees below zero, and dark.

From my window, I could see the houses up and down the street now sported Christmas trees, in windows, in front gardens or further in the house, with the lights twinkling out through the dark. I wondered what I would do for Christmas.

Last year, of course, it had been Gareth and I, and our first Christmas alone in our new house. We hadn't quite got the heating sorted and the oven was broken, but none of it seemed to matter; we'd stayed in bed and then I'd cooked – at Gareth's insistence – an approximation of Christmas dinner on the gas hob, and we'd drunk too much and played some stupid game. The worst of it was I'd wondered, secretly, in a well-hidden place in my heart, whether he would propose.

He hadn't. At least, not to me.

And now I remembered washing up alone while he phoned his brother for an hour's chat and I planned the colour scheme for the kitchen, and wondered if I could afford new tiles for the splashback.

This year... I stared, unseeing at Miriam's files. I could go to Eva's, of course, with Mum and Dad. She and Didier always laid on a good dinner, and I'd referee the boys, while Mum helped cook and Dad and Didier talked work.

I slammed a sudden fist into the mattress beside me. It wasn't *fair*! I'd had the house and the boyfriend and the plans and now – I looked around the slightly bleak little room. We weren't allowed to hang pictures, so the only ornamentation on the walls was a mirror, supposedly designed to make the room look bigger, but in reality it just reflected three walls simultaneously and enhanced how tiny it was. The magnolia colour scheme made it look chilly and the narrow bed emphasised my single status.

I punched the mattress again. I didn't mind the being single part. In fact, the further I got from Gareth, the more I realised what a chauvinistic, undomesticated pig he'd really been. He was just interested in sex and food in that order and had absolutely no desire to be an equal partner. He'd had no interest in the house or what needed doing to it.

I felt a flame of horrified realisation burn its way up my face. Gareth hadn't really wanted to buy a house. He'd been happy with a peripatetic renting lifestyle, moving every year of the three that I'd known him, keeping all his possessions in a huge old army kitbag that had belonged to his dad. He had gone along with my desire to buy, my love for the little terraced house on the edge of the city, my desire to decorate and make the place ours. I had, in effect, talked him into the purchase. He must have known, even then, that it wasn't for keeps. He was always on the lookout for something, some*one* better. Thinner, prettier, blonder, more acquiescent.

If I'd had anything to throw, I would have thrown it, but the bed was too small for anything other than me and a hot-water bottle, so I kicked that instead, and it fell off the end of the bed and onto the floor with the sound of a hundred empty stomachs sloshing.

'Gareth, you *bastard*!' I shouted, at the chintz curtains.

The house went suddenly quiet. Ed stopped thumping and, after a second, Sophie's voice drifted up the stairs. 'You all right, hun?'

'I'm fine!' I called back. 'Just thinking.'

'I hope he gets syphilis and his willy rots off!' Sophie called back cheerily, and went back to her phone call. She only knew the outline details about my break-up, but she was still prepared to swear that Gareth had been 'a nobber' and was fully on my side, which was encouraging. Although it was beginning to dawn on me that the relationship had been, pretty much, all on my side.

I did a quick mental audit of the state of those walls which kept my feelings in check. I relied on them to keep my emotions from spilling out and overwhelming me, shored up with the medication my doctor had prescribed. I sometimes pictured those emotions as towering blocks of stone, threatening to become ruinous but kept propped into walls by huge white buttresses. They seemed firm.

Miriam's buff file was spread on the duvet in front of me. It was against policy to take files home, for confidentiality reasons, but I figured that, after yesterday's late email, they thought I *should* be working from home, so I would. And it wasn't as though I had anyone else in here who was going to see it, was it?

The file was rucked and tattered at the edges. It had clearly been in circulation for some time at Back To Employment in Leeds, and sending it over when Miriam continued with us hadn't done its cardboard outer layer any favours. It was mostly full of photocopies of handwritten application forms. Every shop, it would seem, in Leeds. Some supermarkets. A couple of cleaning agencies. Schools and a bus depot and the local council offices. I flicked through, my mind only half on the task as I now started to wonder about what Zac had said. *Were* they deliberately trying to make one of us look bad? And, most importantly, what if it was only me they were trying to sabotage?

I couldn't ignore the fact that the email telling me about the presentation had come in long after I'd left work. Deliberate, or just bad timing? Surely not calculated, *surely* not.

Then the horror of unemployment crept up my spine. I was qualified. I was experienced. But that word 'cutbacks' whispered itself into my ear, and my mind started to whirl with images of unpaid loans, of phone calls and desperate attempts to pay; men turning up on the doorstep to take away everything I owned...

I gave an unintended snort of laughter. All I owned right now was some furniture, currently in my parents' garage, and a ten-year-old Skoda. Good luck, bailiffs, with getting much for that lot.

Quick check – walls, shaky, but holding.

I couldn't help but wonder about that look on Zac's face, that lonely, shadowed look when he said he needed the job too. How desperate could *he* be, compared to me? Surely, if he needed out of his marriage, he could move in with friends? My need was greater.

I tried to focus, but the thoughts wouldn't go away. Did I have that same, haunted look? The anxiety had given my eyes a slightly hooded look and the medication made my skin break out in dry patches now and then, but – did I? Did that fear that the worst was bound to happen, that fear that stopped the breath in my throat and pulled the air from my lungs, show on my face?

Breathe. Breathe. Breathe.

I needed a distraction. In the absence of anything useful in here, apart from Miriam's overworked buff file, I went downstairs and helped Sophie tidy the kitchen.

10

A few days later, Michael caught up with me as I escorted Samantha into the office to fill in her application for funding for her Domestic Budgeting course.

'Ah, Ruby!' He always seemed so surprised to see me, as though I hadn't worked here in a decade and was just visiting. 'A word, if I may?'

'All right, Michael.' I waited. The offices were busy, everywhere seemed to be full of people buzzing with activity and I wondered what the sudden rush was, until I realised that it was probably the presence of Michael and the possibility of having your job rationalised out of existence.

'Ah. In my, er, office, if you would. Finish seeing to your client first, of course.' Michael turned his smile on Samantha, who, despite having sworn off all things male in front me, many times, turned pink and giggled. In comparison I felt pale and mirthless. Being called to the office never boded well.

I took Samantha through and left her with Sally, who was accurate and never sent forms to the wrong address, wrongly completed and with, sometimes, the incorrect contact information. I'd been here long enough to know who was reliable, although, looking around the office, most of those whose performance had been less than optimal seemed to no longer be here. It gave me a chilly feeling in the pit of my stomach. As though we were being picked off, one by one, vanishing one day never to be seen again. It was either a ruthless management style at work or ritual sacrifice.

Michael's office was small and guarded by his fierce PA, but she wasn't at her desk when I went through, and there was no sign of activity in the outer office.

'Where's Rachel?' I asked casually, sitting in the chair Michael indicated. 'Is she having a day off?'

'No. Er.' Michael looked a little shamefaced. 'I made a good case, of course, but, well, it's been decided to drop her hours. She's only in three times a week now.' He looked, almost wistfully, at the door between his office and Rachel's. 'She makes the most marvellous coffee,' he said, longingly. 'But, apparently, well, cost-cutting, you know the drill. And,' he added with an audible touch of pride, 'I can send my own emails now.'

That chill in my stomach solidified, as though glaciers were moving in my abdomen. Rachel had been forced to go part-time. She'd run the office and Michael like some kind of military project for years, and I would have sworn that he wouldn't even know how to take his coat off without Rachel's detailed step-by-step guide. Things were bad. It could explain the late email about the presentation, though. It may have taken Michael all day to type and work out how to send.

Michael looked at his fingers for a while. Finally I had to say something. 'Michael? What did you want to see me about? Only I've got a few phone calls to make, another couple of training courses to set up for some clients...' I tailed off, hoping that he'd pick up the hint that I was working, I was *Being Successful*. The implication that I was outperforming Zac hung woven through my words like the paper chains that Michael had wound around his office ceiling.

That would have been Rachel too. Michael didn't really notice that sort of thing.

'Ah. Yes. Little bit, um, awkward.'

Another pause while my stomach sank even lower. My knees had started to shake and those walls in my head were ready to go if given a hefty enough push. Or, possibly, a slight poke. They were beginning to feel more like soggy cardboard than York stone.

'It's, well, look, it's like this. You and Zac Drewe, you're up for the same position in our new, affiliated company, yes?'

I couldn't speak. My mouth had gone dry and I would have given anything for Rachel to have come stalking through with her tray of coffee and the superior biscuits that lurked in the tin up here. I just nodded.

'I have to tell you, um, Ruby, that Mr Drewe is edging slightly to the fore on this particular one, I'm afraid.' Michael went back to looking at his fingers, which seemed to have taken on a life of their own and be twiddling away on the edge of his desk. With the way he was watching them, I half expected them to crawl away independently into a corner.

'Oh,' was all I could say.

'But obviously, Ruby, *obviously* I would prefer to keep you on. Your work has always been – well, apart from your extended leave last spring – you've always been reliable and efficient and your results are top-notch.' Such a long run of words seemed to exhaust him and he lapsed back into the detailed hand study again. I began to realise how essential the coffee was.

My whole job relied on me being positive. Enthusiastic. I fixed a smile across my mouth that was so broad it brought my cheeks into my line of vision. 'I've got a couple of excellent prospects for getting two very long-termers into work or training,' I said in a tone so brilliant that it had facets.

'Good, good.' Michael sounded vague, as though he was not listening. 'It's just that, well, obviously, I'd prefer to keep you on, but other forces are at play here and they are keen on keeping Mr Drewe in his position.' He glanced, almost involuntarily, upwards. I wondered if the mothership was hovering. 'So I wondered,' he dropped his voice to a murmur, 'if there was anything you could do.'

For one, tiny, almost jaw-dropping moment, I wondered if he meant that if I slept with him he could keep my job for me, then I looked at Michael and dismissed it. He had all the sex appeal of a Golden Retriever and, I suspected, a similar attitude to the act, plus a very lovely young wife. 'What do you mean?'

Michael leaned forward so that only a small strip of desk separated us. 'I wondered,' and his voice was almost inaudible now, 'if you could, you know, get any *inside information* on Mr Drewe. Anything we could use to help our case? I mean, obviously the *other lot*,' another glance upwards, 'know things about him, but they are going to brush any indiscretions under the carpet, aren't they? If there's anything you can find out and bring to me that I can use to gain leverage for you over him, well...' He sat back and nodded speculatively. 'It could only be to the good,' he finished.

I left Michael's office feeling simultaneously terrified – Zac was ahead of me in the job; mildly elated – Michael wanted to keep me; and slightly appalled – surely this was a 'dirty tricks' campaign. But overall I settled on a feeling of hopelessness. Zac hadn't let any sign of weakness slip. He arrived early and left late, he was reliable, friendly, approachable. The only thing I could possibly raise against him was the fact that he had a tendency to be a little bit harsh with some of his clients. But then, he thought I was too soft on mine.

The awful, horrible creeping started around the back of my neck, as though I were wearing an itchy scarf. *What if his bosses had asked him for inside information about me?*

I mentally audited as many of our conversations as I could remember. I'd always been bright, sparky, positive, hadn't I? Forward-thinking, upbeat, bordering on the jolly at times. And then, crashing into my head came the memory of the café when Zac had walked in to hear me talking to Priya about the anxiety and depression.

I broke my determined stride towards the office and wheeled around into the ladies' toilet behind Reception, where I could lock myself in a cubicle and rest my forehead against the cool wall.

Shit. Of course, management would have all my records, but all those showed was a three-week absence, taken as sick leave. Apart from that first day, when I'd tried to come in fresh from the screaming argument with Gareth, and Priya had had to lock us both in the interview room for two hours and then take me home, I was pristine. I had come back to work, firing on all cylinders and so overly cheery to make up for my one-day lapse that I had heard it rumoured around the main office that I'd won the lottery.

And three weeks sick was nothing, was it? Could have been – I dunno, shingles?

My medication, the fact that it kept the walls from caving in on me and the terror and fear from cascading over me like someone dropping liquid lead on my head, that was my own private affair. Only known to myself and Priya.

And, now possibly, Zac.

Or maybe he hadn't heard? Or hadn't picked up that I was

talking about myself. Yes, it had been noisy in that café, and he'd only just arrived, Pri and I could have been discussing *anything*.

But then I'd walked out, hadn't I? I had had to get away from the crowding and the influx of sensation into the fresh air and quiet. Was it possible that Zac would have put two and two together?

I headed back to our shared office, determined to give absolutely no hint of any kind of negativity. I brightened my eyes, nailed on a grin and thought 'sparkle, sparkle' to myself all the way down the corridor and in through the narrow doorway.

I needn't have bothered, Zac didn't even look up as I went in. 'She's running rings around you,' he said, hidden away behind his keyboard.

'Who?' Everything I had was focused on Michael and his words. I'd almost forgotten that I had an actual job.

'Your last client.'

'What, Samantha? She's just a bit lost and confused. She was married and dependent on her husband for a long time; it's natural that she feels cast adrift and out of her depth.'

Zac jerked his head up so he could see me over his laptop. 'She's using you as cheap therapy,' he said. 'I can hear it when you're in there.' Another jerk of his head, towards the interview room this time. 'All she seems to want to talk about is how crap and untrustworthy men are.'

I stared over at where he sat, my sparkle slowly fading from me, like a fire having water thrown on it. 'Well, yes,' I said. 'Counselling *is* why we're here, isn't it?' I could feel my grin starting to slide and nailed it more rigidly back into place. 'That's our brief. To get to the bottom of why clients feel they can't get back into the workplace long term?'

Zac harrumphed. Michael's words about Zac edging ahead in the job competition stakes repeated in the back of my head, and I wondered what it was that he was doing to gain that edge. Apart from never going home, he and I seemed pretty even in the number of clients, time we spent with them and the number getting back into work. What did he have that I didn't, apart from a Land Rover Discovery and a proper parking space?

'Sometimes it really isn't about the jobs, it's about *them*,' I said, although I wasn't sure why. This was the 101 of our job; that people were sometimes kept from working by personal hang-ups and fears. 'They've had years of being told they're stupid or incapable or badly organised or whatever, usually through someone *else's* sense of inadequacy or need to feel superior. Some people have to hand that kind of crap down and down and the people we see are like Patient Zero, the ones that all the crap has landed on, who don't have the tools necessary to shrug it off or say "bugger you, I'm going to succeed anyway".'

'Maybe.' Zac rattled the keyboard a bit more. 'And yes, you're right in some cases. It doesn't explain Miriam though.'

I tried to imagine anyone calling Miriam stupid or incapable and could only conjure up images of the resultant bloodbath. Miriam would not take that kind of talk from anyone. 'Maybe not. But Samantha, Grace, Krystoff, Taylor – all those clients, they've all got backstories that would make your hair curl. And sometimes they just need someone to believe in them.'

'And some of them are only coming so they don't get their benefits sanctioned, and they reckon talking to us means they can get at least another year of not having to apply for anything.' He sounded odd. Sceptical. I knew Zac was less inclined to get involved with clients than I was, he didn't see them out of hours, for example. But maybe it was just that he had clients who didn't have emergencies like Taylor had had.

'Maybe. A few. But in the scheme of things, not that many.' I was having to fight really hard for my sparkle to reignite in the face of his utter pragmatism. 'What's the matter, did someone send you a copy of the *Daily Mail* or something?'

Zac sighed. 'I've just had half an hour of Bob trying to wangle his way out of an interview. They're opening a paint factory over near him, lots of new, non-specialist jobs and he's pleading some kind of mental health crisis.'

Sweat sprang into my palms and I sat down rather hard behind my desk. 'Maybe it's real,' I said, and my voice sounded a bit hoarse.

Zac snorted. 'Nah. Bob plays the "mental health" card whenever he wants to get out of doing something. And, of course, it's impossible to prove, all he has to say is that he's got "anxiety" and that's it, we can't touch him.'

My hands were now so wet that I couldn't type. In contrast, my mouth was dry. 'If he has a diagnosis...' I managed to force out.

'Once. Years ago. He's not currently on medication and he hasn't seen a doctor in months. But the diagnosis stands forever, apparently.' Zac sounded bitter.

I wasn't totally surprised. I'd met this kind of prejudice before. I'd even carried it, slightly, myself, prior to my own breakdown. But now, with my first-hand knowledge, I could safely say that, yes, anxiety, panic attacks, were real. They were awful. And they could strike out of nowhere when you felt perfectly all right. That was the really scary thing. Plus, they were invisible. So many of us carried this fear, like an invisible weight strapped to our backs. The fear that we might suddenly be overwhelmed and carried away on that unreasoning tide.

Of course, I couldn't explain any of this to Zac. Not without handing him the agency of my own destruction.

'I think, possibly, you are being a bit harsh,' I said, carefully. 'Depression isn't a life choice, you know.'

Zac kept his head down. Kept typing. As though my words were just bouncing off him, unheard.

I stood up, hoping that my chair made enough noise that it would indicate my opposition to his opinion and stalked off into Priya's office because otherwise I was afraid that I might throw something at him.

* * *

The next day, it snowed. And the day after that. And the day after that.

The novelty wore off very fast. At first, it was very Christmassy, walking in to work through streets made clean by the recent fall and with outlines fuzzed by the current one. I was in early, mindful of Michael's words, and also because parking was becoming a nightmare and getting in an hour early was the only way I could ensure I could park within walking distance of the office.

Shop lights beamed out, colouring the snow heaped outside their doors and making the offerings inside their windows look mysterious and enticing. I crunched my way down Petergate and there was the Minster, looking even bulkier rising out of a snow-bank, like a large man getting out of an untidy bed. Lights played over the medieval stonework and glinted off the snowfall that was settling in nooks and statues. Several gargoyles wore jaunty caps of snow and the whole building looked complacent, solid amid the blizzard's impermanence.

Inside, our offices were hushed and steamy. People were ringing in to work from home, unable to get through the resulting traffic chaos or, in some cases, out of the villages where they lived. For all that we got a fair bit of snow in winter, the infrastructure still seemed to collapse every time. Karen was fielding calls whilst shrugging out of her enormous coat and unzipping boots, and every corridor I walked down echoed to the sound of unanswered calls from the outside world.

Zac was, of course, already in. His coat, hanging on the rickety coat-stand, looked dry. I'd come through the front door so hadn't seen his car, but I bet you could have made an entire snowball fight from the amount that had settled on his roof and bonnet.

He looked up when I came in. 'Thank God. Miriam's here and I daren't give her any more coffee in case she rips down the blinds and uses them to build a scale model of her unhappiness.'

I stopped, arrested in the act of taking off the spare layers of clothing that had bulked me and made me sweat my way through the blizzard. 'What? What's she doing here? It's not even dawn yet.'

'I didn't *listen* to her, I just caffeinated her. Besides, she hates me.' He slumped in a defeated way onto the corner of his desk. 'Something to do with an early train so she's got a full day to... I dunno, do whatever she does.' His shoulders slumped a little bit more. 'She talked at me a lot. And now she's got possession of the coffee machine.'

'Okay, okay, I'll see what she wants.' I hung up my damp outerwear over the top of his coat. 'Go and make coffee from the machine in Reception.'

'Oh, is there one there?' Zac jumped up. 'I never knew that! Why did nobody tell me that?'

'Because Karen guards it. She counts the spoons too, you know,' I called after him as he dashed out of the door and headed off through the building. A small tickle of smugness teased at the back of my mind; Zac *didn't* know everything. I still held some advantages. Then I wished I'd kept the second coffee machine secret, just to have a one-up on him, and hated myself a tiny bit for having that thought. If the competition between us was going to come down to things as petty as knowing where you could get coffee in an emergency or how to sweet-talk the café next door into letting us use a table for hours – well, maybe it wasn't a job I wanted to keep, after all.

Actually, I thought, as I took deep breaths and straightened my spine to go into the interview room, did I really want a job where they tried to use personal information against us? Where they tried to get us to 'dig the dirt' on one another, just to gain advantage? It was an uneasy realisation, that YouBack2Work may not ethically be a place I wanted to stay. But what choice did I have? The anxiety wouldn't even let me contemplate the complexities of applying for another job, let alone learning new ropes with new people.

Miriam seemed similarly unsettled. In deference, hopefully, to me, she hadn't lit up, but a packet of cigarettes lay on the top of her voluminous bag, ready to be snatched up in a moment. She was circling, uneasy as a spooked horse, and, presumably, containing enough caffeine to jet-propel her through the ceiling.

'Well, you took your time.' She wandered around the desk, running a finger along its bevelled edge. 'I've been waitin' an hour.'

'Miriam, we aren't even open yet.'

'Yeah, well, this is an emergency, in't it?' Her fingers twitched around an imaginary cigarette. 'They reckons I can be a post-woman. Me! Walkin' the streets at stupid o'clock in the snow! What does they take me for!'

I had to bite my lip to refrain from pointing out that she'd already done that in order to come to our office before the shops were even open, but I managed to restrain myself, although I internally squeaked.

'It's not bad earnings though.' I tried to sound rational. 'And they need loads of people this close to Christmas, to make sure there's no backlog.'

Miriam looked, for want of a better word, shaken. 'They tried to make me do it last year, but I got swollen ankles before the interview,' she said. 'Can't walk up and down with swollen ankles.'

Zac's words about my being too soft on my clients whispered into my ear. Miriam didn't want counselling. I'd listened to her talk about the laziness of her daughters and the loudness of her grandchildren and the intransigence of the local council offices already. She didn't want opinions or solutions. I wasn't sure what she *did* want. 'Well, you could give it a try,' I said, feeling a little bit hopeless. If Miriam got into work – well, that wouldn't just be a feather in my cap, it would pretty much be an entire aviary roosting on my head. 'You might enjoy it.'

She sucked in air. 'No,' she said, without a shred of doubt. 'I wouldn't.'

'It would get you out of the house. Away from the computer games and arguments.'

'I can do that anyway. I goes up my friend's. And *she* don't expect me to walk for miles carryin' a bloody great bag.'

I couldn't help it. My eyes travelled to her enormous and over-laden handbag even though they tried not to. 'Um,' was all I said.

Miriam, to my surprise, laughed. 'Yeah, yeah, I know.' She looked younger when she laughed, it ironed out the tight skin and wrinkles of someone who exists on roll-ups and coffee. 'Next year. Maybe next year. I just need your help *this* year, to keep them off my back.'

'Miriam, that's not what we're here for,' I said, with a feeling that I might as well be shouting into that overloaded bag. 'We're trying to get you back *into* work, not help you avoid it.'

'I thought you was here to counsel us through the problems

that holds us back from applyin'. That's what *he* always said, anyway.' She jerked her head towards the door and I supposed that the *he* in question was Zac. 'Fuckin' tosspot,' she muttered. 'Bloke like him with his fancy talk, he's never known a minute of worryin' about the bailiffs or kids. Charmed life, he's got!' She raised her voice, presumably so that Zac, wherever he was, would be under no illusions as to what she thought of him.

I thought of his voice, weighted low with worry, during that overheard phone call. The way he'd never say anything other than 'it's complicated' about his home situation. 'Oh, I don't know about...'

'Right, so I wants counsellin'.' Miriam stopped pacing like a caged animal and plonked herself down in the comfortable chair. 'I can't be expected to work until you've counselled me, right?'

'I'm not quite sure it works like...' I tried, feebly, but she'd already settled herself.

'I've got four kids to four different blokes; one beat me, one raped me and one's still in prison for what he did to a security guard,' she began, with a tone that was half confessional and half daring me to say anything. 'That's the blokes, not the kids,' she finished, with an admirable attempt at clarity. 'Wouldn't stand for crap like that from the kids.'

It was less like one of my usual sessions and more like reading one of those true-life magazine stories. Miriam's life had contained pretty much every form of abuse going, and when she got to the bit about the vodka, I had to stop her. 'Okay, okay. Look, I've got another client coming in soon, so we'll have to carry on next time.'

Miriam sat back. There was a look in her eye, a look of challenge, as though she expected me to disbelieve her. 'But you'll shove a note on me file? You're counsellin' me, so I'm not able to work?'

I thought back over some of what she'd told me. It was amazing that she was still walking and talking, never mind looking for employment, and her pulled-back face and gaunt appearance made a lot more sense now. 'I'll see what I can do,' I said. 'But I probably won't be able to see you again before Christmas.'

'That's fine.' She began gathering up her bag and coat. 'It's not goin' anywhere. And, y'know, actually it *is* quite good to talk about it, you're onto somethin' with this counsellin' lark. I've never told anyone about that stuff with the bloke in the shed.' She went to the door and then leaned back in to pat me on the cheek. 'Don't have nightmares, now.'

Then she was gone. Leaving me feeling as though a hurricane had passed over the top of me, only for a tsunami to snatch me up and hurl me inland. I'd thought that *I* had problems, when all I had was an ex-boyfriend and a bit of debt? Miriam was a walking Reddit forum of problems, and it made me feel weak and a bit of a fraud.

'Did Miriam tell you about her life?' I asked Zac when I went back into our office. He was half-hiding behind the coat rack.

'Has she gone?'

'Yes. But I think I just promised to excuse her from work searching until after Christmas.'

'You got away lightly. She didn't claim your firstborn or try to make you eat an apple that was suspiciously red and shiny?'

'Her life...' I said, and stopped as mental images crashed down on me. I caught my breath. 'She told me about her life.'

'Miriam tells *everyone* about her life.' Zac pushed a mug of slightly cold coffee at me. 'She likes to complain about her grand-children to anyone she meets. I would *not* like to sit next to her on a bus.'

'I don't mean that. I mean, her life growing up.' I sipped at the coffee, its bitter smoothness was a good steadying influence. 'Her parents and...' More images. 'That,' I finished.

Zac frowned at me. 'Oh no, she's never talked about that. She's always been a bit private about that kind of thing. You got her to open up? That's actually pretty amazing, Ruby.'

'It was *horrible*,' I said softly. 'It just made me remember what goes on in some people's lives. People who look sorted and confident on the outside. Well, some of them are just hiding a lot of really awful crap.'

He didn't say anything. He just looked at me, steadily, a pile of forms in his hands. The pile shook, very slightly.

'I mean, yes, I hear a lot of bad life stories in this job.' I sipped again. Zac was still watching me, and there was a hollowness, an expectancy in the air. 'But Miriam goes above and beyond anything I've heard before.'

I waited for him to speak. He opened his mouth a couple of times and tapped at the papers, as though words were building up inside him and he was just trying to put them into a kind of order that would make sense. I could feel myself tensing. There was something, something he wanted to say, but he didn't know how to, and his uncertainty was there, in every line of his body, every crease in his informal jacket and T-shirt combination. So when he said, 'It's not what's happened to you, it's how you deal with it,' in a low voice that was only just audible over the computer fans and the background noise of phones ringing and people talking, it was an anticlimax.

'I think Miriam still being *alive* is pretty surprising, never mind dealing with it.'

We made eye contact. His eyes were surprisingly dark, given that the overhead lighting in here was of 'operating theatre' intensity. Very brown, no back-hints of green or flecks of amber. Dark and shadowed. I realised how infrequently we looked one another in the eye; how we slid past each other even though we worked so closely and we'd spent time outside the office together, and I wondered why. Were we trying not to show our true selves to one another?

Then I remembered. He was the competition. Neither one of us could afford to show any chinks in the armour.

But I was pretty sure now that there were chinks. And I was slowly coming to realise that I'd started to look at Zac as a whole human being, not just the opposition. As a man, with thoughts and feelings and opinions, not as some cartoon baddie with an outsize moustache and an unlikely propensity for throwing mothers out into the snow. Someone with a life that held things he didn't want to talk about. And that thought disturbed me.

'Ruby!' Sophie's yell up the stairs made me jump and I scattered papers out of the file across my duvet. 'You'd better come down!'

'What?' I leaned over the bannisters, which she'd hung with a selection of baubles that meant grabbing hold of the rail was like being assaulted by ping-pong balls. 'What's up?'

Sophie was standing at the front door talking to a man in a uniform. At first I thought it was the police, and immediately felt guilty, but a quick audit of my life to date didn't turn up anything that might get me arrested on my own doorstep. Was it too much to hope that Gareth had died a horrible death and they were letting me know? Yep, Gareth hadn't even admitted my existence to his workmates or new girlfriend, I'm sure, so nobody would bother to tell me of his demise. Unless they thought I'd caused it, of course.

But the uniformed man turned out to be a bus driver.

'Look, here's all our company stuff, I'll get on to the insurance lot in the morning,' he said, as we froze, inspecting the damage his bus had done to my car, trying to avoid a cat on the icy road. 'I'm really sorry.'

Sorry. Right.

I stared at what had previously been the front end of my Skoda. It was now more like the side of my Skoda, having taken a swipe left more decisive than a woman seeing her old maths teacher on Tinder. The bus, currently full of people who were all staring at me out of their comfortably steamed-up windows, was completely undamaged.

'Do you think you can still drive it, Ruby?' Sophie hugged my arm.

'Only around very very tight bends.' I crouched, but the car didn't look any better from lower down. 'Oh bugger.'

The bus drove away, all the faces swivelling to watch my continuing misery.

How was I going to get to work? Priya couldn't give me a lift, she lived on the other side of town. Nobody drove in past our awkwardly placed suburb and it was too far to walk. I could get the bus, but I'd still have to walk from the bus stop and taxis were too expensive for daily use. The car probably wasn't worth fixing anyway, and the insurance payout, when it eventually arrived, would most likely only be enough for an old banger, if I could find one.

Oh, bugger.

'You can borrow my spare bike,' Cav said, kicking at the jutting tyre. 'If you want.'

I looked at the snow-laden roads. 'Is it safe?'

'Course. Safer than this thing, anyhow.' He kicked again and the bumper fell off. 'Quicker than the bus too.' He made 'weaving' motions with his hands. 'And I know you can ride a bike.'

I'd gone out for a 'Sunday jaunt' with Cav, when I'd first

moved in. What I had envisaged as a leisurely cycle out into the countryside, with possibly a pub lunch thrown in, had turned into something like the 'Tour de Yorkshire'. Cav had got so far ahead of me that I'd had to keep phoning him to find out where he was, and we'd found the steepest range of hills outside of the Alps, every one of which only, apparently, went up. Another couple of climbs and I swore we'd be in orbit.

'Thanks, Cav.' There were no other options, but I'd need to leave early, to miss the traffic. Probably literally, as the roads were slippery and I didn't fancy cannoning off every commuter vehicle all the way in.

'No prob.' He picked up the bumper, completely unashamed. 'You might get to like it. Honestly, bike over car, every time.'

That's what I'm afraid of, I thought, looking at the tiny frame and skinny wheels of the bike he'd just pulled into the drive. Because Ed and Sophie had been home first, the driveway had been full and I'd had to park on the road. Hence the bus-car interface problem. I wondered if I could sue the cat.

'You'll have to wear proper gear.' Cav seriously handed me his helmet. 'And change when you get to work.'

'I am *not* wearing lycra,' I said firmly.

'Nah. I mean the fluorescent stuff.'

Oh Lord. I was going to have to arrive at the office looking like Mr Bean. Just when I thought things couldn't get any worse.

I slowly cycled in to work the next morning, so early that even the roadworks hadn't started, looking like a fourteen-year-old off to do her paper round. The oversized helmet tightly strapped to my head was pulling all the skin of my chin into folds so that I could feel them ripple when I went over cobbles. I was wearing enough fluorescent gear that I was probably visible from space, and a set of lights strapped around my body, which gave me the appearance of one carrying an arsenal of halogen-powered weaponry.

And, because I drew the line at bicycle clips, I'd had to wear leggings.

I caught sight of myself in shop windows as I cycled past, down the pedestrianised streets because there was nobody to stop me, apart from pigeons, who took half-hearted flights to shoulder level and then settled back behind me. The enormous amount of clothing on my top half, teamed with the necessary streamlining below the waist, made me look like a half-inflated balloon that's had all the air pushed into the top. The helmet forced my cheeks and chin forwards, so that I bore an astonishing resemblance to the Human Cannonball, and I was pink and sweaty from the effort of propelling myself over the ridges of snow. The bike skittered and slid and only the fact that I was going at walking pace stopped me from several nasty accidents.

'Are buses really that bad?' I asked myself as I cycled past one, idling its engine while people boarded into the brightly lit relative warmth. Okay, it meant a bit of a hike at both ends, and money I couldn't really afford, but it would be better than this undignified progress surely. Plus, I wasn't going to be able to sit down for a week. Cav, apparently, didn't believe in saddles, and just tacked a bit of razor wire down the middle of the frame. That's what it felt like, anyway.

I swung sharply left into the Minster yard and wobbled over the picturesque but not comfortable cobbled surface, past the brooding hulk of building replete with austere snow in its crannies. It seemed disapproving of my arrival, too early, too brightly lit, and I was sure it turned to watch my legging-clad bottom wobble its way into the YouBack2Work car park with a raise of its Gothic arches.

I had to get off in the car park and push the bike. The overnight snowfall hadn't been disturbed by the arrival of cars and it lay too deep to easily pedal through. There was only one car in there.

Zac's Discovery was parked in its usual spot. There were no tyre tracks blemishing the smooth metres of snow around it, nor footprints leading to the side door. He'd been here all night. Or, at least, I reasoned to myself, his *car* had. He may have got a lift, or gone back to Leeds by train, not wanting to brave the blizzards or risk not being able to get through today.

The car looked dark, cold and deserted. So at least he wasn't living in there, which had been a thought which had crossed my mind. 'It's complicated,' he'd said. I had allowed myself to conjure him an imaginary life, which had consisted of sleeping in his car, using the facilities in the offices, and eating breakfast in the next-door café before turning in to work.

Or, he could just be getting the bus.

I looked down at the sweaty handlebars of the bike. 'Very sensible,' I muttered. Then it occurred to me that Zac wouldn't need to sleep in the car, he could have slept in the office, or the interview room, in the warm, so all that half-dreaming thought of him curled in the back of the Discovery had been total fantasy.

I distracted myself from feeling sorry for Zac by turning off the million points of halogen light from my jacket and locking the bike to a downpipe with the space-age padlock that Cav had made me promise to use.

I suppressed the urge to write an obscenity in the snow on Zac's windscreen with difficulty; after the bike ride, my inner fourteen-year-old wanted to come to the fore. Instead, I settled for peering through the windows, just on the off chance that he was lying, wrapped in a sleeping bag, on the back seat. He wasn't. There was nothing on the seats apart from a tangle of what looked like scarves and jumpers, all in that same hand-knitted pattern that he'd been wearing in the café, all heaped together in one corner, like a woolly sulk. The jumpers looked child-sized, and I wondered again about Zac's home life.

Reassured, if a little annoyed, that he wasn't frozen to death in his own vehicle – even if it would have solved the 'who gets the job' problem – I used my key fob to open the side door into our corridor. Only the doors bore alarms. There was no point in running an alarm system through the whole building, so Michael had said. The downstairs windows were barred anyway, so we were safe from any burglars who didn't have ladders or helicopters and it gave the place the look of a genteel workhouse.

All this meant that I could stride through the darkened building without being disturbed, and it was rather pleasant, even though it was *ridiculously* early, hearing only my footsteps, soft in the trainers, squeaking along the boards. No background hush of machinery or muffled phones ringing. Just the slightly dusty dark, lit by the multicoloured glint of illuminations reflecting off snow and shredded by the window bars onto the floor in front of me.

Down the old-tobacco smell of the hallway, turn right up the two steps past IT and their cheese-and-onion scented office. I could have found my way through the building using only my nose. Now I was outside the interview room, where the smell changed to cheap polish and air freshener overlying that faint whisper of retouched paintwork. I hoisted my bag higher onto my shoulder. I was going to change in the interview room, with a huge mug of very strong coffee and, I looked at my phone clock, possibly a nap.

Under the door to our office, there was a faint glimmer. Not strong enough to be our overhead light, more like the blueish light from a computer screen. There was also a strong smell of coffee. I tiptoed up, pushed the door with a fingertip, and jumped.

In the middle of the floor was a hunched shape. Illuminated only by the light from a screen saver, it resembled nothing so much as a pile of clothes that had been formed into the rough approximation of a human form. Adrenaline flashed through me, then died on wondering why someone would want to scare me, then seared back into my veins again when the huddled shape moved.

'Zac?' I dropped my bag.

The shape went still. I could see now that it was Zac, hair flattened to his head and his face on his knees, sitting on the floor with his big coat drawn up over him. He looked as though he'd walked in and collapsed, huddled down on the rough-weave flooring.

'Zac?' I said again, more gently now. I took two steps towards him and kicked over a mug of coffee that had been sitting on the floor near his hunched shape. It spread a cold pool out over assorted papers and the carpet and the mug clanged away into the darkness beneath the desks, but neither of us remarked on it. 'Has something happened? Are you all right?'

At the back of my mind, a tiny flag waved in triumph for a second – *he's not perfect. He's not always the cheery, upbeat in control person you see every day!* – but I shot it down. This wasn't the kind of advantage I was looking for.

'Hey.' Zac's voice sounded tired. Lost. 'You're early.'

The car. The cold coffee. 'Have you been here all night?' I bent down to sit beside him, my body lights clattering against one another like chattering teeth.

'I...' he tailed off and slumped further forward, cheek against his knees as though he lacked the strength to raise his head. 'Complicated,' he muttered.

I shouldn't touch him. I was well aware of staff policies and the possibility of accusations. But he looked so lost, so forlorn and empty, with his back against the legs of his desk and the spilled coffee like a lake of blood at his feet, so I put an arm around him. He was shivering.

'*Zac.*' I did the brisk arm-rub thing, showing no sexual intent, just an innocent desire to warm him up. 'You're freezing.'

He laughed, a throaty, almost swallowed laugh that turned into sobs. And then his head was down on his knees and he was sobbing, proper, heavy sobs that sounded as though they'd come from his soul, and I was hugging him tight.

'Zac.' It was all I could say. I would try to use his name to keep him anchored. I'd been here, this awful sadness that felt as though it was all-encompassing, when the world flew to pieces around your ears and you couldn't focus on anything except the misery. 'Zac. Listen. Whatever this is, we can work on it, okay?'

My mind was running the possibilities. Was he being fired? Some gross misconduct? No, someone would have given me a heads-up. Gossip ran through this place like norovirus. Not work then. Some personal tragedy? But the Zac I knew, the contained and measured Zac, would have phoned in on compassionate grounds, taken time off to deal with it. *This* had all the hallmarks of an emotional overload, finally coming to a head.

The sobs stopped being audible and mutated into sudden jerks of his shoulders. Then a muffled 'sorry'. A deep intake of breath. 'This isn't me. This isn't *me!*'

I knew that feeling too. When the emotions and the fear and the hopelessness overwhelmed you and you felt as though you existed as a tiny seed of your original self, buried deep under the mourning and the grief and the awful, awful despair. As though anguish laid thickly over the top of the real you, wearing your face and using your words, imitating you without letting you out to speak.

'No.' I held him tighter. 'But if you let this go, you will come to the surface, eventually.' Tears of sympathy threatened behind my eyeballs. *I've been here. I know how this feels.* 'Breathe.'

So I held on. Slowly the sobs became the occasional twitch of his body and the deep involuntary indrawn breaths. The tension ebbed and even the air in the office seemed to become warmer, but then I realised that was because Maintenance had turned the heating on. People were arriving for work. Far down the hallways, there was clattering, voices, a half-laugh cut off by a closing door.

Suddenly, and without warning, the door to the office flew open and a dark shape hurtled inside, then stopped. 'Oh.' A bit of a pause. 'Sorry.'

'Can you come back later, Sam?' I didn't even look up. Caretakers tended to fly around the building in these before-work hours, tweaking heating systems and mending torn carpets; it was rarely urgent.

'I been told to bleed the radiators.'

'Can you bleed them tonight?'

I could feel Sam's baffled gaze travelling from Zac to me and back again.

'Why are you on the floor?'

Zac gave a shaky, almost-laugh. I could feel his breathing returning to a steadier state, with the odd gasp. I kept my arm around his shoulders.

'It's nothing, Sam. Just come back later, okay?'

'Weeeellll...' When I half-glanced up, Sam was scratching his scalp and wrinkling his face. 'I dunno. I'm supposed to bleed them radiators today. That's what it said on the calendar, "bleed radiators", so here I am.'

'Can you cross it out and write it in again for tomorrow?' I chanced a quick look at Zac and was reassured to see that he'd drawn his head up from his knees a fraction. 'The radiators will still be here.'

'S'pose.' Sam gathered his brown janitorial overall around him, like an evil villain about to make a cape-twirling exit. Sam could be nearly as single minded as Cav, but with variable focuses.

'But I'm supposed to do it today.'

'We won't tell if you don't.' I gave him a grin, which wasn't returned, but at least he went out.

He closed the door carefully behind him, but I couldn't tell if he'd gone. He was surprisingly quiet-footed, and we'd not heard him arrive.

'Do you want to go home?' I asked Zac gently. 'I can cover for—'

'No.' The words were sudden, snapped out. 'No. I've got Bob at nine o'clock.'

We fell into silence again, but the emotion was gone. Zac was returning to himself.

'I'll make some coffee then.' I gradually eased myself away from him. 'And I'd better get changed. I look like a Christmas tree.'

He raised his head. 'You do, a bit. Why the...?' He waved a hand at my peculiar clothing choices. 'Leggings? It must be bad.'

Yes, Zac was back. Whatever had caused the misery, the momentary lapse in his normal cheerful self, was gone. Pushed back. I didn't kid myself that it had vanished, I knew too well how this sort of thing worked. You could keep it underground, but it would burst up at every point of weakness. This kind of thing was like playing Whack-A-Mole without a mallet.

We both stood up. Without acknowledging it, Zac peeled his

coat off and hung it on the hook, then began collecting up the coffee-splattered papers from the floor.

'Sorry about that.' I nodded towards the soaked-in stain. 'Didn't see the mug.'

Zac stopped for a second, frozen in the act of piling papers back up onto the corner of his desk. 'I'll clean it up properly.'

'Can't we just cover it over with another rug? That's pretty much standard behaviour for this place. Or we let the sheer volume of paper drift over it. I think that's how glaciers form, you know.'

'By someone spilling a cup of coffee?' We were both injecting so much lightness into our voices that it was going to sound like a helium party soon.

'Layers forming.' I watched him stack those papers and then tap the corners so they were precise. Distraction technique. 'Anyway. I'd better get changed.'

I didn't want to be caught looking like a Glo-stick. It hadn't bothered me when it was just Zac, but some of the office staff would tease me into the New Year about this jacket and the associated lamps. I didn't want to think what they'd say about the leggings.

'Yes. I ought to get ready for my nine o'clock.'

Fine. Clearly we weren't going to talk about it. I supposed that was probably for the best. I'd been within a breath of telling him I knew how he was feeling, but it was information I didn't want him to have about me. Or – I shut the door to the interview room and began to change out of my cycling clothes – did I? It had helped me to know that other people suffered General Anxiety Disorder too. To know that all those people I passed in the street, laughing, chatting, holding their lovers' hand and looking as though they led charmed and perfect lives, could also have episodes where the world seemed too much.

But if I told Zac that, he had ammunition. Although, I thought, peeling off that awful jacket and stuffing it into my bag, *now, so did I.*

The morning was busy, with lots of courses closing for the Christmas break, so phone calls to make to clients to check that they'd be attending in January; new courses would be starting up so there was much form filling to get people moved onto them. Stuff to check, chasing up to do, and I was grateful for it, because it kept me from thinking too hard.

Outside, apparently, it was still snowing. Staff from outlying regions, and some of the Leeds contingent, went home early. Roads were closing over the moors and high hills, trains were affected and nobody wanted to be trapped in the office by snowdrifts and nightfall. So, by lunchtime, the place was relatively quiet.

Priya brought her sandwiches into our office to eat. 'Hmm. Hummus, mung beans and something,' she said, peeling back the top layer of bread. 'Nettie made lunch this morning and she doesn't believe in peanut butter and chocolate spread.'

Zac barely looked up. 'How can she not believe in them?'

'Oh, she knows about their existence. She just doesn't believe their place is together between two slices of bread. They're an ingredient, apparently, not a standalone substance.' She looked sadly once more upon the damply green filling in her sandwich. 'Love her to bits, but she's a barbarian about food.'

Priya sat on the end of my desk. I usually popped to the café next door for lunch but it was closed due to the snow at the moment, so I was making do with a KitKat and coffee. Zac wasn't eating at all, I noticed. He was working normally but there was a jerkiness to his movements that told me he was running on empty and the reflection of the snow through the window was giving his skin a yellowish tinge.

I got up and went into Priya's office. The confectionary cupboard was still as well stocked as ever, despite the fact that we'd been grazing our way through it for weeks. Priya was evidently restocking, there were two boxes of mince pies that hadn't been there a few days ago. Perhaps she was afraid that Nettie was going to start a healthy-eating regime, and these were defensive baked goods? I chose a box and went back into our office, where Zac was talking to Priya about the weather forecast.

'Supposed to snow right up to Christmas,' he said. I wondered if he was talking about normal, routine, down-to-earth things, to stop darker thoughts from breaking through.

'Oh great.' Priya munched at her sandwich, which did, I had to admit, look pretty boring. 'I'll have to get the bus tomorrow then. If it turns up. The roads were bad this morning. How the hell did you get in on a bike, Rubes?'

'Carefully. Very carefully.'

Zac stared at me.

I held out the box of mince pies. 'Here. We may as well get seasonal.'

He took two and gave me a faint smile. 'Thanks. I didn't think about – I mean, I've not had anything yet today. You came on a *bike*?'

'You didn't think that there was absolutely no other reason in the world that I would have dressed like that? I mean, *leggings*?'

'I wasn't—' he broke off. What had he been about to say, that he wasn't in any state to notice how I was dressed or wonder about why? 'I just thought it was your version of snow wear.'

I told him about the car. I'd already had a lengthy discussion with Priya about it, in case she had an obvious solution to my getting-to-work problem, but she didn't. It looked as though the bike and I were going to be an item. Going forward, as Michael would have said.

'That's a bit of a bugger.' He stuffed a mince pie into his mouth, whole. 'Do you want a lift home? The bike will go in the back of the Discovery if we take the front wheel off.'

I hadn't even thought about the journey home yet. Every time I peered out of the window, the landscape looked more Siberian and even the pigeons which usually flocked and pecked around the area outside the Minster steps were sitting on the statue of Constantine, who, in consequence, looked as though he were wearing a cloak of fluffed up feathers and misery. It also occurred to me that getting Zac to drive me home would mean he'd need to leave the car park and therefore might not end up spending all night in the office.

'Thank you,' I said. 'That would be great.'

'No problem.' He ate another mince pie. Whole. 'I owe you one anyway.'

I looked up sharply, to meet his eye. He wasn't going to talk about earlier, was he? With Priya here?

'For bringing the mince pies.' He raised one to me. 'I was seasonally starving.'

But there was a darkness behind the words, a weight that Priya wouldn't have noticed, but I did.

11

The office emptied even more during the afternoon. Michael actually ventured out of his office and stalked the corridors, popping his head round doors, seemingly astonished to find a workforce still there and still actively working.

'Not all gone home yet, then?' he asked jovially to the general office at large, whilst I was in there photocopying some paperwork.

'No,' came the dull assent. Nobody was brave enough to point out that, with jobs on the line, many people would stay until the last possible minute.

'And you're still here, Ruby.' Michael sauntered up to me with the confidence of one who drives a 4x4 vehicle and can afford a hotel room in one of the best establishments, should the snow worsen.

'Apparently.' I hugged the machine-warmed paperwork to my chest like a flimsy hot-water bottle.

'Ah. On your way back to the office?' He fell into step beside me. The draught caused by all the eyebrows in the room raising at once, made the paper chains swing. 'I'll accompany you, if I may.'

Oh great, I thought, clutching my bundle like my firstborn and being forced to pass through the door he held open for me. Now what?

We got as far as the first set of doors before Michael's motivations became clear. 'Any, ah, any follow-up to our conversation the other day?' He had his hands behind his back and a fixed geniality to his expression. 'About our Mr Drewe?'

I made a business of pushing open the door, juggling my paperwork and pretending to slip on the polished boards a little, to give me thinking time.

Do I do it? Do I tell him about Zac's breakdown this morning? It might give me the edge – and I need this job...

'No,' I said, and I sounded more breathless that opening a door and a misstep should have made me. 'He's squeaky clean at the moment.'

Zac's unhappiness was not a weapon.

'Ah.' Michael sounded disappointed. 'Oh well. You keep trying, Ruby.' Then he peeled off to go up the main stairs, back to the safety and warmth of his office, where Rachel would baby him through the rest of the day with good biscuits and careful management. Despite my envy over the proper chocolate coatings and the working heating, I wouldn't have had his job for anything right now.

I heard the familiar, strident tones as I approached the office. 'Hello, Miriam. I didn't think you were due in today.'

'I weren't. But I got this letter and my Angel told me to bring it to you.'

I had a brief moment of picturing Miriam communing with heaven, before I remembered that Angel was the name of her eldest daughter. 'So you came all this way to bring me this? You could have phoned and read it to me.'

'Nah.' Miriam fidgeted outside the interview room door. 'You goin' to let me in, or what? I needs a coffee, it's bloody cold enough out there to freeze your tits off.'

I unlocked the door, remembering our last conversation, where Miriam had spilled her life story to me, and I looked, with a new respect, at this thin, edgy woman. She'd had the kind of life I had only ever read about in those awful books that Gareth had left piled in the garage when he went. Misery Lit, they called it. Gareth had called them 'Daddy, No!' books, but then he'd had all the sensitivity of a walrus. Miriam was a survivor.

'Plus, I had to come in to York to change this top I got for our Lewis. It's too small, apparently, well, not surprisin' now he's a fat bastard. He wants to knock off them computer games and do some exercise, I told him.'

I held my hand out for the letter, while Miriam poured herself a cup of coffee and took a handful of the biscuits.

'It's all right.' I scanned the paper quickly. 'It's just a follow-up letter to remind you that you're expected to be applying for jobs in the New Year.'

'But you're counsellin' me! I thought I didn't have to apply for nothin' while you was counsellin' me!' Miriam raised her head from her mug to wail.

'Yes, but you only get so many sessions before you have to show willing and get back out there. Counselling doesn't put a stop on applications, it's to help you have the confidence to accept jobs you may be offered and to apply for the most suitable positions.' I sounded exactly like I had when I'd given my talk to the management. It felt like months ago now.

'That's what *he* used to say.' A jerk of the head towards our office. 'The tosspot.'

'You've worked before.'

'Yeah. Some cash-in-hand stuff. And I used to clean, up to Woolworths. That was great. Used to nick the Pick-n-Mix of an evenin'.'

'They won't keep paying you indefinitely, if you don't show that you're looking for work.' This was what it boiled down to.

Miriam stared around the room for a moment. 'D'you like doin' this?' she asked sharply. 'Makin' people do stuff?'

'I like helping people, yes.'

She sniffed. 'Thought so. You're a bossy little cow, ain't you? There's more than one way to skin a cat, my mum used to say.'

'Your mum was probably technically correct, but cat skinning isn't one of the courses on offer,' I said, straight-faced. Calling me 'bossy' had stung. My sister was bossy, I was – what was it Gareth used to say? Persistent. Not bossy. 'You need to read through that prospectus again.'

Miriam tipped her head on one side. 'You're very keen. Why're you so bothered about me workin'? I thought this was one of those "soft option" things – I keeps comin' in, you keeps talkin' to me, you tick your boxes and I tick mine.' Her blue eyes were sharp. 'Why are you suddenly so up and airy about wantin' me to get a job? Even the tosspot basically gave up after a bit.'

There must have been a touch of Christmas hypnotism going on. Maybe it was the swinging prisms of the foil star that someone had stuck with tape to the light fitting, doing a Derren Brown on me. Before I knew what I was doing, I had told Miriam about the merger, about needing to keep my job, about Gareth leaving me to pay the house debts, about being in competition with Zac to keep this position.

Miriam seemed happy to listen, but then she was indoors with free coffee and biscuits and the faint background sound of Christmas carols being piped through the music system, presumably to keep us all in seasonal spirits and to stop us killing one another. It was like being in a particularly liberal church.

'So you both wants the job but management thinks he's the best,' she précised, when I stopped talking to drink my now luke-warm coffee.

'Maybe he is, though.' In the interests of fairness, I felt I had to put this view forward. 'He's quite forthright with clients.'

'Forthright! That's one word for it,' Miriam snorted, inhaled biscuit crumbs and then coughed her smoker's cough for a few minutes. 'He's a dictator, is what he is. Makes that Hitler look like, well, like you.'

That was the second time she'd insulted me. And now she'd compared me to Hitler?

'But I see now why you're so keen to get me off the books,' Miriam said, thoughtfully. 'It'd give you one-up on tosspot.'

'He's not really a tosspot.' I thought of Zac's cheerful attitude, even his hair was upward-looking. And then, almost reluctantly, of that vulnerability that had shown through this morning, like the earth showing through a wind-scoured patch of snow. 'It's just that his way of doing things doesn't chime with everyone. His success levels are pretty good.'

Miriam nudged me. 'But us girls have to stick together though, eh? Can't let them blokes get the upper hand on us. You've been through it too, with that prick Gareth.' She frowned for a second and pursed her lips, as though an invisible cigarette had made its way between them. 'Yeah,' she said, slowly and thoughtfully. 'Okay. Look. I'll give you this one. Check my applications.'

'I'm sorry?'

She was collecting up her bags and coat now, tutting at the damp hems of her jeans and trying to put on her scarf without getting encrusted snow in her hair. 'That's all I'm givin' you. If

you're smart enough to work it out, then you deserve it. If not –
well.' She wound the bright red wool around her head. 'Then
maybe Tosspot should get to keep the job.'

I stayed sitting after she'd bustled her way out. I had that
slight sense of relief that I often felt when I'd confessed something to someone, but underneath it bubbled an annoyance.
Miriam thought I was bossy? But I *had* to be assertive, it was part
of the job, even though Zac seemed to think all I did was listen
and reassure, I still had to encourage people to look for work and
not take feeble excuses as an answer. *That* wasn't bullying, was it?

Was it?

I liked helping people reach their own conclusions. I didn't
tell them the answers to all their problems, but instead I laid
things out in a way that helped them see for themselves. That was
definitely not bullying, it was doing my job.

But then I had a flashback. I'd got used to them now. At first
they'd been part of the anxiety and depression, reliving past
events as clearly as if they'd been happening in front of me. I'd
relived that finding of the earrings so often now that it had taken
on the quality of a repeated TV episode, harsh but part of the
overall story. The pain wasn't so sharp any more. But this flashback was different, it was something I'd nearly forgotten.

We'd been sitting, Gareth and I, in the packed-up remains of
the rented flat. I was doing a last clean through, Gareth was –
well, Gareth was doing what Gareth usually did, sitting down in
front of the TV.

'Come on, we've got our moving out inspection this afternoon!' I waved a cloth in front of his face.

'Yeah, yeah. Plenty of time.' He looked up at the ceiling. 'I like
this place. Wish we could stay here.'

'But we've bought the cottage now. And buying is much better
than renting! We can decorate and do our own thing, and we'll

have a garden and all that.' I noticed a spot on the carpet and set about it with the damp cloth.

'But this is right close to town and all that. I can walk home from the pub, no taxis or anything.' He'd caught at me as I'd got up from the carpet and pulled me onto his lap. 'One last shag in the old place?'

I wriggled free. 'We get the keys tomorrow, we've got to get this place ready to leave today!'

He'd let me go, and gone into the kitchen to pour himself a beer that was warm because we'd already turned off the fridge. 'I dunno about this moving thing,' he said again. 'I like it here.'

'But you like the cottage too! It's cosy and it will be ours!' I playfully flicked him with the cloth as he came back in. 'On the property ladder at last.'

'Yeah, yeah.' He sat down again, thwarting my attempts to push a window-cleaning spray into his non-beer-holding hand. 'You're a bossy cow, Ruby, you know that?'

Then he'd laughed and I'd laughed and I'd not really thought of it again. Until now with the scene playing in front of my eyes so powerfully that the cleaning spray smell burned my nose and I could feel the echo of the ache in my muscles from all the scrubbing.

Had I bullied him into buying the cottage?

I thought back over my relationship with Gareth. We'd met through friends and drifted into a relationship after seeing one another out and about with our various groups. I'd been living in the tiny flat in Acomb, he'd been sharing with a bunch of rugby friends, and we'd found a place to rent together near the centre of town, 'cheaper with two', as he'd said. But, if things were left up to Gareth, when he was home from Europe, days would consist of me phoning in sick to work, all-day sex sessions and then ordering a pizza, sides and beer delivered to the door. We'd never have left the flat. We'd never have gone on holiday, or out for walks, or visited parents. There would never have been any housework done or washing up and the bedsheets would have been unchanged for a year.

Somebody had to take charge of all that. *Somebody* had to get us outside in daylight, to actually be a couple and not just two people who lived together and never got out of bed. Was that bossy?

And surely, buying a house was the next step? I'd haunted Rightmove when Gareth had been working away so much. Evenings had been long and often lonely, unless I went to visit my family or to Priya's, to eat Nettie's excellent cooking and to play board games and drink too much wine. I pretty much sorted the mortgage application and the surveys by myself, Gareth had just signed things and moaned about the necessity of having to move furniture.

Was *that* bossy?

With the benefit of that perfect clarity that hindsight lends, I could see that he'd done his best to put the brakes on the house purchase all the way through the process. Complaining about location, about how he'd have to spend his 'downtime' doing household maintenance; that the takeaways were too far away. When none of that had worked, he'd taken to working longer hours, not being around much for the actual moving, even though I'd timed everything carefully for his annual holiday.

I tried to keep my thoughts from veering into what he'd *really* been doing during those 'extra working hours' that he'd told me would help earn enough to pay for things for the house. The new windows I'd ordered and not managed to cancel in time when he'd gone – that I was still paying for. The carpets and the curtains I'd bought and had to leave behind. The reasons I was still in such debt.

I'd thought there would be two of us to cover the costs. I'd been stupid. And yes, bossy, apparently. But he had tried to stop me. Admittedly, without using the words 'sorry, babe, but I'm seeing other women when I'm not with you, so it would be stupid to buy a house together. I'm never going to commit to you. In fact, I'd be planning to leave you if I weren't so lazy and unmotivated, but, hey.' Which would at least have concentrated my mind and stopped me blithely planning for a life I was never going to have.

I sighed deeply. This room smelled of defeat. It smelled of people who were, for one reason or another, never going to live the lives they wanted. People so beaten down through circumstance that they were going to bob along under the waters of life, only breaking surface when absolutely necessary. It wasn't the job I had thought it would be when I'd applied. I had thought I could make a difference, change people's perceptions, help them overcome fears. Change lives. Help people.

Really, *was* this job worth doing? Were we doing any good, or were we just bossing people about who would be better left alone?

I gave my mental walls a little shove. A mixture of medication and the hope that Miriam had given me was keeping them firm, although the prospect of being without a car for the foreseeable future was putting little cracks in the base.

The broken-down car *and* it was snowing. *And*, if I wasn't mistaken, Kylie Minogue was launching into the fourth round of 'Santa, Baby' over the sound system. But at least I wouldn't have to wear the leggings or the illuminated jacket to go home, so there were positives in the day.

* * *

It got dark very early, although it was a peculiar form of darkness. Light vanished from the sky, but was trapped on earth in the form of the snow, which reflected every tiny incidence of illumination. Under the huge overhead decorations, which swung slowly in an unfelt breeze, the snow glistened an iridescent blue and red. Outside the shop windows, it gleamed a promising gold. Beyond the office windows, in the shadow of the Minster, it lay heaped and bulked by people shovelling pathways clear, as though the Minster were a huge castle rising from a motte and bailey entirely comprised of blood-dark snow.

'Ready to go?' Zac appeared in the office where I was sitting behind my computer, and he was already wearing his coat. 'I think everyone else has tunnelled their way out. Or possibly they are all currently holed up in a self-built igloo out the back, playing poker.'

I tore my eyes away from the window. The room instantly looked too bright. As did Zac, now I knew he wasn't quite the 'what you see is what you get' guy he purported to be. He looked too animated, too cheery, as though his clockwork was wound too tightly.

'Gosh, the afternoon got away from me a bit,' I said, pulling my eyes away from him because I didn't want him to think I thought about him at all. 'I'll just get my stuff together.'

'Well, you did have to deal with Miriam,' Zac said, carelessly slouching down on the edge of his desk. It was a very convincing performance, I had to admit. 'That tends to throw the rest of the day off by about ten light years.'

'She's not so bad.' I remembered what she'd said about her file and gathered it up to stuff into my bag. Zac noticed.

'You're taking work home? But it's nearly Christmas! Haven't you got – I don't know, mince pies to bake and carol concerts to avoid?'

'Avoid?'

'I've heard Sophie sing,' he said, darkly.

'Oh, yes.' An aural hallucination of Sophie squeaking out the descant to 'Oh Come, All Ye Faithful' played in my mind and I shuddered. 'It's not too bad if you don't sit next to her. Or even in the same county.' I found the fluorescent jacket strobing to itself in the corner where I'd discarded it this morning, and looked at it. 'I should have brought a proper coat.'

'The car heater works. Come on, I think we're practically the last to leave.'

We walked out into the car park. Some people had decided not to risk driving and had left their cars, which now looked like children had been building car-shaped snowmen around the outside of the building.

'Wow,' I said. 'It's deep. No wonder so many people went home early.'

The snow made squeaky, tortured noises under our feet as we trudged out towards the Discovery, like a couple of polar explorers. The wind whipped snow from the surface and hurled it into our faces to add to the stuff that was coming down from the sky, breaking our surroundings into barely illuminated fragments.

'Yes. It's worse than I thought.'

Zac opened the back of the Discovery while I unlocked the bike, which was now just a series of humps and bumps under its icy covering.

'Thanks for this,' I said, having to carry it to the car. It was surprisingly light, I expected Cav could tell me exactly what type of carbon fibre the frame was made of and how many miles the tyres could be expected to do, had I been interested enough to ask. 'I'm just realising it would have been mad to try to cycle home in this weather.'

Zac unclipped the wheels and put the bike carefully into the boot. 'I've got a feeling that driving in it isn't going to be much better,' he said. 'Let's hope they've cleared and gritted at least the main roads. The Discovery can handle most weather conditions, but I'm not sure she's got an Arctic setting.'

He gave me another one of those grins, squeezed between the upturned collar of his coat and the knitted brim of his pulled-down hat. Still bright. Still convincing. But now I knew, I could see the slight brittleness around the edges.

I hopped into the passenger seat and we made our cautious way out of the car park. The roads beyond were quiet. Snow-ploughs had been down and swept a single lane clear, piling the left-over snow up around the edges in mini mountainous peaks, so cars ran along the track, making the inner bypass look like a giant Scalextric set. When two cars met heading in opposite directions, one had to pull over onto the virgin snow and there was much slithering and wheel-spinning going on. The drivers seemed all to be wearing enormous grins under stress tight eyes, so I gathered that everyone was having a whale of a time in these unaccustomed conditions.

The pavements were almost empty. Only the most deter-mined shopper still struggled on, booted and coated into animated heaps, through the snow. An escaped ball of tinsel blew past, briefly decorating a drainpipe, a car bonnet and a surprised pigeon as the wind hurled it along, a flock of panicked glitter fleeing the storm.

'It's a bit like nuclear winter, only with more cake,' I said, as we slithered slowly past a still-open Sainsbury's, which had piles of Christmas food in the window.

'Yes.' Zac corrected the natural inclination of the car to bounce gently off the snowbanks lining the road. We were zigzag-ging our way along a deserted stretch of carriageway, very, very slowly. 'Not sure I'll make it back to Leeds tonight.'

'If the guys agree, you can sleep on our sofa.' I looked out of the window again. 'It will be warmer than the office and cheaper than a hotel, although we don't do much in the way of cooked breakfasts.'

'Ah.' A shuffling pedestrian passed us on the outside, then we hit a patch of grit and managed to overtake them again. 'Yes. This morning.'

'You don't have to talk about it, Zac. Honestly.'

He was a huddled shape behind the steering wheel. Despite the fact that the Discovery was blasting warm air at us, he'd kept his hat on, still pulled low over his forehead. Behind him, the pile of little knitted jumpers swayed and rocked. I didn't know if I wanted him to talk about this morning or not. Explanations might make it all make sense, but if I knew – then it all became real. 'If it's all right with everyone, I would very much appreciate the sofa, thank you. I'm not sure I can keep this level of concentration up for a return journey. My eyes are starting to swivel.'

I know he looked at me, because I saw his head turn, but it was too dark, even with the snow beaming back every kind of light, to see any expression. I decided not to push it. Besides, I didn't want him to get annoyed and stop the car, because I was afraid it may never get started again. Even four-wheel-drive was making heavy weather of the snowfall.

Outside the centre of town, the roads were worse. Only the main roads had been cleared, so side roads were just two lines of barely traversed snow. Some gardens were growing a crop of snowmen and small gangs of snowball fighters, who at least made the dark less empty, even if the soft thud of snowballs hitting the bodywork as we drifted past did carry a slight implicit threat.

Further out, there was nobody. The streets were dark and empty, only a passing bus, lighting up the snow with its windows, like a mobile advent calendar, showed any sign that people were still moving about. I imagined trying to cycle through this and knew that I'd have ended up walking and pushing the bike. Zac had, at the very least, saved me from that.

'Thank you,' I said, at exactly the same time as he did.

A confused silence followed.

'Why?' I asked cautiously, in case we were going to end up speaking at the same time from now on, like some kind of fairy's curse.

'This morning. And not asking.'

'Oh.' We were turning, drifting gently over the edge of the pavement which was invisible under the eighteen inches of snow, into my road. I could see the Christmas trees in the windows of the houses, the pinpricks of lights in porches and trees. 'I was just saying thank you for saving me from trying to cycle home.'

More uncomfortable silence. Well, relative silence at least, as there was a small, shouty group of local children lined up behind a garden wall, poised and ready to bombard us with snow as soon as we got out of the car. I could see various-sized heads and the tops of bobble hats crouched in the bare undergrowth and hear the whoops and yells of potential horrors to come as we parked on the road outside the house. Sophie's car was at an angle in the driveway. There was no sign of Ed's, but I remembered he'd headed out to his parents' for Christmas yesterday morning. Cav was in the covered side return, with his bike upside down, doing something to the pedals. My car had clearly been towed away by the bus company's insurers at some point in the day. The snow had obliterated any tracks.

I gathered my bag to my chest. 'We'll have to make a run for it. Those lads out there are armed.'

'It's unfair. It's like the Charge of the Light Brigade, only without horses.' Zac slid the driver's side window down. 'I'm arming up.' He scraped a couple of handfuls of snow from the outside of the car. 'I'll cover you.'

I tore down the driveway and skidded my way into the porch, while Zac pelted snowballs back in the direction of the hiding crew. There was a lot of shrieking and laughing, and I think he deliberately delayed his arrival into the house, because I'd had time to get my coat off, ask Sophie about the sofa and begin the search for some clean coffee mugs before he followed me inside. He was powdered in snow and his cheeks were red.

'Well, that was fun,' he said. 'Two of them have got a hell of a reach on them, but I've got years of experience on my side. Plus an adult's innate cunning, and a really stupid hat.'

'Sophie says you're fine to have the sofa for tonight.' I carried on shifting stuff in the cupboard. The dishwasher was full and actually going, and there weren't many clean mugs hanging around.

'That's really very kind of all of you.'

'She hasn't started on "Oh Little Town of Bethlehem" yet,' I said darkly. 'You may regret staying over, unless you've got very good earplugs.'

My rummaging paid off in the form of two very old and slightly chipped mugs hidden deep in the back of the cupboard where the dried pasta lay, dusty, untouched and unloved. None of us really liked pasta, but we kept buying it for some reason. I began to make coffee.

'Do you mind if I get these wet things off?' Zac asked.

'Downstairs bathroom, through there.' I nodded towards the door, but didn't see him go, as Cav burst in to ask the where-abouts of his second-best bike and then behaved as though I'd performed unanaesthetised surgery on his firstborn when I told him it was sitting in the back of the Discovery with its wheels off. He dashed back out, no doubt to sit and wait for Zac to open the vehicle, murmuring soft words of reassurance through the windows in the meantime.

When Zac came back in, he had changed out of the damp work clothes he'd been snowballed in and into some loose cotton trousers and a sweatshirt.

I stared at him.

'You carry a change of clothes in your work bag?' It was all he had with him, apart from those tiny jumpers in the back of his car.

'Yup, it's just sensible.' He indicated the brightly lit, and somewhat messy, kitchen. 'You never know when you may be stranded by apocalyptic weather conditions in a cross between a squat and a kindergarten.' A hand waved towards the tray of Rudolph biscuits, complete with red cherry noses, that Sophie had cooling on the work surface.

'Sophie's a primary school teacher,' I explained. 'It's the school Christmas party tomorrow. There's probably a load of marshmallow snow bunnies in the – ah, yes, here they are.' I closed the cupboard door again. 'And I wouldn't be rude about the place, because it's this or you're sleeping in the Discovery.'

Zac looked suddenly abashed. More so than I would have expected my jocular tone to have evoked. 'Yeah, sorry, I really am grateful for the sofa offer. It's still coming down out there. Do you think we should send out for supplies or a takeaway or something?'

'Already ordered.' Cav's voice drifted in from the hallway, where he was now in the shelter of the house but still watching the Discovery, presumably in case Rannulph Fiennes decided to come by and turn to bike theft. 'As long as you eat pizza, you're covered.'

'That's very kind of you.'

'Can you unlock the car now?' Cav was almost rotating with impatience. 'I need to check the bike over.'

'He's a bit... single-minded,' I explained, as Zac clicked the key button through the window, very wisely choosing not to venture back outside, and Cav took off through the front door like a terrier sighting next door's cat.

'Are you and he...?' Zac looked from me to the shrouded form of Cav, who was gently stroking the bike as he slid it carefully from the Discovery's boot. 'Only Priya said...'

'Priya once spent twenty minutes trying to persuade me that Cav would make a great boyfriend,' I said, tightly.

'Only twenty minutes? That's not like Priya, she's usually a touch more persistent than that. What happened?'

'She actually *met* Cav,' I said tightly. 'After half an hour of him explaining to her how to strip-clean the gears of his bike, she reported back that he was only suitable to date if you'd already won the Tour de France and, apparently, it's a terrible waste.' Then I rounded on him. 'What do you mean, she's persistent?'

'She, er, she, well, you must have noticed. She keeps trying to set us up?'

'Oh, don't take it personally. She tries to set me up with any available single man. She thinks I just need to meet someone to help me get over—' I stopped. The whole Gareth thing was none of his business. 'She's happily coupled up and not so much smug as totally self-satisfied. She wants a partner in complacency.'

'And you're not so keen?'

'Aversion therapy is a powerful thing.' That was all I was going to say on the subject, so I was extremely happy to see the pizza delivery van slide gently past the house and finally bump to a stop three doors down. 'Food is coming.'

We ate in the living room, pizza boxes on the coffee table. Sophie took a plate of slices up to her room, as she had marking to do. Cav sat with us for a while, but when Zac couldn't take part in any bike-based chat, he sloped back off to twiddle with his pedals outside the kitchen door again. It left Zac and I on our own, amid the discarded pizza and general household detritus.

We ate in silence. Well, almost silence, Sophie was singing softly to herself upstairs over our heads. At least, she may have *intended* singing softly, but as it was mostly off-key it came over as louder than she presumably thought.

'Pizza. Not the best food to eat if you're trying to impress someone.' Zac jerked his chin upwards and a string of cheese stretched to accommodate the movement.

'Better than spaghetti bolognaise.' I was sitting on the bean-bag. I didn't want to sit next to him, it felt unnecessarily intimate and this wasn't, after all, a date, but eating pizza whilst sitting on a surface that is slowly collapsing under your weight was not turning out to be a great move. The plate was virtually under my chin, as were my knees. 'And we don't have to impress anyone, do we? We're just refuelling. Doesn't matter what we look like.'

'You could be right.' Zac licked his fingers and put the plate down. 'Maybe that's it. Maybe we should all care a bit less what people think of us.'

'Is that your excuse for the hat? And the jumpers you wear that don't quite fit?' I meant it to be light-hearted, but I heard it come across as accusatory, and concentrated really hard on my pizza so I didn't have to look at his face.

'No. The jumpers are... Look, Ruby. We really need to talk about—'

I knew he was right, but I just couldn't. While we hadn't discussed his breakdown this morning, I could still kid myself that it was glossed over. Like that chunk in the skirting board that my eyes suddenly found really fascinating, where we'd taken a slice out of the wood moving the sofa and painted over it, pretending that it was invisible, that nothing had ever happened. If we talked about it – then I had to face up to either using it against him, or trying to work out why I *didn't want* to use it against him.

'Look, I've got some work to do. I'll take it upstairs. While I'm up there, I'll sort you out a spare duvet and a pillow, we tend to go to bed quite early in this house because everyone has to be up at the crack of dawn.'

I rushed the words out, giving him no chance to insert so much as a comma between them, and, by the time I'd finished speaking, I was already out of the door and in the hallway, grabbing my work bag and abandoning the pizza. Zac had barely moved.

Up the stairs I went, where I could hear Sophie more clearly, but I was prepared to take that in order to get away, and then into my tiny room, where I changed into fleecy pyjamas and lay on the bed, staring at the ceiling and ignoring the sheaves of paper which protruded, wrinkle-edged with damp, from my bag.

Why didn't I want to hear what he had to say?

But I knew. Deep down. If Zac told me what it was, between the wedding photograph and the small jumpers in the back of his car, between the never going home and the being unable to move from Leeds – it would make it real. It would make his problems something concrete and definite. It would make him a real person.

And if I had to think of Zac as a real, whole person, then I had to stare the competition for my job full in the face. At the moment, I could still just about kid myself that it was never going to happen. That some fluke would mean we would both be kept on and I wouldn't have to peer at the reality of working for an unethical company in a job I was no longer sure was doing any good at all.

Then the thought of having to find myself another job reared into the back of my mind. Interviews. Assessments. Stuff that would stress me into another breakdown, if I wasn't careful. I *had* to stay where I was.

You're fine, Ruby.

My heart rate began to slow again and my hands relaxed from their tight fists.

Now I wanted to go back down and finish the pizza, but I didn't dare.

I hauled a spare duvet from under the bed, which was the only storage space in the room, and flung it down the stairs, where it landed in the hallway with a soft 'flump'. 'Duvet!' I called, and then pushed my door almost closed again.

To distract myself, I pulled the file from my bag. I'd forgotten what I'd brought with me from the office, so the scruffy, hand-written sheets were almost a surprise. They were Miriam's photo-copied application forms and they contained something she thought would give me the edge over Zac. Find Miriam's secret, get her into work – that ought to count so highly in my favour that I'd never even need to *think* about Zac's tears, the hopeless-ness and defeat in every angle of his body…

Yeah. I was thinking about it way too much for something I didn't want to think about.

I switched on my bedside lamp and tilted the papers to throw more light onto those black lined forms.

Date of Birth: *1979*

I sat back, hitting my head on the lamp as I went. I'd pegged Miriam a good ten years older.

Qualifications: *None*

I knew she'd left school early, pregnant with her eldest son, so that wasn't a complete surprise. She'd had no time to take exams, and then, with a small baby to care for and no real help, no wonder she'd slid through the cracks.

Experience: *see following:*

A list of jobs, all temporary, all very short-lived. Cleaning, mostly. Well, that was fine, if I could get her a small job with a cleaning agency, it would get her off our books and she'd still receive some benefit money to top up her earnings.

I tilted the pages again and felt a little dig of sadness under my ribs. These few scratched markings on the form, that was all Miriam had to show for her life. No qualifications, four children. A council house on an estate in Leeds, where she shared a bedroom with her smallest granddaughter.

I gave a short, hollow laugh and looked around my own, four squeezed walls. I may be many years behind and several qualifications ahead, but my life wasn't exactly where I'd planned it either, was it? I couldn't fault Miriam, because I knew how things didn't always turn out the way we wanted. Then I gave a little shudder. Sometimes these thoughts spiralled. This might not be where I thought I should be, but there was always further down to go. Huge debts. Mounting repayments. Bailiffs and homelessness and job loss and...

Breathe.

Miriam's life was not, thankfully, mine.

So, what did she think I would see? I spread the forms out across the bed and moved from one to the next and then the next. All of them gave more or less the same information. I could see where details had been slightly altered, dates truncated or elongated, experience talked up a little, but nothing that would give me pause for thought.

Nothing that would actually tell me anything.

But if I *didn't* find whatever she'd been alluding to, then that only left me with the dirty tricks campaign. I put my face in my hands. I didn't need this kind of moral conundrum. Be nice, be moral, versus play the game and keep my office. Was I the kind of person who would hang on to my job at all costs? Or was I *nice*?

Oh, this was *horrible*.

I rubbed my eyes with the heels of my hands, making the neutral paintwork blur and slide. The knock on the door meant that I pressed too hard and nearly blinded myself and jumped so hard that papers slid off the bed and sprawled onto the floor in an untidy ruckus, with yesterday's socks and old magazines.

'Ruby? I made you a coffee and brought the rest of the pizza. You didn't get to finish yours and—'

I cut Zac off by flinging open the already partly open door. I must have looked ferocious, because he took half a step back and collided with the banister rail. 'You,' I said sternly but mainly focusing on the pizza box in his hand, because, damn him, he was right and I was still hungry, 'are treading on my boundaries, Zac.'

He made a face. 'Sorry. I didn't mean to. I don't want to come in. I just thought you might like coffee and pizza. You know. Because I'm a guest and it's your house and everything.'

He looked out of place, my work colleague standing on the landing in non-office clothing. Unsettled, with his hair flattened by the wearing of the strange knitted hat. Cheery, normal, an easy-going and approachable man with no worries other than how we were going to get the Discovery out of its snow bank in the morning.

'Michael has asked me to tell him if there's any reason I can find that you shouldn't get to keep the job.' The words fell out of me. They'd been so uppermost in my mind, so on-the-tip-of-my-tongue for so long now that I was almost unaware that I'd said them aloud.

'Ah.' Zac shifted his weight.

'Have they asked you to do the same about me?'

'Yes.'

Our eyes met. Level and steady, we held one another's gaze. Was he weighing me up? I was noticing the way his brown eyes seemed more hazel in the muted light from the purple-shaded bulb. How his eyelashes were long and still spiky from the snow. I didn't know what he was looking at, staring so deeply into my face, as though he could pull secrets to the surface if he just looked at me long enough.

'We are working for a bunch of fucking crooks, aren't we?' Zac said, eventually. 'Ethically, I mean,' he added. The question he wanted to ask was there, hovering in the steam from the coffee which rose from the mug which must have been scorching his knuckles. But he didn't ask it. He just stood, head tilted slightly to one side, as though he could get an answer merely by looking at me quizzically.

I didn't ask either. I just stood to one side. 'Come in. But stay sideways. If you turn ninety degrees, you'll get jammed.'

I shuffled back to allow him into my bedroom, and then closed the door behind him with my foot.

'Wow. It's quite small.' He juggled the coffee and pizza. I took them both from him.

'Yes. It's the cheapest room.'

'Well, good. Because if it were the most expensive, I would be asking serious questions, like does that wall fold down to reveal a gold-plated bathroom.'

We both looked at the wall in question.

'No,' I said sadly. 'If it did fold down, it would reveal only Ed's room and, I suspect, a wardrobe of colour co-ordinated workwear.'

'Blimey.' Zac rotated, slowly and carefully. 'You haven't even got room to draw the curtains.'

'It reduces the room space by seven per cent. That window ledge is essential shelving.'

We stopped talking. The unspoken hovered between us.

Eventually, Zac put his coffee mug down on the window ledge.

'I don't…' he began, and then stopped.

Everything pivoted on that moment. In that tiny room, which now mostly smelled of fresh-brewed coffee and bed, with an undercurrent of cold pizza, I could feel myself turning through space. Was I nice? Or was I what Gareth had believed me to be, bossy, self-serving? Which was the real me?

I reached behind me and picked up my bag. Inserted a hand into the secret, zipped compartment.

'This is me,' was all I said. Withdrawing the slim foil packet with the damning words printed on it. My anti-anxiety medication. The pills that kept me from collapsing. Handing him the method to destroy me.

He looked at the pills, then up into my face. 'Okay,' he said slowly.

'I had a breakdown when my boyfriend left me for someone else. Oh, it's not quite as straightforward as that, he also disappeared, leaving me with all the debts and a house to sell at a loss and all that, but that was what started it. I have an anxiety disorder. Stress makes me…' I stopped. That was enough, I could see from his face.

He looked as though he were coming to a conclusion. 'Fair's fair then,' he said and sat, uninvited, on the end of the bed, causing another torrent of paperwork to hit the floor. 'You may want to grab a slice of pizza; when I said it was complicated, I wasn't kidding.'

He didn't attempt to stop me as I reached over him and took a slice of wilting pizza from the box. It was almost cold and had the temperature and texture of cooling flesh. I looked at it and put it back, exchanging it for the still steaming coffee.

'My mum has dementia.' He dropped the words heavily into the air. 'Early onset, she's been developing symptoms since her forties. She was attacked one night, getting into her car, by a man she mistook for an old friend.' He stopped speaking again, dipped his head as though the weight of what he was saying lived on the back of his neck. 'She was never right after that. She's in a... I dunno what you'd call it. A nursing home? Care facility? She comes home most weekends and I look after her then. But I can't move, can't change anything about the house, it has to be as she remembers it.'

'Oh, Zac.' I touched his shoulder and sat beside him. This was so much worse than the various marital situations I'd imagined for him, so much more painful. My chest ached with sympathy.

'She knits, you see.' He carried on talking to the carpet. 'She likes to knit me jumpers. And hats. I think it's how she shows she cares. But...' Another stop. A deep breath. 'She remembers me as being nine years old. When she comes home, she thinks... she thinks I'm her nephew, looking after her.' He gave me a quick flick of a look. 'My cousin is sixty-three now and lives in Australia. I like to think I'm wearing rather better than that.'

A whole load of implications came flooding along with his revelations. Zac's mother didn't recognise her own son. Did that mean she must wonder, aloud, where he was, why he didn't come to see her? But she knitted for him, that absent son, who stood in front of her in his thirties, unrecognised.

'Oh, Zac,' I said again. I couldn't think of anything else.

'Dad died years ago, it's just me and her. And, usually, it's just me.' The word stretched in a way I recognised. He was trying not to cry.

I looked at him with fresh eyes. He wasn't just a smart, bright, overconfident competitor for my job, but a man struggling with an awful burden. It made my 'boyfriend dumped me' look thin and feeble as a reason for breaking down.

'The photograph on your desk?'

'Mum and Dad's wedding. I look a lot like him, apparently.' Then an attempt at humour, trying to drag this conversation back from the depths it was rapidly circling, 'Then, I mean. Not now, hopefully.'

I made a connection. 'And that's why you're so worried about me walking to my car in the dark?'

He raised his head a couple of degrees and looked at me side-ways. 'I can't help it. Sorry. You know one of the worst things?' He reached out and took his coffee mug, cradling it between hands that shook, just a little bit as I watched. 'I have to live with the most hideous wallpaper you've ever seen. I can't change it because Mum would get upset, unsettled. Honestly, I don't know what possessed them. It's got *swirls*.'

There had been swirls in the cottage when we'd moved in, so I could empathise with this horror. 'I was painting our living room blue,' I said. 'It looked lovely.' All those leftover tins of paint I'd just abandoned. Still there, on the floor of the half-painted room when the house had gone back on the market.

Zac nodded, solemnly. 'I've been dealing with Mum since I was fifteen. At first she was just... funny, y'know? Just forgetful and easily confused. She's been diagnosed with a form of Pick's disease.' His voice brightened temporarily. 'It's quite unusual in females and she doesn't have the aphasia. She's being studied. I

think she's the subject of at least one PhD.' A sigh. 'And sometimes, like this morning...' He stopped again.

'It just gets too much?'

'I guess we all just have our own lines. Some people's are
further away than others.' He rubbed his hands over the top of
his head, sending the flat hair back up into its more usual spikes.
'I reach mine every so often. When I just think how fucking *unfair*
it all is.'

'My boyfriend married a thin, rich blonde,' I said, although
why this would help, I had no idea. 'I saw the pictures before my
friends wrestled social media away from me.'

Zac gave a snorty kind of laugh. 'Comparison is the thief of
joy, isn't that what they say? Well, comparison can go get fucked.
My joy got stolen a long time ago. But you can't help thinking
"what if?" can you?'

'My whole life seems to consist of "what ifs",' I said, sadly. 'It's
the feeling that you're not living the life you were led to believe in,
isn't it?'

Zac raised his head fully now. 'I think you've got it there.' A
deep, deep inbreath, like a gasp. 'I'm *fairly* sure that life promised
me I'd be playing for Manchester United by now.' A glance flickered down to my bag. 'Do they work? The tablets?'

I shrugged. 'They seem to. I'm better now than I was,
although whether that's the tablets or just time and space, I can't
tell. But I'm not about to stop taking them to find out.'

Another silence, into which the sound of Sophie breaking
into 'The First Noel' came plummeting. I spared a moment to
think of my parents' bickery, happy health-consciousness with
Zac's upbringing and felt an awkward moment of unearned guilt.

'Does she think she can sing?' Zac looked up the ceiling,
where Sophie, in her attic room, was reprising the same verse
over and over.

'No. She knows she can't and she doesn't care.' I sighed now. 'You were right before, we should care less about what people think of us. I wish I could be more like Sophie.'

'There's the disadvantage that you would have to teach small children, who would, no doubt, advise you of your inabilities continually.'

'That's true. But then, I've got Eva and Albie and Xavier for that.'

Flakes of paint began blistering off the ceiling as Sophie continued to sing.

'So, what do we do?' Zac began drinking his coffee. There was still a slight shake to his hand, maybe the relief of the tension or just the continuing knowledge that we still had to compete for the job.

I pulled a face at Miriam's paperwork, strewn across my left-over socks. 'Carry on? Do the job to the best of our abilities?'

'Let the best man win sort of thing?' Zac scuffed up his hair again. 'I just felt I owed you an explanation for today. I'm flattered that you've told me what you did.'

'It shouldn't be used against us,' I said, suddenly fervent. 'We're both capable of what we do. My being medicated and you being under domestic stress, it shouldn't affect anything. I'm pretty sure that's discrimination.'

'Well, of course it is. But first, we'd have to prove it. And that's going to be hard, with the merger and them only needing one of us – they could frame it as necessary redundancy.'

'There's plenty of work for both of us.' I was still fervent. 'The one that's left is going to be overworked into stress-related absence anyway.'

Zac shrugged. 'But they're looking for any reason to get rid of one of us, it doesn't have to be mental health related. Any nasty habits could get you pushed out; sleeping with your co-workers?'

'You've met our co-workers. I'm pretty sure that *wanting* to sleep with most of them constitutes a mental health related problem,' I said. 'But you're right. They are looking for any reason they can get. They've told me you're ahead, so they obviously expect me to go looking for another job.'

'They've told me *you're* ahead,' Zac said, tiredly. 'So, ditto. I presume you aren't sleeping with anyone I could use to my advantage?' He gave me a cautious grin.

'Sorry, no. What about you?'

'Only thing I'm sleeping with is some truly heinous wallpaper. One of the reasons I try not to go home that often. Just at weekends, for Mum.' The words 'who doesn't even know who I am' were hanging in the still, cold air. They didn't need to be said, his tone was enough. 'That Miriam's file?'

I grasped the change of subject and clutched it next to the mug of coffee. 'Yes. I'm working with her to try to get her into work of some kind.'

Zac chuckled. 'Good luck with that. She's the most resistant client I've ever had. She'd float in, talk at me for an hour, and then bustle off with me none the wiser.' He poked the sheaf of application forms with a toe. 'She seems to like you. I never really gelled with her.'

'I think it's because you're a man,' I said. A distrust of men must run through her like a seam of ore through rock.

'Flattered you've noticed.' Zac flashed me the briefest of grins. 'Priya's finally having an effect.'

'Shut up. And go to bed. Getting to work tomorrow is going to make polar exploration look like a trip to Tesco's, and if we don't show they'll probably fire both of us.' I bent to begin stacking the papers together again.

'Okay.' He slid off the corner of the bed, bumped his hip against the door frame, swore softly and then was gone, closing the door gently behind him as he went. I listened to the socked shuffle that was him descending the stairs, until I heard the creak and grumble of the sofa having someone lie down on it, when I let out a breath.

I knew about him, he knew about me. Now we'd find out. Which one of us would fold and pass that information on?

12

It had stopped snowing next morning when we drove in to work, and the roads were clearing in patches. Little bits of cobble stood clear of the snow, giving the approach to the Minster the look of a head under thinning hair as we rattled into the car park through the shadows of the monstrous towers. Somewhere, piped music from an open-doored shop played an ironic 'Silent Night'.

Zac and I didn't speak. I think we were both lost in despondency, but it could just have been the earliness of the hour; watching other workers clambering over piled snow to get onto buses or trudging grimly through darkening slush had not been conducive to conversation, so I jumped slightly when Zac spoke.

'Let's just forget last night, yes?'

'Do *not* say that in front of Priya, please. She will jump to conclusions so fast that she'll be in the middle of the North Sea before we can hang up our coats.' But then I nodded. 'And yes. We'll forget about it.'

'It's probably best.' He steered the Discovery in through the archway to our office car park and into the parking space that had, until recently, been mine.

Lights streamed from downstairs windows, filtered through tinsel and foil decorations into swinging splinters and odd prismatic shapes. Most of the staff, overcome by guilt for yesterday's early finishes, must have got in early. An unmistakeable smell of mince pies baking floated over from the café next door and a well-trodden path between the two buildings clearly indicated that breakfast was mostly being taken from the pudding end of the spectrum today.

I went to open the car door, but Zac put out a hand to stop me. 'Can I just ask,' he said, not looking at me, but keeping his eyes on the side door. 'Your tablets. Do you think they'd be any good for me?'

'You're not having them.' I held my bag close to my chest.

'That's not what I meant.' There was a little laugh in his voice and it intensified the gleam of light on the snow and the deep, fruity smell of the pies. 'I meant – do you think I should see a doctor?'

'Well, they don't solve anything, Zac.' That pile of little jumpers on the back seat fell onto the floor with a soft sound that made my heart hurt. His mum knitted them out of love, and he kept them out of the same love, even though most of them wouldn't have fitted Tiny Tim. 'They just help you deal with it. Nothing makes it go away.' The walls were holding, though. 'But, yes. I think you ought to see someone. I'm surprised they haven't already prescribed you something.'

Zac began rubbing his hands up and down the steering wheel. 'I said I didn't want them,' he muttered. 'They put Mum on tablets, but they just made her worse.'

'The tablets did? Are you sure it wasn't her condition worsening?'

'It might have been, looking back.' He was still muttering,

almost as though he was ashamed. 'I just got a bit of a... prejudice against taking stuff.'

'Then you're an idiot,' I said, smiling as I opened the door and slithered off the seat down into snow that instantly filled my boots. 'If you had a headache, you'd take something, right? Well, depression and anxiety – that's like an ache in your soul. Someone makes medicine that may help that pain, and you refuse to take it? Yep, idiot.'

I waited for him to get out of the car and lock the doors, and then we both stood together just beyond the reach of the golden lights and reflected ornaments.

'Bit of a metaphor, you reckon?' Zac asked softly. 'Us standing on the outside while there's heating and light and mince pies in there?'

'There are bars on the windows, Zac,' I replied, equally softly.

'That is either very deep,' he began walking and I had to hop through the snow to keep up, 'or such an obvious observation that I should be worried about you.'

'You don't need to be worried about me.' I sounded so cheerful that I almost made *myself* feel sick. But I had to be. I needed him to forget that I may ever have any issues with keeping the overwhelming nature of life at bay. I even grinned.

Zac smiled too. It was a sad kind of smile, that made his eyes look old. 'Okay. Point taken. But I am allowed to think that you are quite brave, aren't I? For not giving in?'

I stopped in the doorway and he stopped too. 'I'm not brave, I'm just keeping going,' I said quietly. 'You, on the other hand – I can only imagine what your life must be like.'

His smile was gone, and the sadness was still there, pulling at the corners of his mouth, tugging lines into his cheeks, as though the emotion put pleats in his face. 'Don't. Please, Ruby, don't even try.'

But I couldn't help it. The thought of a lady somewhere, knitting, knitting endless small jumpers for the son who was, in her head, still nine. Whilst he stood in front of her, cooked for her, cared for her, unrecognised and called by somebody else's name. It made me want to cry.

But then I looked up at those windows, letting stripes of light slide through onto the snow. This was work and I couldn't show any weakness here. Even sympathy or empathy could be the little finger-hold they would grab to show me as unsuitable for my job, so I straightened my face and pushed any thoughts that didn't include paperwork, coffee or vague discussions about the weather to the back of my mind.

We bustled in and had just begun the lengthy business of taking off layers and hanging them up to drip dry and add to the fusty atmosphere of the office, when Priya came in, having entered through the main office and having heard the gossip that Zac and I had gone home together.

'Okay, spill the beans.' She dragged me into her office, where a radiator, totally out of proportion to the size of the room, made the place steamy and subtropical. Even the chocolate was wilting. 'You and Zac? *Well?*'

At least I could let a *little* of that emotional sympathy show to Pri. I thought of the way Zac had stood in my bedroom doorway, carrying hot coffee and leftover pizza. 'It's like he's had "caring" engraved on him at some point.' I knew which point that would be too – when his mother started showing symptoms, when she became too forgetful. He must have had to learn to take on the running of the household very young. The caring must be more habit now than anything else and I wondered what the inner Zac was like.

'That's a good thing.' Priya tugged off gloves and hung up her coat. 'Do you fancy him? Oh, that's a stupid question, of course you do.'

'He's still the opposition,' I pointed out. 'Fancying him doesn't come into the equation.'

'Ah, but he's a nice guy, I keep telling you, Ruby. You just don't recognise nice when you see it, that's why you got caught up with Gareth. You've got tied up in the patriarchy, thinking all men have to be macho rugby players, demonstrating the kind of behaviour that we have, thank God, nearly stamped out after fifty years of campaigning.'

I stared at her. 'I am not *tied up in the patriarchy*, whatever that might mean!'

'Oh, come on. Look at the way you defer to Michael. You get all smiley and "Daddy knows best" with him, even though we all know Michael wouldn't know which way round to put on his trousers if he weren't married and didn't have Rachel in the office.' She was looking at me defiantly. She'd even put her hands on her hips.

'Oh dear Lord, you and Nettie have been talking about me again, haven't you?'

'Well, it's true. We have no idea why, because your mum and dad have role reversal down to a tee, except that your mum has to cook because your dad has learned incompetence. Maybe you're just reacting to that? But you were looking for a man to take control with Gareth, and then when he turned out to be wetter than a towel in a rainstorm, well, you turned into your mum and took over.'

'Has Nettie been letting you loose in the university library or something?' I was a little bit shocked at Pri's confrontational attitude.

'I'm just so tired of watching you dwindle down. The way you reacted to Gareth doing the inevitable, it was scary. Watching you fly into pieces, just because that pile of shit behaved exactly the way we'd been predicting he'd behave, it was like telling you the moon was round and then having to pat you gently when you went out one night and had a breakdown at the sight of the full moon! Whereas Zac is really, really kind and a decent guy and yet you don't even see him because he's not leering at your bum and chatting up every woman he meets.'

'Well, I don't want him.' I was getting a bit sweaty. Maybe it was the heat in this tiny office, or maybe I was getting too much mental exercise trying to avoid Priya's full-on attack. She had a point, I knew she did, but I really didn't want to think about it. Zac was, well, he was just *Zac*. 'I've got to go and do some work.'

It was difficult, but I didn't flounce out. Instead, I gave her a cheery wave and took half a bar of fruit and nut chocolate with me in revenge.

In the office, Zac was sitting at his desk, fiddling with his computer. I watched him for a few moments. Was Priya right? *Did* I fancy Zac, underneath a whole load of my own baggage and barely being able to see past the fact that he might get the job I needed so badly? Well, he was nicely shaped, I suppose. When his hair wasn't doing that sticking up thing that made him look like an anaemic Muppet, he looked quite pleasant. He had large, dark eyes. He didn't suddenly leap up shouting 'phwooooarrrr!' as a result of either his team scoring a goal or a nice-looking woman walking past. He'd thought about me to the extent of bringing me my discarded pizza and a cup of coffee.

Zac looked suddenly away from the cabling and caught me looking at him. 'Stop it, you'll go blind,' he said.

'My eyes have to be pointing somewhere,' I said, nettled.

'Yes, but you're staring at me like I've turned into Harry Potter or something.'

'Harry Potter?'

'I read it to Mum, when she's over. She likes Harry Potter. She used to read it to me when I was younger, but she can't... she can't concentrate to read any more.' He looked away now, fiercely tidying the wiring at the back of the computer.

He was right. I *was* looking at him as though he were a different person. Now I knew what lay underneath that 'complicated' life; how much he was keeping hidden. How much he probably wasn't even admitting to himself. I'm sure he knew a thing or two about those walls in the mind that kept the bad things restrained.

'I am now really worried that your benchmark for romantic intentions is a teenage wizard.' I managed to look away now and back to my bag, where Miriam's file was threatening to escape and spread discord through the entire office.

Zac stopped moving. 'I wasn't aware that you *had* romantic intentions, Ruby,' he said softly.

The heat flared over me as though I'd been sitting on top of Priya's radiator. 'I didn't mean I... well, I was just... it wasn't like...' Unable to justify my slip in any way that could make me feel less pink and mortified, I became very interested in the contents of my desk drawer.

'No, no, you're fine. After last night's, um, revelations, I was beginning to worry that you'd had any kind of inclinations in that direction taken out and replaced with paper clips.' I was studiously avoiding looking even in the direction of his voice, but I noted it had taken on a slightly amused tone. 'Maybe, when this is all over, we might manage to actually go out together in a non-office mandated way? And I can prove myself to be a decent, upstanding representative of the male gender?'

'When this is all over, Zac, one of us is going to be out of a job,' I said, waspishly, still backwashed with a pink glow that was even visible in reflection in my computer screen. I wasn't sure I liked him bringing levity to the situation.

'Out of a job, not chained to a radiator in a basement.' There was a note of good-natured teasing in his voice now. 'We'll still be allowed out.'

'If I can't pay the bank...' I trailed off. The walls were threatening to rock, and his certainty that life would be breezily fine was, oddly, not reassuring.

'Yeah, well, I have to pay Mum's care home fees.' The words had sounded trawled out, as though he kept them very, very deep down and tried not to think about the implications. 'But, even if I get redundancy, there will be other jobs. There are other things I can do. This place isn't the be-all and end-all, is it?'

But I wouldn't walk into a job earning what I earn here! I wanted to shout. Not without having to commute to another city! Don't you think I've looked? There ARE other jobs, but they come with more stress, different stress, and I'm not sure that I could cope with learning new routines and new ways of working without the walls buckling and folding. I'd have to go and live with Mum and Dad in my old bedroom surrounded by Madonna posters and my old school textbooks! 'No,' was what I actually said, in a tone dull and reverberating with the unspoken.

'Ruby—'

He was interrupted from whatever he'd been about to say by his phone ringing. It was a very short call, just two 'yes'es and an 'okay' and then he was hanging up and going out of the office, raising an eyebrow at me as he went.

Released from my obligation to look busy, I slumped back in my chair and tipped my head back to stare at the ceiling. It wasn't particularly edifying, but it was better than either looking at the space where Zac had been, or my own reflection. Overhead, the foil star glinted, sharp points heading my way whichever direction it revolved in, and from outside my office, occasional bursts of sound came and went as doors were opened and closed, as though someone was turning a radio up and down.

Okay. Well, I couldn't sit here all day swivelling and trying to avoid everyone. There was work to do. I got Miriam's file out and put it on my desk. There had just been that *something* last night, that feeling that, had I not been interrupted by Zac and pizza, I was almost getting the point. That there was something – not wrong, but strange, about Miriam's forms. She'd told me as much anyway, that the answer to getting her back into work was in here, somewhere...

I shuffled them, in case that helped, then dealt them out, one by one, in all their scribble-written, stapled glory. Ten – no, twelve, separate forms. Some single sheets, some linked by treasury tags, most given a cursory staple.

Something. There must be something.

Upstairs, over my head, a door slammed and made me jump. I felt itchy, as though my skin was irritated on the inside and every little annoyance was just making it worse. I needed to shout and run and work the needle-catches of peevishness out of me. There was nothing in these forms. Who was I trying to kid? Miriam had resisted work this long, she may be well disposed towards me, but she wasn't going to put herself in the way of a job this close to Christmas. Maybe she was just trying to distract me. Make me *think* she preferred me to Zac, in a sort of 'divide and rule' move. Then she could blame falling out with him and falling out with me, and use a failure to get counselling as another way of pushing back the inevitable stopping of her benefit payments. Then what? Another short-lived cash-in-hand job, and then back to the benefits office to apply again?

I stirred the papers with a finger. Footsteps were banging their way down the upstairs corridor now, and I could hear each angry stride distinctly, the concomitant complaints of the boards. Someone was angry and in a hurry.

I'd just gathered all the forms back up together again and was about to sheave them against my computer screen, when the owner of the angry feet crashed into the office, sending the door flying back to smack into the coat rack.

It was Zac. His hair was so high that it was a wonder he'd got through the door and his shoulders were set in a kind of half shrug that made his head look as though it had sunk into his chest.

'What's up?' I asked, swivelling to face him, but he ignored me.

He dragged his coat down off the rack, which tipped and spilled my jacket, discarded and forgotten scarves and umbrellas and an old cardigan which had belonged to someone who'd possessed the office before even I had arrived. Zac ignored the mess too. He pulled his coat over his arms, turning as he did so, so that the mass of tangled outerwear swirled around his feet like multicoloured surf on a knitwear beach.

'Zac?' I half stood. 'What's happened?'

He stopped now, hand on the door edge, and looked at me. His jaw was set with anger, but there was another, different expression in his eyes. They looked on the point of tears. 'I would have thought you'd have known,' he said.

With a quick twist of his wrist to open the door, he was gone, still struggling into his coat, and I heard the outer door bang as he went outside.

I stood up and followed a few strides, enough to see him through the barred corridor window, striding out across the corn-flake-crunch of the snow. He clearly hadn't taken his car keys, because he faltered momentarily by the Discovery, hand groping in a pocket, then shrugged and slammed a hand against the bonnet, dislodging a crust of snow.

His head dropped and I watched him stand. Two heartbeats, no more. Then he was off again, shuffling the snow aside and moving his shoulders so that the collar of his coat rose almost to his ears.

I should let him go. I knew that. Sometimes, emotional turmoil was best dealt with alone, and the way he was walking, as though the snow was a personal irritant sent just to aggrieve him, I could see there was anger that needed to be worked through.

But it was *Zac*. And the way he'd said that I should have known what was upsetting him, that look in his eyes, that had all held the sharpness of unfinished business. He was angry about something that I had done, when, as far as I knew, I was innocent.

I grabbed my coat from the floor and, calling a 'just popping out!' through Priya's door as I went, I set off after him.

It was snowing again. Huge tufts of snow the size of duck feathers floated down around me, as though some celestial duvet was being plumped onto a bed, and the streets were almost empty. Zac was easy to track, his new footprints lay crisply imprinted, stamped down hard onto the previous snow. He was clearly very, very angry because he'd kicked the head off a small snowman that a shop owner had built out of the snow cleared from their doorway, and the remnants lay in a frozen massacre across the path.

Zac didn't seem to be heading for anywhere specific. I'd thought he would perhaps be making his way to the station, catching a train bound for Leeds. Back to his chilly, old-fashioned house, with the ancient sofa and all the things his mother had surrounded herself with as a newly-wed, as a new mother. Everything held in a stasis from a time she felt she could hold on to.

But Zac wasn't held in a stasis, was he? Poor Zac was ageing in front of her, unrecognised. She talked, apparently, to him, about her son, little Zacchary, who was 'out playing' or 'at school', whilst she knitted and knitted those small sweaters in intricate patterns that her fingers remembered while her mind forgot the death of her husband, her son's twenty-first birthday, his graduation, his passed driving test...

He had told me that sometimes she'd knit a sweater for the man he was. Proudly presenting him with it, 'for his help'. A sweater knitted not with love, but with duty. Her love went into the jumpers that lay piled in his car, that he couldn't bear to get rid of. Those jumpers he wore occasionally, even though they were so small they bordered on the ridiculous.

I was tracking him like a bloodhound, keeping my eyes down on the snow. Seeing where he'd hesitated, walked a small circle – was he lost? – and then headed down one of the small lanes that wove their cave-like way between the old buildings, which arched overhead. Past puddles of golden light from shopfronts, through the blue-shadowed darkness of closed businesses, down Low Petergate, under the unlit illuminations gathering snow like uncared-for laundry on a line, through the square and down to the entrance to the Shambles, where he'd stopped.

I knew he'd stopped because I walked right into him. He was standing, staring down the tunnel of buildings which seemed to be huddling together for protection from the falling snow and I'd been so intent on tracking his footprints that I didn't realise it was him until he spoke.

'You've got some front, I'll give you that.'

Automatically, stupidly, I looked down. 'No, it's just my coat doubled over... Oh.'

He didn't seem to know what he wanted to do. As though he was torn between walking off and staying to let his anger out at me. He was circling, circling, round and round me, treading his emotions into the snow, while more snow fell around us, enclosing us in our own personal blizzard.

'Why did you come?'

'Why did you walk off?' I countered. 'You seemed upset.' I shivered now, realising how cold the air was out here now that I'd stopped walking.

'Upset!' Flakes, turning to water and flew as he threw his hands in the air. 'Didn't you *think* I'd be upset? Alison and Peter called me up to the offices to "have a word" about my...' he stopped. 'About yesterday morning,' he went on. 'About me possibly not being able to cope with the stress of the job.'

I stared at him, his outline shattered into fragments by the falling snow. The implication behind his words sent a little spurt of heat through my veins. 'What? But I never said... It wasn't *me*! I would never have told them.'

But he was on a roll. 'I mean, they already know about Mum as I had to tell them ages ago when I needed time to help her get to appointments, when I needed time off to move her into the home. And they know about the weekends, when she comes home, I can't just... I can't just work at the drop of a hat.' He was rotating now, pacing, pacing, tiny circles, like a caged animal. 'And they've always done that "sympathy" thing – "if you need time off, just tell us," but I've never taken it. Never dared. Because I knew they'd hold it against me. I always kept as much as I could away from them.' There was a break in his voice. The words catching on his breath. 'They didn't know. *They didn't know.*' He raised his face to the sky and the flakes seemed to divert themselves around him, as though his emotion was a force field, shutting him off from the world.

'It wasn't me, Zac,' I said, carefully factual. Emotion wouldn't get through. Only pure rationality could puncture the walls, when they were resisting sense as strongly as his were. 'I thought about it, but I wouldn't do it.'

The snow muffled the sound. Everything was slowed and silenced by those huge falling flakes that brushed like the kisses of the dead.

He didn't look at me, just continued talking to the sky, to the falling snow. 'Well, who then? Nobody else knows. Only you, Ruby.' He lowered his head, so that he met my eyes. 'Only you,' he repeated softly.

Somewhere far down the row of bent and shuffled buildings, a door opened. A burst of Christmas music rang out and was cut off again. 'Do They Know It's Christmas?' Then just the silence again, and us, and the snow.

I shook my head. 'No.'

'Well, WHO then?' Zac shouted, and the words went up the walls, falling back down onto us as echoes.

'I dunno, maybe Sam? He walked in on us, remember?'

Zac went very still. Then he crumpled, leaning back against the conveniently bow-fronted shop behind him. His head dropped to his chest and he dragged his hands up over his hair. 'Oh bugger,' he said. 'Bugger, bugger, bugger, bugger.'

A coldness crept up my spine, edging its way through my ribcage to my heart and drying my mouth. There was such an air of defeat in his words that I feared the worst. 'Did you... I mean, I'd understand if you had, but, oh God, Zac, you didn't tell them about me, did you?'

He snorted into his lapels. 'No, Ruby, I did not. Two wrongs do not make a right.' His head came up and he was looking at me and his eyes burned through the snow. 'Is that what you think of me? That I'd play a tit-for-tat game like that? Shit, I've really done a number on you, haven't I?'

The cold died. Warmth was flaring inside me again now. 'Then why all the buggering?'

He sniggered, such a down-to-earth sound that it gave me hope.

'You know what I mean.'

He blew a long sigh that made the falling flakes flutter upwards on that melting sound. 'I'm cross that I've got it so wrong. That I could even think you had – which is now becoming increasingly apparent that you wouldn't – and I never even considered the caretaker coming in. I didn't register him at all, which is giving me *another* moment of consideration.'

He was standing quite close to me now, although it must have been me who moved because he was keeping his back firmly pressed against the protruding front of the darkened shop behind him.

A man, shuffling his bag-laden way through the snow down the line of the street, detoured around us with a curious look and a preoccupied smile. Once he'd passed, slithering his way out into King's Square, I spoke again.

'I haven't got the faintest idea what all that meant, Zac.'

'It meant I'm sorry. I'm sorry I thought that you'd even *consider* giving me away. I'm sorry that I've given you the impression that I would hand over information about you that was given in confidence. I'm sorry that anything I have done has led you to believe that I am that kind of man.' He took a step closer, so that we were pressed together now, with the snow creating a little broken barrier around us and crunching under our feet. 'I am so, so sorry,' he said.

What was it? The golden streaks that backlit the Shambles, making the street look like a place lost in time? The isolation of the snow, throwing a blanket of quiet over us? The curious feeling that somehow we were outside the real world, caught in this bubble while the white fragments whirled around us as if we were in our own snow globe? Whatever it was, when Zac leaned further in, I forgot all the hurt and doubt that Gareth had left planted in my heart, and I moved towards him. Our lips met in a pressure of heat that made the snow sizzle on our faces. And the way our bodies reacted to each other with a leaping eagerness made me wonder if part of our friendship had been this all the time.

Gradually, gradually we stepped apart, although not far enough for the snow to put a layer between us.

'Well.' Zac looked down to find my face looking back up at him. 'Well, this was... unexpected.'

'We're both under pressure. It's that time of the year. The festive atmosphere and all that,' I gabbled, with the memory of his mouth on mine still at the forefront of my mind.

'Don't be daft. We fancy each other.' A pause. 'Don't we?'

I scanned his face. I would have been hard-pressed to describe it; there was a nose, a mouth, brown eyes and a chin, but all in a configuration so familiar that it had lost any kind of definitive features. It was just Zac.

'We might,' I said, and the realisation escaped in a bubble of laughter. 'We might.' I brushed some snowflakes from the front of his coat, where they were settling. 'You realise this means that Priya was right and we're going to have to listen to her being all smug at us?'

'It's probably worth it though.' A slight, almost shy grin was breaking through now, lightening his eyes as they stayed fixed on mine.

We were still just standing. Still close enough for there not to be much space for the snow between us, but it made up for it by drizzling its dizzy way around us and into our hair.

A woman towing a small curly dog hopped around us, with a

'Sooty! No!' and a tug on the lead which slid the dog past us on braced legs, but there was nobody else about. Lights shone, but the shops stayed deserted and eerily quiet, the buildings leaning towards one another in every direction, like drunks on ice.

'We should go back.' Zac broke the silence. 'It's cold and we've probably got work to do.'

'If we've still got jobs.'

'You should be safe enough.' He slid his arm around me and drew me forward, so we started walking into the whistling silence of King's Square. 'They've got the perfect reason to get rid of me now. Oh, they'll be all sensitive about it, and it will be for my own good and all that. They wouldn't want me under any unnecessary stress, after all.' The arm around me tightened, half hug, half warding off the inevitable.

'But I told you, Michael keeps saying that you are ahead. Why would they get rid of more successful you and be left with – well, me?'

Zac looked down at me and I couldn't read the expression in his eyes. 'Because maybe they are lying to us?' he said and his gaze flickered off elsewhere.

I faltered, one foot slithering on unseen ice. 'I suppose we aren't allowed to dynamite the whole building, are we?'

'Sadly, it would merely be seen as confirmation of our unsuitability for the job,' he said, with what sounded like real regret. 'Otherwise I'd be first up there with the detonators.'

Our bodies bumped together companionably as we crunched our way back towards the office, rounding the corner to see the building still sitting amid the twisted layout of the other ancient buildings, with the shadow of the Minster laying over them all.

Ice crusted along eaves and snow cushioned and pillowed the roofs, merging all the buildings into one entity. The only indication of difference between our offices and the café was the light spilling out of the latter, while ours was barricaded behind the bars on the windows, escaping in meagre stripes onto the precinct. That and the happy Christmassy music that the café let out every time the door opened. It looked like a jewellery box next to a prison.

'So, what do we do now?' I pulled Zac to a stop before we got to the car park entrance.

He sighed. 'I'm willing to bet that they are drawing up my redundancy plan right now.' He jerked his chin towards the office. 'I might as well start clearing my desk.'

I stared at him, aghast. 'But you can't! You need the job, you said so!'

He gave me a slow, sad smile. 'I'll find something else,' he said. 'I'm qualified. Hell, I can work in McDonald's if I have to.'

'But McDonald's won't help pay the fees for where your mum is, will it?' I didn't know why I was pushing this. He knew the options.

'Maybe if I work twenty-four hours a day?' He was trying to sound cheerful. 'Honestly, Ruby, there will be work out there. It might take a while, but...' he tailed off. I knew why. He didn't have 'a while'. Like me, those bills needed paying. Redundancy pay wouldn't buy much more than a month's breathing space, I guessed. 'I'll think of something,' he said.

We moved apart and he went on ahead as we entered the warmth of the seasonally illuminated building, but I could still feel the ghost of his kiss on my lips. That lift in my heart as I realised that this was far, *far* more than friendship.

This wasn't fair. He'd kept my secret. I had to do *something*.

I caught up with him in our office. 'Where are you going?'

'I thought I might go up and see what kind of redundancy package they're going to give me, if I offer to take it voluntarily. It's likely to be better than if I wait to be pushed.' He'd taken off his coat but the steely flecks of melting snow still dotted his hair.

'Don't. Please.'

'Ruby.' Zac smiled a gentle smile. 'It's fine. It will be fine. Honestly.'

'Please. Just give me an hour. I'll come up with something.'

'Something to counteract their belief that I'm one paper cut away from a breakdown?'

I gave him my steadiest look. 'None of us know how far we are from the edge, Zac. I never thought I was particularly fragile until Gareth... well, did what he did. And Priya was right, I *should* have seen it coming, I should have been less demanding, shouldn't have tried to drive a relationship that wasn't a real relationship, but I could never have foreseen it all leaving me with this dreadful anxiety and the panic attacks.'

Zac stared at me.

'What I mean is, they shouldn't judge you or make you lose your job just because you have a problem, should they? Because that's like saying you can't do your job because you broke your leg or because you've got toothache!'

Zac sat down on the corner of my desk. I was reassured that he wasn't immediately ignoring me and stomping off upstairs to throw himself on his sword, but he *was* still staring at me in a way that made me feel slightly uncomfortable.

'You're right, of course you are,' he said. 'But what *should* be doesn't change anything. They want one of us out, they've got stuff on me. All you have to do is keep your head down and the job is yours.'

'Not if I can make us equal.' I looked around the room, desperate. There had to be *something...* My bag lay sprawled beside the desk. 'Miriam.'

Zac twitched. 'Where? Shall I hide?'

'No, I mean, she half-hinted... something...' I tipped all the forms that I'd spent the evening staring at onto my desk. 'If you can do something about Miriam, do you reckon that would be enough for them to keep your job for you?'

'Never mind keeping my job, I'd probably get a knighthood. Or the head of the benefits office will come down and give me a big kiss.'

The memory of that kiss outside in the snow hit both of us at the same time and our eyes met over the top of secretive smiles.

'Then give me an hour. I stared at them all evening, *something* will dawn on me.' I put a hand on his arm. 'Please, Zac.'

He reached out and touched my cheek, I hadn't realised how cold my skin was until I felt the heat of his fingers. 'But what about you? You need this job as much as I do.'

I thought about my options. About my life. 'I do, but I've got more ways out than you. Hell, I can always throw myself on my parents' mercy, move back home and get a job in... I dunno, I can always do cleaning jobs – I'll get by, Zac. Honestly.' I looked around the office, where I'd felt so happily complacent until his arrival. Had that complacency stopped me from realising that the job wasn't worth it? 'I'm just a bit sick of the way this place is treating us. Making us turn against one another to keep our jobs. It's hardly ethical or... kind. And I want a job where I help people, not where I'm forced to shove them into any job going, just to keep my own.'

'Well, the turning against one another thing isn't working out too well for them, at least.' He laid his hand against my face again. 'We might just salvage something rather pleasant out of it all. In the end.' His phone buzzed then and he fished it out of his pocket. 'Oh. Bob is here,' he said, standing up and looking reluctant. 'I bet he's blown another interview. Ah well.'

'You talk to Bob, I'm going to stare at these forms.' I stood too and gave him a little push. 'Go on. Go.' I needed him to leave. I needed time to process what had happened between us, and also, if he didn't go, I was worried I might just start kissing him again.

'You and I—'

'We can talk about that later. Go.'

With a jerk of his head that seemed to indicate a mixture of reluctance, attraction, and resignation, he went out, carefully closing the door behind him and leaving a Zac-shaped hole in the room that I had previously not been aware of.

That kiss. I ran a finger over my lips as though I could recreate the feelings of that moment in the snow. Despite a chilly draught that worried my ankles and the dampness that was the flakes in my hair melting down my neck, I couldn't recapture it. But just remembering it made my heart feel as though it were suddenly taking up more space in my chest.

Okay. Okay. Concentrate.

Last night, looking at the forms spread out, I'd felt that I was standing on the edge of a discovery. All I had to do was recreate that situation. I tipped the papers out of the file and laid them out on the floor like a very neat jigsaw.

'Something. *Something*,' I muttered, walking around and around them, narrowing my eyes as though the resultant blurring of the image would make something significant jump out, like a magic eye puzzle.

'Oh, you're back.' The air from the door opening caught all the papers under their edges and drifted them into a heap. 'Where did you go?' Priya stuck her head and one shoulder into the office. 'It's horrible out there.'

'I went after Zac,' I said, without really listening to myself. 'He walked out.'

'*Oh.*' The rest of Priya came in and she closed the door behind her in a meaningful way. 'Did you find him? Did you snog?'

'The second of those questions is redundant if the answer to the first is "no",' I wasn't really involved in this conversation, I was concentrating too hard on the mass on the floor.

'And why does this place look as though you've tipped up a bin and you're dancing on loads of people's files?'

'Not loads, just Miriam's.' I looked at Priya now. 'And what makes you think I'd snog him?'

'Unresolved sexual tension,' she responded, snappily. 'Forced to the forefront at moments of high drama.'

Nettie lectured in Women's Studies at York University. Sometimes the lectures leaked.

'Well, for your inform— What did you say?'

Priya gave me a Look. 'Unresolved sexual tension. The air was so thick with it in here that I could only get in with scissors.'

'No, not that. The files. Different people?'

She looked down at the paperwork at my feet. 'Err?'

When I looked now, it was obvious. 'I think you may just have got it,' I said slowly. 'I bloody love you, Pri.'

'Don't tell Nettie, she's very territorial. She might pee on me,' Priya replied calmly. 'You carry on your bonkers paper sorting, I'm back off to my own office. I only came in for salacious details, but I'll get those later.' She wiggled her eyebrows. 'When you've got further than the snogging.'

'Shut up.'

'And you still owe me a shirt.' She backed out, her face one enormous grin, and I heard her shout 'I *told* you so!' from the safe distance of the corridor.

But I couldn't worry about Priya's smugness now. My brain had finally made the connection, and I pulled the nearest bit of paper up towards my face, found the telephone number on it and dialled.

* * *

The roads got cleared, despite the near-constantly falling snow, and we all made it to our respective homes that night, although I stayed on late enough to make sure that Zac actually left the building, hustling him out and locking the door behind the pair of us.

'What are you doing for Christmas?' he asked me as we crossed the car park.

'I haven't really thought. I'm more concerned with just getting home tonight.'

'I could drive you...'

But things were different now. Yesterday's Zac had been a workmate, a friend. There had been well-defined boundaries between us. Now – and I flicked a glance at him – now, since that kiss, new boundaries needed drawing up and I didn't think I could do that sensibly if he was in the house with me.

'It's fine. I've got an Uber coming.' I checked my phone. 'It's only two minutes away.' I'd put it on the work's account, I'd rationalise it if I needed to, but, with the way they were treating me and Zac, twenty quid of Uber was the least they deserved.

'So. Christmas?' He was standing very close to me. That boundary had been well and truly crossed.

'I hadn't really thought. Mum and Dad have already gone up to Durham, they spend Christmas with Eva and her family. I could go up there, I suppose, join them once the office closes.'

Zac looked pointedly at the snow. 'Isn't it worse north of here? You'd risk being snowed in with your family?'

'Well, they are my family, not werewolves or something. I'd probably survive.'

'Ah. Only I wondered...' Zac tailed off, staring across the wilderness of the snowy car park. The caretakers had been out shovelling and scraping and spreading and the surface had an odd, piebald look. 'Up until this year... I mean, well, last year Mum came home, but this year, they think it's best if she stays where she is. They don't have the staff to help settle her when she gets back, everyone's on holiday, you see.' He spoke in a rush. 'I can visit her in the morning, but... I mean, I'll give her her present and stay for the carols, but...'

I had a sudden image of Zac going back to the emptiness of his house. I'd never been there, never even seen pictures, but in my imagination it was chilly with lots of deserted rooms and forgotten things. One of them being Zac, of course. *All those tiny sweaters.*

'Why don't we do something? Together, I mean. Sophie and Cav go home – at least, I think Cav goes home, he may just set up camp outside the local bike shop window. We could...' thoughts of what we 'could' do made my face go hot. 'Cook dinner together,' I finished, in case his mind had gone there too.

He relaxed. It was the answer he'd hoped for, I could tell by the way his face creased into that grin that I'd always found a bit annoying before. 'Thank you,' he said, and there was weight to the words. As though I'd rescued him from drowning.

Zac. That kiss. That kiss...

13

The next day, Miriam was there before me again. Haunting the corridor outside the interview room with the smell of old smoke and Chanel, she was tapping up and down as though she were anxious.

'Yeah, okay, I'm here,' she said. 'What's the big hurry? They're not firin' you, are they? You've got to keep your job, I mean, never mind you being shafted by some bloke, you're the only one daft enough to keep talkin' to me. Did you look at the forms?'

'That's why you're here,' I said, shaking snow off the fluorescent jacket. I'd had to come on Cav's bike again and I was still a bit out of breath. 'We need to talk.'

'Long as there's coffee and it's free.' Miriam began unwinding her scarf. 'You're payin' for me to be here and all. Keep goin'; the kids is fightin' over Xbox and it's quieter here.'

'We're waiting for – Ah, here he is.'

Zac came in at the far end of the corridor, bustling along with post in his hand, flicking through envelopes as though he hadn't seen us.

'Oh God, it's Tosspot,' Miriam said, no attempt to keep her voice down.

'Hello, Miriam.' Zac kept sorting the post, didn't look up.

Miriam looked from Zac to me, then back again and her pencil-line of brows rose. 'Oh. Like that, is it?'

'Like what?' I finally got the last of my lights turned off.

'You and him. Bloody hell, lass, he's a—'

'Tosspot, yes, thanks Miriam.' Zac opened the office door. 'Well, this tosspot is wondering quite what we're all doing in the corridor at this time in the morning. Shall we go into the inter-view room?' As we all filed through, he made a face at me and lowered his voice. 'I'm presuming there's a reason you asked me to get in early? You don't just want to batter me to death with Miriam to save me the indignity of redundancy?'

'Well, yes, sort of.' I was newly aware of him, his shape in the doorway as I passed through, the smell of his soap and shampoo, the deliberate way in which he moved. It was as though he was someone else now.

The coffee machine hadn't even been switched on, so there were an awkward few minutes while we circulated around the room like particles in a gas cloud, so widely spread as to be in our own little spaces. Zac fiddled with the coffee, changed the filter. I fetched more biscuits, opened packets, arranged them on a plate. Miriam sat in the comfortable chair, watching us with the air of a regent whose minions aren't quite living up to expectations.

Eventually, when the machine had spat gobbets of hot coffee, I pulled my sheaf of application forms from my bag. Miriam looked nervous.

'Took me ages,' I said. 'But I got there in the end.'

She shifted about in her chair, pulling at the hem of her jacket. 'Well. Yes. I've had a bit of practice an' all.' She flipped a look at Zac. 'You're never lettin' him in on this? I told you, save your job.'

'It turns out that Zac is in more need of saving than I am, Miriam.' I handed the paperwork to Zac. 'Look. Look at the forms.'

He took them from me and casually glanced over first one, then another. 'Yes. I was responsible for putting Miriam up for most of these jobs.'

'Look at the way they've been filled in, Zac. Look at the hand-writing.'

I tapped the topmost piece of paper, looking him in the eye as I did so. *Make the connection, Zac, don't make me tell you.*

'Oh. Oh!'

And there it was. It clicked and I saw his eyes change.

'Miriam.' I sat opposite her on the less-comfortable chair. 'Why didn't you just *tell* us? Or tell someone, at least.'

Miriam shifted about. 'Well.' She looked down at her designer bag and fiddled with its clasp, clicking it open and shut. 'It's kind of shameful, in't it. Leavin' school when you can't read or write proper.'

It was obvious now I knew. I took the forms from Zac's hand and laid them out on the little low table between us. Miriam moved them so that the biscuits were uncovered, and I could see her averting her eyes from the wildly differing handwriting on each form. Some had clearly been filled in by the same person, but some looked as though they'd been filled in by someone who'd been watching TV at the same time.

'Our Angel did those ones. Her Ryder did those,' Miriam tapped a couple with a scarlet nail. 'Donna did those, but she can't write as good as her sister, and our Kiara did that one. I just told 'em what to write.'

'Miriam...' I stopped. She'd had a life I couldn't even begin to imagine, with my middle-class background, two caring parents whose only bone of contention was my mother's special trifle. 'It's nothing to be ashamed of,' I finished gently. 'You should have told us.'

She shuffled her shoulders in a shrug of combined acceptance, embarrassment and pride. 'Yeah, well. Not being able to do what even a five-year-old can do. Luckily they're not ones for havin' their Nana read bedtime stories. I carried it off, though,' she said. 'You never even guessed. I had to tell you what to look for.'

Zac was looking at Miriam with a different expression. Before he'd seemed to regard her with a mixture of dread and resignation. As one of those 'people you just can't help'. I couldn't really fault him, hadn't I also started out seeing her as just one of the work-shy job-avoiders? Even I hadn't suspected that there may be a very good reason for her ducking and diving, her cash-in-hand short-lived employments; nothing too involved, nothing that needed her to fill in forms, read or write. I hadn't spotted it until she'd practically handed me the information. Without, I realised now, actually having to say the words.

'And I'm great with numbers,' Miriam went on, the note of pride strengthening. 'And somehow they thinks if you're good at sums you *must* be able to spell and read long words.'

'Miriam.' Zac leaned towards her. His voice was gentle now. 'I am so, so sorry.'

She sniffed. 'So you should be,' she said, but her voice was similarly lacking its normal stridency. 'You wrote me off. Which is kind of ironic, if you thinks about it.' She gave a grin that backlit her blue-shaded eyes with mischief.

Zac acknowledged her words with a sideways shake of the head. 'Yep. You're right. I did. And I was wrong. I never even considered— You are devious and I am a tosspot.'

'And now Zac is going to work out the best way of getting you on some of those courses that will help you learn to be functionally literate,' I said, and stood up. 'If that's all right.'

Miriam looked from me to Zac. 'What sort of courses?' She'd huddled herself in again over her bag, was clicking and flicking at the catch.

'Courses that mean you won't have to apply for jobs for a while,' he said, and the pair of them smiled a complicit smile at one another. 'Let's get your literacy up to standard before we start thinking about application forms again.'

She relaxed, the bag slid lower on her lap and the catch-clicking stopped. 'Yeah,' she said. 'I was startin' to think it was time I learned. Other day, I gave our Ryder a thing to read for me an' he told me it were a final demand from the council, the little bugger. It were a circular about windows.' She sniffed. 'I knew it weren't a bill, they always comes with loads of big red letters on the top, but it gave me a turn for a few minutes.' A deep breath. 'So, yeah. Reckon it's time.'

I slid out of the room, my cheeks hot with the knowledge that I was doing the right thing, but that it might mean that I had handed over my only hope of triumphing over Zac in the job war. A war that we had never declared and that never should have been.

In our office, I sat at my desk, looking over the familiar mess, smelling that hot radiator and dust smell that had hung in the background for as long as I'd been here. My job. Part of my identity, since I'd come in after a stint for the CAB, after uni. I'd not really known anything else.

Cautiously I let the catastrophes run through my head but managed to stop them before the panic built too far. Yes, I could be out of a job. Yes, it would be hard to find anything similar, particularly if my breakdown counted against me. Yes, the bank would still want their money. But. But. I wasn't responsible for anyone but myself. I'd spent the money, now I had to pay it back, it was as simple as that.

The walls in my head wobbled a little and I diverted my thoughts. *Zac. That kiss.* Had it meant something? It had felt as though it did, and I could still feel the remnants of it on my mouth, like a hot echo. And yes, I did fancy him, damn Priya. Now I was going to spend Christmas day with him...

The phone on my desk rang.

'There's someone here to see Zac,' Karen said from Reception. 'Doesn't have an appointment, just a bucketload of anxiety.'

'Zac's in with Miriam.' I began to scribble a Christmas shopping list on the edge of a bit of printer paper. 'He's going to be tied up for a while.'

'Oh. Poor love.' Karen had clearly fallen for Zac's charm and Miriam's assumed air of brittle ruthlessness. 'Well, this lad's come a fair way, any chance you could see him instead?'

'Who is it? I'll look out the file and give him a ten-minute talk-down. We'll have to go to the café though, Zac's taken possession of the interview room, and the other one's out of commission being repainted.'

'It's Bob,' Karen said. 'I'll tell him you'll come up here and collect him.'

Bob. Bob. I called up the computer files. Luckily Zac only had the one Bob, so I skim-read his file, hoiked out the paper copies of his applications, a file nearly as thick as Miriam's, but with consistent handwriting. I couldn't imagine never checking that detail again. Then I bustled down to Reception, where a large bloke with bulky shoulders and a lumberjack shirt was hunched against the main doors.

This was Bob, of the mechanical tendencies. Bob who was

avoiding getting any jobs in the machine fitting he was qualified for. I had my suspicions already as to what he may prefer.

* * *

We sat in the café in silence. Bob had failed yet another interview and been told to report back to us, although I wasn't sure why. I think his local office thought he may be throwing the interviews on purpose and wanted to make counselling him out of doing that our problem. But I thought there may be other reasons, I just didn't know quite how to raise the issue.

In the end, I decided to bite the bullet and go for it. 'Bob, are you *sure* that mechanical engineering is the career you want?' I sat back with my coffee held tightly, in case he exploded – he was six foot three and any anger would at least tip the table. 'You haven't considered doing something else?'

Instead of any kind of display of temper or frustration, I got a quiet nod and a raised eyebrow. 'You know, don't you?' he said, in a very low voice. 'How do you know?'

'Tell me what you'd *really* like to do with your life,' I said, neatly ducking the question. 'I might be able to help you. To achieve it, I mean, not talk you out of it or anything,' I added quickly.

Under the table, he tapped a foot. Impatience? Or it could have been following the beat of 'Merry Christmas, Everybody' which was playing over the café sound system. 'Dunno if I can,' he muttered. 'Sounds stupid.'

'My job,' I said, as quietly as he was speaking, 'is to get people into work doing things they want to do. Not just a quick fix, not just a six-week placement. I want everyone to be doing what they love. And I don't think you love mechanical engineering, however much Zac might think that's what you're qualified to do. Now, if you tell me, I might be able to help you not spend the next thirty years hating every second of your life. So?'

Bob's large, smooth face relaxed a little. 'Can you do that?' he whispered. 'Are there jobs? I mean, things that pay?'

'I'm sure we can find something.'

'Only I've done a couple for free, just for a laugh, couple of pub parties, that kind of thing.' Bob squared his shoulders, and the table rocked. 'But what I'd really like, one day...' he leaned forward and his voice lowered to a conspiratorial whisper, 'is to be on that *Ru Paul's Drag Race*. I can sing,' he added, a little louder, sitting back in his chair. 'And dance.'

'You'd like to work in the world of entertainment.'

Bob gave a shy nod. 'I know it's tough. I know there's a lot of competition, but it's what I've always wanted to do. But Dad said – Anyway, I went into his trade. Only, my heart's not in it.' He fiddled with the sugar bowl. 'I'm not gay,' he'd gone back to a whisper. 'I just like the dresses.'

I was so relieved that I'd guessed right that I swallowed almost the entire contents of my coffee cup down in one. It hadn't been a *total* guess, of course, the very close shave, the shaped eyebrows, manicured hands and the slight traces of mascara still clinging to his lashes had given me a heads-up.

'I may be able to find you some Musical Theatre courses; we can put it down as retraining,' I said, once the coffee had slid past my windpipe. 'What about that?'

Bob's face relaxed again. 'Can you do that?'

I felt a sudden, unaccustomed elation. *This* was what my job was meant to be like. Helping people. Reassuring them that they weren't bad people for not wanting to be doomed always to work away the edges of their square peg, weathering them down in that tight round hole they'd got nailed into. Why couldn't it always be more like this?

'Yes,' I said, and the certainty in my voice made him smile. 'Yes, I can.'

'Cos Zac never... he never picked up on that. Even if I told him about performing and all that, he just thought it was, like, a hobby. He got hooked up on my qualifications and my experience, like. But I don't want to do that any more.' He looked wistfully at the café speakers, now belting out Wizzard, and his foot tapped again. 'I want to *sing*,' he said. I just hoped it wasn't right now. The café was not the place for a six-foot bloke to stand up and belt out 'I Wish It Could Be Christmas Every Day' without repercussions.

When I got back into the office, I felt like a fairy godmother, as though I'd tapped my magic wand and sent Bob to the ball, even though all I'd done was raise his spirits a bit and given him several application forms. But maybe that's all it took, I mused, wandering down the corridor, feeling the dampness of my shoes. Maybe people just wanted to be heard and their choices appreciated. Not to be judged.

Priya lurked louchely through the door, eating a Twix. 'I hear you did a swap,' she said, chewing caramel. 'He's got Miriam and you took his client?'

'I think I got the best out of that deal.' I sat down and twiddled my seat round. 'I'll have Bob on a course by the New Year.'

'Nice work. Should give you some brownie points. By the way, Michael wants to see you both upstairs, day after tomorrow. The fact he's giving warning means it's going to be big.' Her eyes narrowed in concern. 'You okay about that, Ruby?'

I'm going to lose my job. This is it. 'Well, at least he's given me a couple of days to get over the shock,' I said.

'I think that's why. You know Michael, he won't want anyone breaking down in his office.'

'He's the king of the stiff-upper-lip.'

She looked at me through narrowed eyes. 'You're very chipper for someone who might lose their job. I mean, compared to how you have been.'

'I'm not, Pri. I'm really not. It will all get to me at about–' I looked at the clock on the wall '– about three o'clock in the morning. Anxiety doesn't just get displaced.' I twirled the seat around a few more times. 'It pads along at your shoulder just waiting for you to weaken.'

'Yes, yes, very poetic,' Priya shoved the rest of the Twix into her mouth and leaned towards me across the desk. 'But what are you going to *do*?' she finished, somewhat muffled around the flakes of biscuit and chocolate.

'I'm going to let Zac have the job.'

Priya recoiled, her chin tucking back into her collar. '*What? After all this?*' She waved an arm to indicate the office, although I wasn't sure why that qualified as 'all this'. It was just a small dusty office with dreadful heating and not enough storage. 'What about–' she lowered her voice '– you know. All the debts?'

I shrugged. 'I don't want to work somewhere where they behave like this. It's unethical, making us try to get the dirt on one another, just to score points. And anyway,' I looked around the office again, 'I think I want a change.'

'I'll miss you.' Priya sat on the edge of the desk. 'You'll still come over though, won't you? You're the only one who eats Nettie's vegan loaf.'

'Of course I will. You're both still my friends. And Zac...' I wanted to say that Zac would still be here and maybe, just maybe, Zac and I could have something that wasn't based on competition. 'I *like* her vegan loaf,' I finished instead. 'You should give it a proper go. Just because it doesn't come with buttercream icing on doesn't make it horrible.'

Priya was not convinced. 'Yeah, you and Zac.' She fiddled with a Post-it pad. 'I knew you'd be good together.'

'We haven't really been *anything* together.' *That kiss.* 'But he's not as bad as I thought when he first came, that's all.'

'Despite the fact that YouBack2Work have been trying to set you at one another's throats ever since we merged? And you still managed not to hate one another? That's got to mean something.'

'There were moments,' I said darkly. 'But he's actually a really nice guy.'

'And he's hot. That doesn't hurt either.'

'I shall tell Nettie you said that.' I twizzled my chair a bit more. It squeaked its protest.

'I'm just being heteronormative,' Priya said complacently. 'I'm the Gay Best Friend, remember? My job is to make sure you know your worth.' Then she sighed. 'And it's a bloody hard job sometimes. I'd be delighted to see you go and work somewhere that appreciated you with more than a vague smile and some of Michael's top-class biscuits.'

'Yes, all the fries I can eat, probably.'

She gave me a sudden, very direct, look. 'You're better than this place, Rubes. You have to know it. You could make a difference out there if you got the anxiety sorted. Don't let it keep you trapped in this place.'

'Oh.' I hadn't realised that she felt quite as strongly as that. 'I wasn't aware that I was trapped.'

'Well, as Gay Best Friend I am here to tell you that you need to move on. I never thought you'd stay as long as you did, but once you got with Gareth and then you got all complacent and settled and everything – well. And then he went and you couldn't cope with change, but now...'

'I still have the anxiety, Pri.'

'But you handle it better now. You know what to expect from

it.' She slid down off the desk, causing a shower of sticky labels to hit the floor, and swept off to the door. 'If you don't find somewhere better than this, more *useful* than this, I'll donate the whole of my confectionary stash to... to... someone who will appreciate it!'

She swung her way out and closed the door.

'The Gay Best Friend is supposed to be a man!' I yelled after her, my emotions buoyed up and bobbing on a rising tide of someone believing in me. 'Who gives me fashion advice!'

'That top is horrible!' she called back and then I heard the sound of her door close. It opened again a second later. 'And stop wearing leggings!'

* * *

Of course, pep talks were all very well, and during the rational hours of daylight I could convince myself that everything would be all right. When night came, however, it was different.

Without the external stimulus of other people, without the distractions of work or even TV, when I was closed into my tiny room – *that* was when the fear came out to play. When I *knew* that, for all my bolshie talk of not staying with a company who had such dreadful ethics, I'd work there until I retired or they got rid of me. When I was convinced that my qualifications wouldn't get me anything and I would end up on a permanently renewing temporary contract, no sick pay, no redundancy protection, probably selling skimpy tops to people thinner than me. It was when I absolutely knew that I'd have to move home and cope with Mum and Dad's misguided kindnesses, Eva's constant questioning and comparisons, as though she'd won the life lottery by marrying a doctor and producing two badly behaved children.

I wrapped the duvet round my shoulders and went to sit at

the open window. The air in the room was too thick to breathe, too concentrated with regret and self-doubt, and the cold of the outside kept my heart from trying to drill its way through my ribs. I still felt sick and incapable of thinking anything that wasn't on the circuit of despair and loathing, but at least I knew I wouldn't suffocate.

I went through all the exercises my doctor had given me, but none of them helped. Concentrating on my breathing was the worst, it just made me aware of how fast my heart was beating and how likely it was that it would shortly give up and stop altogether. When my phone pinged a message, I was torn between being grateful for the distraction from dying and knowing that it was probably Michael firing me from my job. Somehow, in my head, Michael, at three o'clock in the morning, was aware of my current mental state and was dragging himself from his warm, and no doubt luxuriously oversized, bed, to let me know not to bother coming in tomorrow.

A brief flash of rationality told me that Michael didn't know how to text, and it was unlikely that Rachel was sitting at his marital bedside to instruct him. I picked up my phone in my sweaty-palmed hand and turned it over.

There's an emergency with Mum. I might not get in tomorrow morning, are you all right to make your own way to the office? I'll update you when I know more. Zac x

The sudden inrush of emotional overload made me pull the duvet over my head. So, Zac's mum was having a three-o'clock-in-the-morning level of emergency. That wasn't good. He'd thought to let me know he couldn't give me the planned lift, which made him a good guy. And then he'd finished it with a kiss.

I shuffled away from the window and flopped onto the bed,

falling into a tortoise configuration with my arms and legs tucked in under the carapace of duvet. The weight of it, pressing me into the mattress, was comforting and my heart rate started to steady, which, in turn, stopped the feelings of nausea and the hyperventilating. Slowly, slowly, I returned from that wilderness of panic and back to a place where hope at least had a foothold.

Zac was a good guy. Priya was right. He seemed to genuinely like me, we had a good working relationship, and we'd saved one another from the worst that management could throw at us. So far. He'd coped with my family, had driven me over when Mum had her accident, and he hadn't attempted to throw Albie and Xavier in the coal shed and nail the door shut. He was, to all intents and purposes, a nice man.

And I liked the way he looked. I had to admit that much to myself, even when the admission that he was a nice person made my teeth itch. I liked his leggy, wiry body. I liked his brown eyes and his smile. The hair was something I could work on.

My heart was going fast again, but without the driving whips of panic behind it now. This time it was the heating effect of lust and that tiny splinter of hope.

I fell asleep to uneasy dreams of Zac turning up at work with a big bunch of roses which turned into a tent, and him telling me that it was my new home.

The next morning, despite my sleepless night, I was awake and up early enough to strap on all my luminescence and peel on the leggings again for the ride into work.

The roads were mostly clear now, and I was only prone to the occasional wobble when I had to ride over heaped and frozen snow that had been piled up on the sides of the road so as not to inconvenience car drivers, but instead massively inconvenienced anyone *not* in a car.

Dawn was breaking as I rode through the city, lights on in windows and the early starters trudging along parallel with me, all of us giving one another sympathetic glances. Purple and gold strobed out from between curtains as people turned on their tree lights, countdowns of shopping days until Christmas were emblazoned across lamp posts and swinging in the cold, blue air.

I still hadn't got a present for Zac. On impulse, I propped the bike against some railings and threw myself on the mercy of two guys unlocking a menswear shop, waited while they fired up the till and then gift-wrapped my purchase. I stuffed it into my saddle bag in a way that destroyed the whole point of having it professionally wrapped, before hopping back into my pedals and pushing fast though the awakening city to the office.

Again, I was first in. There was no sign of Zac's car, and the space looked oddly naked without it. I padlocked the bike, wary of Cav's wrath should anything happen to it, and hobbled inside, handicapped both by my speedy pedalling on a bike with no discernible saddle and the tightness of the leggings. Neither of these things were conducive to a walk of any grace.

I changed in our office, which was steaming hot. The radiators only seemed to have two settings, boiling and off, and today it was clearly our turn to roast. Once I'd got respectable clothes on, I did some paperwork and then wandered around the room. I looked again at the photo on Zac's desk, the smiling, pretty woman and the tall, handsome man, and tried not to see my unslept face reflected back at me from the glass. There were shadows under my eyes and my skin looked dry and tight from the cycle ride in. What the hell could Zac see in me? *I* wouldn't date me.

I heard Priya come in and go straight into her cubby-office, but I didn't pop out to see her. She'd take one look at me and know I'd had a bad night, and I still felt a kind of shame about it all. I didn't know why, I couldn't *help* it and it wasn't my fault – nobody would choose to have random anxiety attacks, after all – but there was still a tiny tickle of *you aren't as good or as strong as everyone else* fidgeting away in the back of my mind. Priya didn't have panic attacks. Rachel wasn't reliant on medication to keep her from catastrophising until she was incapable of movement. Karen didn't sometimes feel that she just wanted life to stop for a while to let her catch up.

As far as I knew, anyway. I often reassured myself with this thought. Just as I didn't have a big arrow on my head that said 'poor mental health!!!' neither did anyone else. I probably wasn't alone. No, I knew I *wasn't* alone. There was Zac. And remembering that Zac, who always looked in control and even of temperament, could also have moments of breakdown, of being overwhelmed by life, made me feel better, even though I wished that he didn't struggle too.

The door creaked open a slice, letting in a gust of more normal temperatures, and Michael put his head into the room.

'Oh. Ah. No, er, Zac, yet then?'

'He's... he's around somewhere.' Nope, I was not going to choose now to stick the knife in. Zac and I were in this together. 'I'll tell him to come and see you when he turns up.'

Michael swayed, as though his mind had gone visiting elsewhere and his body was just propping his head up. 'Oh. No need, no need,' he said vaguely. 'Just wanted to congratulate him on getting Mrs Tate onto an education course. Bit of a bane in our stats, that lady.' Then he smiled at me, slightly sadly. 'Of course, that means he's running ahead of you in the employment game, I'm afraid.' He laughed, and I joined in, although I guessed neither of us knew what we were laughing at.

'I've got Bob Lassiter to agree to retraining,' I said, and I could hear the note of desperation in my voice. 'He's been on the books a while too.'

'Mmmm.' Michael's head was withdrawing. 'We will bear that in mind, of course.' The door closed behind him with a gentle click, and I heard the ghostly sound of his moccasinned feet treading the corridor back towards his office. It was like being haunted by the politest ghost in history.

'Oh bugger.'

Actually, oh bugger didn't even begin to cover it, but this constant high-level uncertainty, calculated, as I was *almost* sure it was, to unsettle us both, had ground away at me for so long that I had no vacillation left. I'd swayed so much between the 'everything will be all right' and catastrophising that I'd be living on the streets by summer, that I had nothing left to give.

I could smash up the office and storm up into Michael's, full of fire and sparks, tell them all to sack me now, I could do better than this. I could walk out into the snow, get on Cav's bike and ride away into the distance; start again. But the down-to-earth thought that Cav would hunt me down to get his bike back made me giggle and grounded me. I would do none of those things. I'd get my head down and work sensibly and cheerfully until I was told the worst was actually happening. Then I'd deal with it.

Zac came in around lunchtime, looking pale and strained.

'How's your mum?' I was eating a slice of Christmas cake, baked by Karen and brought round by one of the girls from the main office. She'd been wearing an elf outfit and I didn't know whether it cheered me up or made me more depressed.

Zac sighed and flopped into his chair, then shook his head. 'I dunno. She'd got out of her room without anyone seeing her and she was out in the grounds half the night. No one knows how she got past the alarms, she must have followed someone out.' He sighed again. 'She was hypothermic when they found her, just sitting in the snow. She was waiting for me to come out of school, apparently.'

My heart squeezed with concern. 'That's heart-breaking on so many levels.'

'I know.' He dropped his face into his hands. 'I know.' Another huge sigh that sounded as though it caught on words he wanted to say.

I got up and went over to him. 'Hey.' I touched his shoulder. 'Michael came to congratulate you on getting Miriam off our books. Looks like you win the "job" competition.'

Without looking at me, he put his hand over mine where it lay on his arm. 'There's just so much going on in my head,' he said. 'They're going to move Mum to a more... secure place. Still within the care home, of course, but she'll get some extra funding. She's not going to be able to come home at weekends any more though, I can't keep the place secure enough.' He flashed up a quick look. 'So now I need to sell the house, find a place to live, work out how to keep seeing Mum, all whilst working somewhere that seems to set Taskmaster challenges just to make me keep my job.'

I couldn't think of anything to say. Hoping he would take my physical presence as reassurance, I turned my hand and interlaced my fingers with his and squeezed gently.

Zac took another deep breath and raised his head. 'Okay,' he said. 'Okay. We can do this, Ruby. We really can. I think I might have a plan.'

'A man with a plan.' His level tone and the way he squeezed my hand in return was hopeful. 'If you've also got a van, I think Doctor Seuss may want a word.'

'Would you... would you come with me to visit Mum tonight?' The question was hesitant, as though he thought he would be tearing me away from a night of threesomes with the Hemsworth brothers after drinking champagne and dancing in some exotic club.

'Of course I will, if you'd like me to.'

He stood up sudden and tall, smelling of damp wool and anti-septic. I found myself in an embrace, his face against my hair, and realised that I quite liked it. 'I don't know what I'd do without you, Ruby,' he said. 'You're so wonderfully sensible, it's very grounding.'

'I have my non-sensible moments too.' I relaxed into his hold. 'Don't forget that. Anxiety isn't always great for being sensible.'

The hold around me tightened. 'I know. I know. But knowing you're fighting your own demons and yet you can seem so together; it gives me hope.'

I didn't like to say that I'd been thinking the same about him. Were we just two fragile people, both believing that the other one was going to save us? Were we clinging onto one another in the lifeboat as the ship went down?

'I don't just like you because you're suffering along with me, by the way.' He gave me a little squeeze. 'I like you because you're a genuinely nice person.'

'You're not privy to what I'd like to do to my sister,' I said, slightly muffled because he was very close up against me. 'I'm not *that* nice.'

'I've seen you, you really like helping people. You glow when you've made a difference to someone's life. It's really lovely. I'm more worried about what you could ever see in *me*.'

I took a half-step back, forcing him to move his head, and I looked up into his face. 'Well, you're tall,' I said. 'And that's always a good thing.'

Zac laughed. 'You're right,' he said. 'This isn't the time or place for this kind of introspection.'

The door opened and Priya was standing there holding a tray

of steaming mince pies. 'Brought these over from the café,' she said, then noticed us. 'Oh. It's like that, is it?'

Zac and I stepped further apart. 'It's been a bit of a day,' he said.

'And we're looking down the barrel of Michael and the Aliens making their decision as to who stays and who goes tomorrow,' I added. 'We're feeling a bit highly strung.'

'Fair enough.' Priya came into the room. The smell of hot pastry and steaming raisins was mouth-watering. 'But if you could unstring yourselves to give me a hand with eating these? The café is closing early today and these were left over, so they've given them to us. And if I eat them all I'll never get into my sexy reindeer outfit for tomorrow.' She looked at our blank expressions. 'Last day before we close for Christmas? Wear your Christmas outfit? Did all joy to the world and seasons greetings pass you two by?'

'Sorry.' I took a mince pie. 'It's been...'

'... A bit of a day, yes, I heard.' She put the tray down. 'By the way, you two make a great couple. Just thought I'd throw that one out there. And now I'm leaving you with the calorific baked goods and going to finish clearing my workload.'

Primly, like an understairs maid, Priya turned and walked out, leaving Zac and I staring at one another.

'Clear her workload!' I snorted. 'She's gone to phone Nettie and tell her the gossip.'

'What does she *do*, exactly?' Zac was staring at the carefully closed door.

'I'm not completely sure.' I ate another mince pie. 'Something they can't get rid of, obviously. Do you think she's right? Do we make a good couple?'

'I don't see why not, do you?' Zac took a pie in each hand. 'They've been trying to force us into competition all this time, but we've resisted. That and me being tall, it's got to mean something.'

'Well, I'm going to concentrate on "clearing my workload",' I said. 'Because tomorrow the news is going to be bad for one of us, whichever way things go, and if it's me, I don't want to leave you with a scrabbled mess of files and half-completed notes. Actually, no, that's not true, nothing would delight me more than to walk out of here and leave ineligible stuff for everyone to sort, but as the person doing the sorting would be you and I... quite like you, I shan't.'

'Then I suppose I should ditto.' Zac looked at his computer screen and sighed. 'But if one of us goes, we can still see each other, can't we? I mean, we can go out and all that?'

Solemnly, I screwed up some spare pieces of paper. They didn't even have writing on, but I wanted to make a point. 'Your presence will probably be the only brightness in what will be an otherwise pretty pointless existence,' I said.

'Don't overdramatise.' He didn't even look up.

'Well, I'll probably be living in Scarborough—'

'I like Scarborough. Now I've met it.' He was typing, one-fingered, which, as I knew he could touch-type, was being done for as much effect as me screwing up the blank papers.

'With my parents.'

'I like your parents too. Your family life is a nice counterpoint to mine.' He said it with no inflection, but I instantly felt bad.

'Sorry, yes. I didn't mean...'

'I know you didn't, Ruby.' He flashed a smile in my direction. 'Honestly. If we really want to, we can make it work. If people only ever dated people they worked with, then institutions every-where would become one huge incestuous mass of no work ever getting done and a *lot* of shouting. Other people manage to meet and form relationships with people at a distance. We will be fine.'

I kept my head down over my desk and didn't continue the conversation. I was still a little bit concerned about getting into anything with someone who lived and had ties nearly seventy miles away, particularly when I had no car and there wouldn't be the money for train fares. And I definitely didn't think I'd be cadging lifts off my dad at weekends, those days were twenty years behind me. I needed independence. And money, obviously, but the two were practically synonymous.

Plus, he'd be doing my job, I'd probably be selling ice cream from a handcart, and the temptation to push him into the sea might get too much for me.

14

Zac and I drove to Leeds through the late evening.

'I'll take you straight home afterwards.' Zac steered us out onto the practically deserted A64. Apart from late-night shoppers taking advantage of long opening hours, there weren't many people out and about in the snowy landscape. 'I really do appreciate the company. It was... tough, this morning.'

I touched his hand. It felt a little strange to be able to do it, but nicely strange. 'It's okay. And you can always put me on a train, you know. You don't have to drive me back.' *Just please don't make me buy my own ticket*, I added, but only inside my head, where the walls were having minor wobbles at the financial implications.

'No, it's fine. I don't mind.'

'Well, maybe if you're good, I can put in a word for the sofa again.' I looked out of the window at the fields flashing past. Between the outskirts of York and the suburbs of Leeds lay a flat, winding mass of snowy scenery, lit only by a cold moon. Occasional farmhouse lights illuminated paddocks and gardens, the odd well-fed and rugged-up horse, some huddled sheep straight from a Christmas card. Garish outdoor decorations stained the snow like multicoloured murder scenes and our headlights showed the road ahead to be a stirred-up mess of browning slush.

'Mum won't even know who you are,' Zac said conversationally, after miles broken only by swooshing tyres and the flash of occasional Christmas lights. 'But I want to introduce you. Visiting hours are different at the more secure unit and I'm not sure how I'm going to...' he tailed off. 'I usually try to get to see her three times a week, and then we had the weekends of course, but things might be... well...' He dropped his head and drummed his fingers on the wheel. He swallowed hard.

'You could ask to change your hours? Start early, leave early?'

'That wouldn't really go down well with the counselling, unless I can get our clients to agree to come in mornings only.' A half-grin. 'And you know how much some of them hate mornings.'

I sighed. 'Why does life have to be so *complicated*? Why can't we all live nice tidy lives with regular hours and no paperwork?'

'Because that's not a life, that's a children's TV programme.' Zac swung the wheel. 'Here we are. It's down here.'

The nursing home lay at the end of a long track which ran across fields on the outskirts of the city. The fields were scrubby and poor and even the snow looked half-hearted, but the building itself was a big old house with lights shining from practically every window, and it had a lot of effusive decoration going on around the front door.

Zac's mum was in the hospital section, behind several doors which required us to show identification and use passkeys. The carpeted hallways were plush and there were framed paintings on the walls.

'It's like a hotel,' I said as we walked through the last set of doors.

'An expensive one.' Zac looked around. 'Mum has additional

funding provided, and she had insurances that are paying quite a large proportion of the fees. I just have to make up the rest,' he added, glumly. 'Ah, here we are.'

Zac's mum, Debbie, was in a bed in a small room which contained one other patient. There was a hushed bustle going on and a lot of starched uniforms. It looked like a hospital in a 1950s drama.

'She's resting,' a nurse informed us. 'She's doing better than she was this morning though, and her temperature is coming back up to normal. Go and say hello, but don't keep her talking too long.'

We went over. Debbie was still the pretty woman from the photograph, ageing had barely touched her, apart from greying her blonde hair and adding some fine lines to her face. She lay sleeping, her hands wrapped in some kind of thermal thing, and the bed covered in cellular blankets.

Zac sat on the chair beside the bed and gently took a gloved hand. 'Hello, Debbie,' he said quietly. *He can't call her Mum*, I thought. *She doesn't know he's her son.* And my heart ached a little more for his situation.

Eyelids flickered. A brief smile hovered for a second, and was gone. 'Simon? Did you bring Zac? Did you fetch him from school?' Her speech was slow, she seemed to grope for words.

Zac's face betrayed only a momentary flicker of pain, but my eyes were filling on his behalf. 'Zac's fine, Debbie,' he said. 'He's really, really fine.' He smiled at me over the bed, where I stood awkwardly, feeling too big and too out of place. 'Yeah, he's doing very well.'

Debbie opened her eyes. 'I don't like it here,' she said. 'I want to go home. Zac will be home from school soon.'

'You just have to stay until you're better. Look, I brought someone to meet you. Debbie, this is Ruby. She's my girlfriend.'

Girlfriend. Yes. I liked the sound of that. It added a little bit of sweetness to the situation.

Deep brown eyes, very much like her son's, met mine. 'You can't marry your sister,' Debbie said.

A small wince of pain creased his eyes, but I supposed he was used to this kind of conversation. 'And I don't intend to. Anyway, we just looked in to say hello as we were passing. Make sure you're all right.'

A lady who wasn't wearing a nursing uniform, but instead had about four different lanyards around her neck, popped her head into the room. 'Ah, here you are. Zac, can I have another word with you? About–' she looked at Debbie, then at me '– what we talked about this morning?'

Zac stood up and indicated the chair to me. 'You sit here and have a chat,' he said, despite me making 'don't leave me' faces. 'I won't be long and this is important.' Now he gave me a significant look, as though I was supposed to know what he had to talk about. The moving of his mother to this new unit, presumably. Oh dear.

When he'd gone, Debbie looked at me again. 'Who are you, then?' she asked.

'I'm Ruby. I work with Z... Simon.'

'Oh. On the buses?'

I had no idea how to handle this. Did I just go along with her beliefs or did I challenge them? I had no real experience with talking to someone with dementia and my brain felt hot with the mixture of embarrassment and a kind of fear. I tried to remember my training. It had been quite a while since I'd needed to wheel it out. *Her beliefs are real to her.* That was what it boiled down to.

'Er, well, we don't work on the buses any more. It's in an office now.'

'Oh. Have you seen Zac? He should be home from school soon.'

I had another pang, thinking of Zac, never being recognised for who he was. 'Yes, I've met him once or twice. He's lovely.'

Debbie showed me the pictures beside her bed, which all seemed to be of Zac up to the age of about ten. She didn't have any more recent ones, presumably it upset her. In her mind, Zac was still a little boy.

'I like the jumpers you knit for him,' I said, when she had mired herself in a swamp of altered reality and was trying to explain how the pictures could be both old, and also current. 'I've got two nephews, would you knit some jumpers for them?'

She looked pleased for a moment, smiling softly at the photo of Zac wearing an obviously hand-knitted bright yellow jumper that made him look as though he was sitting in the centre of the sun, but then her eyes narrowed with suspicion.

'Who are you?' she asked. 'I don't know who you are. Did you break in?'

Just then, the door opened and Zac came back in and I nearly threw myself at him.

'We have to go now, Debbie,' he said. 'We'll come and see you again soon.'

'When are you coming back?' Her tone was forlorn, as though we were abandoning her in an empty room; there were at least three nurses in there, all busily sorting equipment and updating records on the, I couldn't help but notice, very state-of-the-art computer.

'I'll be back tomorrow. Now, you have a good rest.' He kissed her forehead.

'Will you bring Zac with you? When you've fetched him from school?'

Zac smiled. 'I'll see. He might want to stay at home and play games.'

Debbie's face relaxed from the worried frown. 'Oh, that's right. He loves those games.' We left whilst she still seemed happy to let us go.

We got halfway down the entrance corridor before Zac stopped me. 'So, that's my mum,' he said, catching me by the elbow to stop me walking. 'What do you think?'

I looked at his earnest face. There was a little crease of anxiety between his eyes and his mouth was drawn down at the corners, as though he was sucking something bitter. 'I think it must be very, very hard for you,' I said, trying to sound gentle but without being condescending.

'It's always worse for the relatives.' He gave me that look that seemed to be significant again, but I wasn't sure why. 'When you don't know what to expect, or how to behave. At first, I used to argue with her, when she got me mixed up with Simon or when she insisted on things that were obviously... well, she was confused.'

'Current thinking is not to challenge beliefs.' I sounded as though I was reciting from my training handbook or my textbooks. 'What she thinks is absolutely real to her. It would be like me telling you that you drive a Mini and you're deluded to think otherwise.'

Zac nodded slowly. 'I hoped you'd say that,' he said, enigmatically. 'Now, let's go back to the house of dreadful singing and a near-terminal sofa. I really don't want to be alone right now.'

'No. I can see why.'

We walked on a few more strides along the thickly carpeted floor, past a doorway through which I could see a very elderly lady being helped to walk to a chair, and a woman in uniform arranging flowers in a wall niche. There were subtle, understated decorations everywhere and a large tree with a silver and gold colour scheme in a corner.

Then Zac caught at me again. 'You understand, don't you?' He sounded almost breathless. 'Please understand, Ruby.'

There was such feeling in his voice, such an echo of loneliness and despair that I, once again, felt vaguely guilty about my own anxiety issues. What, after all, did I *really* have to feel anxious about? No money and a precarious job? Pah, practically *everyone* has that and they don't all resort to all night panic attacks and medication. Here was Zac, struggling to carry all this worry.

But then I thought, *My beliefs are just as valid.* The thought caught me by surprise. I'd got quite used to feeling that my anxiety attacks, the general feeling of panic that those walls in my head tried to keep suppressed, weren't legitimate. That they weren't somehow serious enough to be 'a thing'. As though something in my personality had built up my natural background fears of being alone forever, in debt forever, and turned what other, normal people dealt with on a daily basis into some kind of huge drama. As though I was somehow showing off by living with this personal dread.

My beliefs are just as valid. What Debbie believed was real to her. What I believed was real to me. It didn't matter that my anxiety was triggered by something others may see as trivial. It was *my* anxiety. They were *my* panic attacks. And I was entitled to feel terrified. It was real *to me.*

In this overlit hallway that held a faint scent of disinfectant beneath the expensive infusers, beside the tasteful tree, I held that revelation to me as though it somehow proved something. *I am allowed to believe what I want. This isn't a competition.*

'Yes.' I reached up and laid my hand against Zac's cheek, trying to show, through touch, that I understood. I may not really grasp the complexities of his life, but I was here, alongside him. 'Yes.'

He let out a sigh that was a cross between a gasp and a sob. 'I was worried for a minute there. You went very quiet.'

'Oh, no, that was... something else. Me realising something. It's fine.'

'Good. Only... look, I've had a couple of girlfriends, in the past.'

I looked at him. Tall and slightly flushed from the heat in here, dark pencil-lines of stubble forming across his chin and those large, intelligent eyes. I couldn't believe that I'd ever thought he looked smug or complacent. I could see the tracery of worry around his eyes. 'Only a couple? You disappoint me. I thought I was going to have to fight off hordes of disappointed women, I was going to buy a special stick.'

He laughed and it sounded as though he was shedding years' worth of tension. 'I can probably muster up a crowd, but I don't know about a horde,' he said and he was smiling into my eyes now. 'But–' and the smile died '– they've not really been able to grasp the situation with Deb— with Mum. That I can't move halfway across the country for a "really good job", not now she's settled here. I can't take long holidays because she gets distressed without visitors after a few days. I'm not loaded with cash, because I have to help pay her bills.' He opened the inner front door and we emerged into the snow and strobe effect of the front of the home. 'And it's pretty expensive,' he went on, in a low voice. 'It just about leaves me enough to cover my bills and buy food. If I think about it too much, well, that's when I... well, you saw, the other morning.'

I took his hand. 'I'm still paying for my expensive tastes in interior design for a house I only lived in for a few months,' I said. 'So I'm in no position to judge.'

Zac looked down at our hands, fingers wound around one another. 'We've gone blue,' he observed mildly.

'It's these lights.' I swung our arms up and out of the electric blue effect that the multitude of outdoor decoration was causing. 'Look.'

'I've been wondering,' he carried on, still looking at the anoxic tinge of our skin, 'why your ex isn't liable for half the costs? His name was on the mortgage too – why are you carrying all the debt?'

Slowly we walked down the ramp towards the Discovery, which was the only car parked in the visitors' car park, I noticed. I wondered about the other residents, and how often they were visited.

I tried to think of the best way to frame my answer. 'Partially guilt,' I said, when we'd negotiated the ramp and trudged over the slushy grit. 'I was the one who talked him into buying when he clearly, as I now know, had no intention of staying with me.'

'And the rest of the reason?'

The inside of the car was still warm, but cold in comparison to the hospital-level heating in the home. 'Stupidity, really. And stubbornness. Gareth didn't leave an address when he moved out. I never asked him where he was going and once we'd blocked each other on every device known to man, I couldn't get in touch to ask. Without knowing where he is... well, the bank don't care who pays. They go after the person whose address they *have* got, and that's me.'

'And that guilt stops you looking for him?'

I nodded, feeling a bit feeble. 'It sounds stupid, I know. And now, with hindsight, I know that he is as culpable as I am. He could have said no. He could have walked away. But I made his life so easy, why would he?' I shrugged. 'So. Yeah. My fault.'

Zac looked back over his shoulder at the huge house as we

pulled out of the car park and onto the wet snow of the lane onto the main road. 'Guilt,' he said. 'I get that one. I *could* get Mum into a fully NHS-funded place now, she's reached the level of not being able to care for herself. But there was only her and me, and I can't bear to see her in a place set up for bingo and all-day TV-watching, with people thirty years older than her. She's only sixty-three. I can't help think about your mum and all about her running and the dogs and the trifle.'

'To be fair, the trifle is Dad. Mum would happily never cook again,' I said.

'It's the contrast, though. I know how Mum's life *should* be, and I want to keep it as close as it can be for as long as I can.' He steered the car out onto the road, which was still mostly empty, only one other pair of beams coming carefully through the slush at us. 'Though I am aware that I'm losing that battle, with what happened last night.'

'She's going to stay in the hospital unit?'

'Pretty much. They've got a more secure section, round the back, she'll move in there once she's recovered. We can recreate her room exactly, she won't even notice.' He swallowed the last three words. 'But this place,' he indicated with a jerk of his head the place we'd already left, 'caters for all kinds of long-term nursing needs. So it's not just for people who... for those with memory loss. It's full of rich people's relatives who are *inconvenient* in any way.'

'Don't be bitter, Zac. You can't judge people for the choices they make, you know that. No doubt everyone who has their relatives in there feels they are doing their best by them, the same as you with your mum.'

He shrugged and carried on driving.

I kept my face turned to the snowy fields and hoped that Zac never realised that the true reason I didn't want to look for Gareth was that I couldn't bear the comparison. I couldn't stand for Gareth to look at my life as it was now, with no real home, the same job as I'd had when we were together, a dependence on medication to help me sleep and stop the panic from rising. How was it fair that *he* had left *me* and yet he'd prospered and I was floundering around in the ruins of my previous life?

I caught Zac's eye and we smiled at one another and I realised that I'd rather have him, here and knowing everything about me than a rich blonde and having to keep up appearances. Gareth was doomed now to a life of depending on his wife's family money and being dictated to, and it served him right.

Oh, who was I kidding – that life would suit him down to the ground.

And me? Well. This life may be precarious, and I may be out of a job, but at least I had Zac.

15

The house was in chaos when we arrived. Sophie was packing to leave for Christmas with her family whilst simultaneously preparing what looked like a hundred costumes for the school Christmas play which was tomorrow. She kept putting things down in bags and then realising that they were for the play and unpacking them again in an increasingly distracted way. Cav was sitting by the window like a cat waiting for a squirrel, and he leaped up to paw at the Discovery until his bike was released from the boot and he could coo over its safe return. He was heading out to Dublin in the morning to spend Christmas with his sister, so the hallway was full of cycle bags of gear.

'Is he going to pedal to Dublin?' Zac whispered to me, when I told him why they were there. 'The sea is going to be a bit of a problem, isn't it?'

'Sssh. He goes by taxi and train, but he'd bike it if he could. And he wears his bike gear all the way so nobody mistakes him for a non-cyclist. Which, to him, would be worse than drowning.'

We stared out of the window at Cav, who was replacing the

wheels we'd had to take off the bike to fit it in the boot, and adjusting the chain.

'Does he meet many girls?'

'A surprising number. But it's all right, they're all cyclists too.' I poked my head into the kitchen, which was a whirlwind of Sophie. 'Is it okay if Zac has the sofa again tonight?'

'Mmmm? Oh, yes. Course.' Sophie shoved an inflatable snowman into her bag, sighed, and took it out and put it in the carrier bag of school costumes. 'Oh, Ruby, really sorry, but the landlord is putting the rent up in the New Year. I got a letter this morning.'

'How much?' I felt the snatch of panic that caught at my breathing.

She stopped with a tin of biscuits in her hand, clearly undecided about whether they were destined for family or school, then named an amount that seemed horribly high.

'Seriously?'

'Well, he's going to redo the kitchen, apparently, to make it worth it, and paint the bedrooms. Of course, as he says, we can always find somewhere else if we don't like it.'

We both laughed, hollowly. 'I hope he's repainting the bedrooms in solid gold and putting in a cooker that orders the food, prepares it and then cooks it for us,' I said.

Sophie shrugged. 'Maybe we could turn the living room into another bedroom, get someone in to share the rent five ways? It's probably illegal, but...' she waved a hand at Zac, who was replacing a string of lights which had become detached from where they'd wrapped around the curtain pole and now hung limply across the window like a fallen shop sign. 'Maybe he'd take it?'

Well, I thought, as we all filed around the house, packing or preparing for bed, Zac might end up taking over my room, if I had to go back to Scarborough and move in with the parents. I said 'goodnight' to Zac and went up to stare around the tiny space of my bedroom. Zac wouldn't even be able to have a morning stretch without punching holes in both walls beside the bed. This wasn't so much a 'room', it was Jenga with furniture.

I felt the familiar gripe in my stomach that told me the anxiety was getting a hold, that wobble in the mental walls allowing the worry to take centre stage. I couldn't afford that raised rent. Even if I was the 'lucky' one who got to keep the job, things were tight enough already. I'd have to find somewhere cheaper to live, and since this had been the cheapest place available when I'd had to find somewhere last year, and now I didn't have a car...

Breathe.

Distraction. I needed distraction. The reason that the panic attacks didn't strike so often during the day was that I could find something to busy myself with, something that stopped them getting stuck in. Sometimes it didn't work, of course, but lately I'd got better at diverting the attacks. Like an oncoming freight train of worry, during the day I could switch them to another track by finding something more immediate to sweat over. It was the darkness and relative quiet of the night that was the enemy.

I got up from where I'd sprawled on the bed and tiptoed to the landing. Sophie, in the attic, was a series of thumps that told me she was still packing. Cav's room was utter silence. I didn't know whether he slept or just disconnected his chain, but he never made a sound once his door was closed. A narrow strip of light told me he was in there though.

Downstairs was dark and silent. I crept into the hall and through to the kitchen. Pouring a glass of water would help. Maybe there was a newspaper in there that I could read, kick my mind away from the circling thoughts that hovered like vultures, ready to swoop in and pick over my entrails if I gave them chance.

The light ticked and strobed into life, revealing the sad chaos of the kitchen. The landlord was right, it did need updating and a sensible work surface put in, but unless he was going to extend it into the garden and put a swimming pool in, it still wasn't going to be worth what we'd have to pay for it. But then, it was worth what someone would pay and *someone* would cough up to have a convenient roof over their heads without having to travel in by train every day.

'Can't sleep?' Zac's voice made me jump. He wandered into the kitchen behind me.

'I don't know yet, I've only been in bed for five minutes. I just needed...' I trailed off. Unless I needed some emergency green crepe paper, there wasn't a lot of inspiration.

'The nights are the worst.' Zac sounded as though he was agreeing with something I'd conveyed without words. 'When you just lie there running through all the things you can't do?'

I sighed and picked up some bits of silver foil. It looked as though a dog made of tinsel had wandered through and had a good shake. 'Yes.'

He was standing by the fridge, wearing a fleece and jogging bottoms. He looked as though he was off for a run. 'Ruby,' he said and then stopped.

'What?'

'I need to talk to you about something.' He came towards me, his feet sticking slightly to the vinyl flooring. 'About tomorrow.'

I knew I had to stop him. I couldn't bear to even *think* about tomorrow. About what was going to happen when Michael and the Aliens delivered their verdict. When one of us had to go. How would the one left feel about that?

'Can we not talk about it, please?' We were squeezed up

together in the corner by the fridge, keeping our voices low so as not to disturb anyone who may be sleeping. 'I can't think about it. Not yet.'

Zac looked down into my eyes. Whatever he saw looking back at him made his mouth twitch up at one side. 'Yes,' he said slowly. 'I can understand that.'

Beside us, the fridge purred into life.

'I was going to have a drink of water.' For some reason, my voice was thick in my throat. Zac was so close, smelling of shower gel and something dark and mysterious, like a really rich fruit cake. 'But I've gone off the idea now.'

'Don't let me dehydrate you.' He reached out a hand and very gently brushed a curl of my hair away from my face. 'You might unravel and blow away.'

'Fairly sure I won't.'

'Don't be so prosaic, Ruby.' The hand lingered on my cheek. 'You make me think of cobwebs, you know that?'

'Grey, dusty, full of spiders?' My voice had gone a bit shaky now as well. His look was so direct, so heated, and his touch against my skin was making all my erogenous zones perk up and take notice.

'Fragile-looking but really as strong as steel,' he corrected me, raising his eyebrows. 'But, yes, there's the dusty spider thing going on too.'

I giggled, which made me raise my internal eyebrows. I was not the giggling type, but something about the proximity of Zac, the intoxicating scent of him, the feel of his fingers on my face – it was turning me into a cartoon version of myself. If he kept this up much longer, I may even go as far as a simper.

'You really aren't used to the chat, are you?' Zac went on. 'Has nobody ever told you how gorgeous you are? Nobody ever kissed you in dark corners or ran down the road after you with flowers?'

He was so close to me in that little space, with the fridge motor vibrating all down one side of me and the floor cold and tacky under my bare feet. It was like some kind of romantic fantasy suddenly materialising in Real Life Land – that mix of heady, breath-holding potential combined with the smell of stale pizza and bike oil. The closeness of him and the whispering was making this all feel rather intimate, although it was possibly the most unromantic place in the world for a tryst.

'Too dusty and too many spiders,' I half-whispered.

'I know exactly how you feel.' His voice was a whisper too. Then he leaned just that little bit further and kissed me, and it was a very different kiss to the one we'd exchanged in The Shambles in the snow. This one was hot. It made my veins burn and my body expand.

I ran my hand along the hem of his fleece and up under the edge until I could touch his skin, warm and smooth and rimmed with the bone of his ribs. Then higher, feeling the scatter of hair across his chest, spreading my fingers across the lean firmness.

'Come upstairs.' My voice was more of a growl.

'Won't the others notice?'

'It's a bike-obsessed Irishman and a primary school teacher, not The Pre-Marital Sex Obliviation Committee.' I sounded a bit fierce now. 'Who cares?'

'Well, all right, if you're sure.'

Still kissing, we tacked our way across the kitchen and hallway. He let me lead the way up the stairs and then he let me lead the way from there on. He was gentle, but deft and sure and he followed my cues until the pair of us were breathless and sprawled side by side on the narrow little bed. I was pressed against the wall and he had one hand looped through the headboard to prevent himself sliding off onto the narrow strip of floor.

'That was unexpected,' he said, pulling the duvet up to cover us both. 'But I am not complaining.'

'High tension.' I wiggled to be less flattened against the cold plasterboard. 'The worry about tomorrow and everything else, it's making us behave uncharacteristically.'

'Oh, was that uncharacteristic?' Zac made a comedy-disappointment face. 'I was hoping we'd have sex like that from now on.'

I nudged him with my elbow. 'You know what I mean.'

He planted a gentle kiss on my forehead. 'Of course I do. Just, well. It was pretty good from my end.'

'Yes. Yes it was. Oh, I mean from my end too. We're surprisingly compatible in bed.' I was gabbling, trying to cover that I didn't really know quite what to say. Events had taken me utterly by surprise and I had no reaction ready.

'But we ought to go to sleep.' He slotted the headboard arm under my shoulders. 'If sleep is possible in this bed. Because tomorrow is going to be tricky, and the last thing we need is to be behaving like a pair of zombies. We'll need our wits about us at this meeting.'

I shuddered beside him, and it wasn't from pleasure this time. 'I don't want to think about it or I'll never sleep.'

Another soft kiss. 'Things will be all right, Ruby,' he whispered. 'I promise. One way or another, things will be all right.'

The panic made a brief resurgence and tried to snatch my breath, but my body wasn't having it. It was just too tired. 'I'll hold you to that,' I said, the words almost too heavy. 'I really will.'

And then I dropped into a warm pit of sleep, whilst the walls strained to keep the horrors contained.

16

Priya was waiting for our arrival the next morning, almost levitating with anxiety.

'Michael said I was to let him know when you arrived.' She gave me a rather sharp look. 'I don't think he expected you to arrive together.'

I raised my eyebrows at her until she blushed.

'Well, sorry, but Nettie and I live our lives vicariously through you.'

'You both have perfectly good lives of your own.' I couldn't help it, I felt slightly – no, not smug, that was too rounded a description for how I felt. But when Zac, hanging up his coat over in the corner, looked at me and gave a tiny wink, I couldn't help but feel a certain degree of comfort. After last night, after waking this morning to Zac's arm still around me and his sleepy breath ruffling my hair, there were little twinges of hope twanging.

Okay, the debts would still be there, whatever happened with us, but just knowing that there was someone on my side, someone who actually enjoyed my company and could find me physically attractive without 'parping' my boobs or shoving his hands down my top like a just-weaned baby hoping for a last chance – it was a pleasant feeling. Quiet reassurance that there was still a life for me out there.

'I know, but yours is just so much more riotous. Our biggest excitement is deciding how to cook the turkey this year,' Pri shoved a mug into my hand. 'Tea. Make the most of it.'

I grinned at her, despite the fact that the uncertainty was beginning to revolve in my stomach again. For all Priya's talk about me being her equivalent of reality TV, I knew her life wasn't as straightforwardly domestic as she made out. Her parents were resolutely traditional and had cut her off for being a lesbian; she hadn't seen her beloved brother for two years and she had a baby niece that she'd never met. There were sadnesses in her life, but she lived for the moment and didn't dwell on them. I wished I could be like that.

'Right, better let him know, then,' Zac said. 'Release the hounds.'

Priya blinked at him. 'Sorry?'

'We might as well start running now.'

'Oh!' She laughed. 'I really hope it's not going to be that bad. I've got used to having you two around.'

'But you'd prefer it if Ruby stayed.' Zac gave her a small smile. 'It's fine. You've been friends for longer, I understand. But you'd still be friends if she went somewhere else, wouldn't you?'

'We have to stay friends,' Pri said, giving me a serious look. 'Ruby knows too much about me to be allowed to live as my enemy.' Then she sighed. 'I know, we'd still see each other, *someone* has to come over and eat Nettie's spinach whirl and Ruby is the only person I know who can pretend well enough. But I just don't like change.'

'Would you be happy if I kept the job?' Zac had to bend down to see her face properly.

'You're all right, I suppose.' Priya averted her eyes. 'But it wouldn't be fair.'

'No. No, it wouldn't.' The way Zac said this gave me a momentary lift in my midsection. If he *were* offered the job, did that mean he wouldn't take it? But then I remembered his mother, that well-equipped hospital wing in that big, expensively decorated home. He *needed* this job. At least I had a supportive family and somewhere else to go. If he had to sell the family home to provide for his mother's care, where would *he* live?

The tiny glimmer of hope that I'd felt died into ashes again. There really was no way out of this one.

Zac gave my shoulder a little squeeze. 'One way or another, it's going to be all right,' he said. 'We can do this.'

'And we're still on for Christmas, whatever happens.' I tried to find something good, something to look forward to other than the gaping chasm opening at my feet.

'Well yes. I'm far too rubbish in the kitchen to be allowed to cook my own Christmas dinner.' Another squeeze.

'At least you won't have to contend with the spinach whirl,' Priya said in her most depressed tone. 'Right. I'm calling Michael. Gird your loins, whatever that means, and head on up to his office. I'll have the coffee on for when you get back and the shouting starts.'

She gave me a little grin, that my imagination inserted a tiny bit of sadness into as I felt my heart push its way up towards my throat. This was it. I either kept my job or I was out in the wilderness, flailing around to find employment in Scarborough, with no transport and not a whole lot of hope.

But I'd have Zac. And as a consolation prize that rated pretty highly.

We walked up the polished stairs to the offices without speaking. Below us, a general air of mince pies and exuberance was breaking out as everyone prepared for the last day of work before Christmas. Any exchange between departments was fraught with the risk of fruit cake and cards, Secret Santa had come into play in Reception and there seemed to be a giddiness out of proportion to our usual serious jobs. Perhaps people were just glad to be keeping their jobs into the New Year, I thought, watching the festoon of paper chains swinging in a draught along the approach to Michael's office.

Zac tapped on the door and we went in.

Michael and the aliens were sitting behind the desk. I wondered if they'd got a mental force field in action in case we threw things.

'Sit down you two,' Michael sounded his usual avuncular self. No hint of preference in his voice, no winks or knowing looks at either of us. 'Coffee? Biscuits?'

'No thank you.' Zac spoke for both of us, which was fine by me. My voice had gone to hide somewhere underneath the solidity that was my heart and stomach. All my organs seemed to have fused into one complete unit and everything under my throat felt rigid. I wasn't even sure I'd be *able* to sit down, but by copying Zac's easy slide into the chair, I managed to bend in all the right places.

All three on the other side of the desk had papers in front of them. The alien twosome held theirs with the edges square and the pile tidily stacked. Michael's were askew as though he'd been reading through them recently.

'We've reviewed your progress jointly and separately,' Michael seemed to be spokesperson for this particular unpleasantness, 'and we have to say that we've been very impressed with how both of you have reacted. Under the circumstances.'

Zac threw me a wary little look. I made the tiniest 'I dunno' face in return, widened eyes and a twitch of the mouth.

'But we have to make a decision,' Michael went on. My heart was drilling its way downwards through my stomach. I was surprised that the whole chair wasn't shaking. 'It's been very difficult, obviously.'

He paused again, like a presenter on a TV talent show, building the tension before the final results are announced. All three were watching our faces, switching attention from Zac to me and then back again. I was sweating.

'And we'd like to offer the position on a permanent basis to you, Ruby.'

First came the flash of relief. The loosening of the tension that held all my muscles taut in that chair, so I nearly slid down onto the floor.

And then my subconscious cut in. 'No,' I heard myself say. 'No, thank you.'

My mouth had gone dry now. *Where the hell had that come from?* It was as though my brain was empty of anything apart from a coalescing knowledge that it had been the right thing to say.

Michael blinked once or twice, then frowned. 'Oh. Oh, I understood that... oh. Well. In that case, Zac, we are able to offer the position to you.'

Here came my heart again, beating so hard that I felt sick.

'No,' I heard Zac say, with a lot more assuredness in his voice than mine had held. 'Thank you, but, no.'

We dared to look at one another now. He looked composed whereas I just wanted to giggle hysterically.

The three on the other side of the desk were consulting now, their heads pushed close together and a frantic amount of whispering, pointing at bits of paper and hand waving was going on. Zac gave me a small smile and raised his eyebrows.

'Apparently,' Michael said, after a moment and some throat

clearing, 'we can offer you *both* the job. On a job-share basis, naturally, which will entail a degree of negotiation regarding salary.'

My subconscious opened my mouth and began to speak. 'You don't understand,' it said. 'I can't continue to work for a company that employs methods like the ones you've used on us. Getting us to try to outdo one another. Trying to get us to gain information on each other to give us the upper hand. It's unethical and isn't behaviour that I want to be associated with, whether it gets me the job or not. So I'm handing in my notice.'

I was torn between being impressed with myself for actually laying my reasons on the line so cogently and wanting to strangle my subconscious. These were all thoughts that had been in the back of my brain for a while, but thoughts that I'd sat on, hard, in the interests of, oh, the usual bill paying, living and the rest.

Beside me, in his chair, Zac nodded. 'And that's how I feel as well,' he said. 'I'm handing in my notice too.'

Michael looked shocked and his coffee cup rattled back into its saucer. '*Both* of you? I mean, who's going to take over the counselling role?'

Zac and I looked at one another, grinned, and then turned back to the now clearly panicked people behind the desk.

'Not us,' I said.

'I'm sure you can recruit someone.' Zac stood up. 'But for now, we need to go and clear our desks. Will you want us to work out our notice? Or finish at the end of today?'

Michael came out from behind the protective mahogany. 'I... err... I, well, the legal team, of course, I will confer, but... well, yes. Probably best if we call it a day now.' His voice was shaky. 'I, err...' He walked us to the door, opened it and, when we stood outside, he pulled it closed behind him so that our view of Beehive woman and Grey Man twittering together over paperwork was cut off. 'I have to tell you,' Michael said, quickly and in a half-whisper, 'that I'm taking early retirement. None of this was my doing.'

Zac patted Michael's arm. 'Of course not.'

'But, you two – you will be all right? From here on in?'

I gave Michael a smile that I could feel didn't extend beyond the immediate area of my lips. 'We'll think of something. Going forward,' I couldn't resist adding.

I got an equally stiff smile in return and he fumbled behind him for the door handle. 'Good. Well, ah. Good.' Then, with an almost balletic pirouette, he turned and went back into the office, leaving Zac and I on the polished boards of the landing, staring at one another.

'That was great.' Zac put his arm around me and guided me to the top of the staircase. 'I'd got something similar prepared, just in case, but yours was better.'

'Was it?' I sounded shaky. Only that arm tucked casually around my shoulders was stopping me from slithering down the mirror-finish of the stairs like a sack of liquid.

'Oh yes. I didn't have the word "unethical" to hand, for a start.'

'I don't know where it came from.' At the bottom of the stairs, I turned to him, the panic was beginning to build now. 'I was angry at the way they behaved and I just...' I tailed off. 'What the hell do we do now?'

Priya was standing outside our office door, two mugs in her hands. 'Well?' she asked, shoving the mugs in our direction as we walked towards her. '*Well?*'

Zac told her what had happened while I sipped at my coffee. I didn't feel as though I had any words left to give and, although the hot drink helped, there was a confusion starting behind those walls in my head that spoke of tears to come.

'Wow.' Priya looked at me through wide eyes. 'That was brave, Ruby.'

'It was *stupid*,' I said fiercely. 'They didn't give me any thinking time.'

'No, no, it was amazing,' Zac insisted, opening the office door.

Priya and I filed in after him and I looked around the cluttered chaotic room. I'd never thought how much I would miss this space, the smell of hot radiator, wood polish and history. This was the last time I'd be in here. The last time I'd...

I had to stop this. I was spiralling and I needed to stop. I needed to *think*.

'I don't know what to do now.' I could hear the rising note of panic in my voice. I tried really hard to stop it, but if simply not wanting to panic was enough to stop panic, then nobody would ever have panic attacks. My breathing was getting faster. I was overwhelmed by that feeling that there isn't enough air getting into my lungs, and that I might be sick and suffocate as a result. I needed to get out of there into space and run from this huge black cloud that tumbled behind me and wanted to steal my oxygen and press me to the earth with its weight and...

'Ruby.' Zac's voice was firm and startled me into looking up at him. 'We need to talk.'

Priya was looking at me, concern on her face. 'Do you need to take those tablets from your bag?' she asked. 'I'll get you some water.'

'I'm... It will be okay, Pri.' Zac's words had jumped me out of the immediate pit of despair and restarted sensible breathing. 'I'll talk to Zac now and take them later if I need to.'

She hovered, dithering about at the door. 'I don't want *either* of you to leave,' she said, finally. 'It's not fair. I've just got you both trained to turn on the coffee machine first thing and give me all the gossip. I don't want to have to start again with new people!'

Then she hustled out into the corridor and I heard the sound of a stifled sob and nose blowing begin before she closed the door to her own office.

'You okay?' Zac came and hugged me.

'I think so.' The words were wobbly but I meant them.

'Good. Because we need to talk. This is important. It's what I wanted to talk about last night, before, well, before things got away from us.'

I had a momentary flash of how far things had got away, and my body heated up all the way from my toes to my forehead. 'All right,' I said, turning slightly so he couldn't see the way my face was reddening. From the feel of it, I was glowing like a meteor entering Earth's atmosphere.

He squeezed slightly, then let me go and walked over to his own desk. I perched on the edge of mine and he hooked a hip up onto his, so we sat like a couple of budgies in an aviary. 'I've got another job,' he said.

'Already? Wow.' I *wanted* to say 'bully for you,' but I knew it would sound sarcastic, as maybe it would be intended to.

He jiggled a leg and gave me one of his broad grins. 'Yeah. Even if they'd offered me this job first, I wasn't going to take it. Mum's place – well, they need a counsellor for the patients coming in with early memory loss. They're starting up an outreach unit – I mean, still private, still a little bit elite, but we can work on that; work on bringing it down into the public sector and making it more generally available. The job will entail working with those who are starting to get confused and frightened, thinking up coping strategies, trying to make the whole process a little easier for them.' He flashed me a look, it was suddenly full of pride, more intelligence than he usually let me see. 'It's what I trained in, you see. When it was obvious Mum was... well, I wanted to help her.'

'So you'd be able to see more of her?'

'That's the idea. Plus discounted rates and a *much* better salary.' He took a deep breath. 'And I want you to come with me. When I talked to their Board, I put forward a case for counselling for the relatives of those with Early Onset Dementia at first, moving on to perhaps helping those who have to... well, who find that they can't care for their relatives at home any more.'

I felt myself blinking rapidly. Was he suggesting what I *thought* he was suggesting?

'I thought of the way you work with the clients here, how, for you, it's more about getting to the bottom of their feelings than about jemmying them into the first job that comes along. How you actually *care* about them being happy. And it just seemed...' he trailed off and stared at me. 'Are you all right?'

I was blinking away as though I was trying to signal to ships at sea. 'I... don't... know.' The words came out staccato, coupled with the blinks.

'Okay. Take a couple of deep breaths and stand up. It will help.'

I did, and it did, I stopped feeling stuck in 'strobe mode'.

'And there's even accommodation with the job,' Zac said gently. 'One flat, or two, depending on how we decide to work things. Maybe start with two, and if we... well. We can think about that later. So that we are on site if we're needed.'

I flopped back onto the desk again. A job and a place to live? I began to feel like the closing credits in some of those wish-fulfilment fantasy-land films that Sophie watched on Channel Five at weekends. All pink-cheeked pretty girls winning their hard-working rugged man, often amid snow in the Rockies or Central Park. There was usually skating involved. 'This is... I mean, I can't get a handle on this.'

'But would you? Could you? I realise that it's the answer to my prayers, but for you it may be different. You don't have to say yes. You can do whatever, we can still see one another.' He sounded anxious, and, when I looked at him properly, the stress lines were back around his mouth and pulling between his eyes. He looked older and slightly scared, and with a loneliness coming down around him like fog.

My mouth twitched. 'I think it sounds brilliant,' I said. 'In fact, I think it sounds amazing. You'd be there for your mum, we'd be doing something really good for people. Yes. I think I'd love it.' *Love it?* My thoughts bounced up and down like Xavier on aspartame. *Come ON! This is practically your dream job!* There was a tiny hint of waiting for the downside, but I recognised that as my anxiety refusing to let me believe in a future. Helping people. No 'end goal results' being judged. Just good, old-fashioned counselling.

There was an instant brightness in his eyes now. 'Plus,' he said, the lift in his voice sounded like relief as well as humour, 'and I can't stress this too highly a salary that's a distinct improvement on this place. Enough for us to save for somewhere of our own to buy.'

'You think it could come to that? Us having our own place? Together?' My heart started racing and I had flashbacks to half-used tins of paint. I refused to give them head room. This wasn't Gareth. This was Zac and things were different now.

'Well, we're dynamite in bed, and that's always a good start.' He raised his eyebrows at me and I felt the laugh start somewhere in my chest.

'Plus, I quite like you.'

'And someone has to save you from Nettie's spinach whirl whilst overindulging on your mother's special trifle.' He moved so fast that I wasn't ready for the embrace and it knocked the wind out of me, leaving me breathless and gasping, but in a really good way this time. 'So, to answer your question, yes, I think it could come to that.'

'My family like you.' I felt his body stop, the catch of his breath. 'And you seem to like them. Apart from Eva's boys of course, but we can always lock them in the shed when we go round.'

Zac pushed me gently back a step so he could look into my face. 'Ruby,' he said slowly. 'Dad died when I was seven. Mum got ill when I was fifteen. I'm an only child. I've never had much of a real family, so your batshit crazy nephews, manic running mother, trifle-obsessed father, your sister and the spaniels – it's all like a little slice of heaven to me. A tiny bit of the normality I've never had.'

It was a statement that didn't need a reply. Instead, I stretched up and kissed him and for a while that was enough. Beyond this little space, the corridors began to fill with the slightly over-loud celebrations of the final day's work before Christmas; the incongruity of 'Silent Night' being sung loudly and even more tunelessly than Sophie could manage, gift and card exchanges between offices, and trays of fruit cake and mince pies slowly migrating their way through the building.

Zac and I stayed in our bubble for a while before we joined in.

17

Christmas Day was unlike any of the Christmases I'd known so far. Zac came over on Christmas Eve and we sat under Sophie's over-decorated tree, illuminated only by the multicoloured string lights that hung in loops from its branches. We drank wine, cuddled and watched awful television before going to bed.

Then, in the morning, we drove over to Leeds to see Debbie, across the wasteland of rapidly browning snow, through tribes of children playing with Christmas toys. The sun came up and stretched itself along the snow, melting random trackways through fields and making the approach to the big house look like a giant game of noughts and crosses.

Debbie had no idea it was Christmas, although she was delighted with the new dressing gown and the perfume Zac had bought her. She kissed his cheek. 'You're very kind, Simon. Will Zac be along later? After school?' We assured her that he would, if he could tear himself away from his computer games, and left her happy, eating a generous and beautifully presented dinner.

Afterwards, Zac introduced me to some of the team who

managed the premises and we talked about working terms and conditions and pay in a very un-Christmassy discussion.

Then we went back to my place, feeling lighter and happier than I had in months. Sitting beneath the tree when we got back, I sprang up. 'I've got a present for you,' I said, finally remembering. 'Here.'

I'd put it under the tree the day before, hoping that he'd take it in the right spirit. I almost chickened out and dashed to the late-opening Tesco's to look for something more... more what? More appropriate? More neutral? But then I decided to stop over-thinking things and just give him what I'd bought. The look on his face when he opened it made me glad I had.

'Oh, Ruby.'

'I thought it was about time that you had one that fitted.'

He held the fisherman's sweater up against himself. It was cable knit, quite plain, but thick and, when he shrugged it on over his head, it fitted him like a dream. It actually made him look rugged and like one of those Rockies-dwelling lumberjacks from Sophie's films.

'I don't want to upset... I mean, it's not meant to replace the ones Debbie knits, I don't want to do that, but...' I tailed off. 'I just want you to wear something that fits,' I finished, slightly feebly.

'I know.' He wrapped his arms around me and pressed me in for a long kiss. 'I know, sweetheart. And thank you. Thank you for understanding, but most of all, thank you for not wanting me to go out looking like I got dressed when I was nine.'

'I didn't...'

He laughed. 'I *know* you didn't, Ruby. Don't worry. It's just dawning on me how great it is to have someone who cares about things like that. How I look, how comfortable I am. I mean, I wear Mum's jumpers, yes, but I can feel close to her in other ways. It doesn't have to be with my sleeves halfway to my elbows and unable to move my armpits.'

He hugged me again. Red and blue fairy lights twinkled in his hair.

I opened my presents from my family. My mother had given me another cookery book, and Eva, in an uncharacteristic burst of generosity, had bought me a beautiful silk camisole. 'I'll call them later,' I said. 'To say thank you. And to see how much inter-family warfare has resulted from me buying the boys musical instruments for Christmas. What?' Zac had raised his eyebrows at me. 'They *asked* for them!'

'I've got something for you, too.' Zac pulled a tiny box from his pocket. 'I'm sorry, but I had to ask Priya what you might like. I half suspected she'd say something huge and impractical just to see if I'd go along with it, something like "a stag with golden antlers" or something, but she was surprisingly restrained.' He handed me the box. 'I hope you like it.'

It was a little bottle of really quite expensive perfume. One I wore, occasionally, and was making a small bottle of duty-free last for as long as possible.

'That's lovely, Zac, thank you.'

I was about to discard the wrapping paper when he stopped me. 'There's a bit more to it,' he said, peeling a folded piece of card from the inside of the wrapper. 'Here.'

'What's this?' I unfolded the card. There was an address written on it. A house name and a rural Suffolk location. I frowned at it. It meant nothing to me.

Zac flicked the card as it lay loosely between my fingers. 'That, beautiful Ruby,' he said, 'is where your ex-partner is now living. And very nicely too, if my research is anything to go by. He certainly intends to marry into money.'

'Oh.' I stared at it. I really wasn't sure what I was supposed to do with this information. Was it meant to help me move on from Gareth? I'd done that a while ago.

Zac laughed. 'Ruby. You pass this information on to your bank. There's absolutely no reason why you should be carrying all the financial weight of the break-up, you've nothing to feel guilty about. He could have refused to sign the mortgage agreement. Everything you were doing to the house, it was to make it nice for *both* of you to live in.'

'But I didn't give him chance to say no!' I was still staring at the card. It did sound like a pretty posh lifestyle Gareth had moved on to.

'Unless you talked at him non-stop during the entire duration of the purchase process, yes, you did,' Zac said, gently. 'He could have left the relationship at any time. He could have told you it wasn't working and stopped you going through with the house buying. But he wanted to have you, convenient for him, and he also wanted to have whoever is bankrolling this.' He tapped the card in my hand. 'He made his decisions too. And he should help to pay for them.' Zac pulled a face. 'Although I suspect he will get whoever is helping to pay for this very fancy detached residence, four acres of land plus stables, to pay it off for him.' He gave me a sideways smile. 'I looked it up on Rightmove.'

I could be paying off only my half of the debts.

Silently, above us, the tinsel and lights glimmered. From across the road, I could hear an impromptu carol concert breaking out, feet crunched their way through the snow, as it iced over again in the cold air of the dark. The house smelled of cooking, of pine trees and chocolate.

I stood up. 'Well, I suppose I'd better start getting you trained in the kitchen, then,' I said. It was a prosaic statement, one that didn't even hint at how my heart was suddenly full of hope for a future. I'd always be prone to the panics, it wasn't all going to go away, but the medication and exercises were helping now, and they would continue to help in the future. And I was daring to imagine that less stress may mean less chance for the walls in my head to rock and crumble.

I looked at Zac, clambering to his feet to share in the peeling of potatoes and poking of the roast, and I knew I didn't have to make any promises. Zac knew and understood. He had his own stresses and panics, but, maybe together we could help one another through.

Plus it was Christmas. There was food to eat and *Die Hard* to watch on TV. And a long, dark night to spend with Zac, before we started packing.

Life. Sometimes it could be a bitch, but sometimes it could surprise you too.

EPILOGUE
EIGHT MONTHS LATER

The sun streamed in through the large windows of the Residents' Lounge as Bob, resplendent in blonde wig, blue velvet and his own bodyweight in sequins, blasted out 'I Will Survive' with evident relish.

'This is wonderful,' I said to Zac, who was sitting beside me. 'Thank you.'

He took my hand. 'I just wanted your birthday to be different,' Zac said. 'And you've got to admit, this is different.'

Bob segued into 'R.E.S.P.E.C.T' and batted his eyelids at us, grinning broadly. This was, I'd been told, his twentieth paid gig and he was clearly enjoying it immensely. His manager sat, handbag tightly clasped to her chest, mouthing the words along with him. Their eyeshadow was exactly the same shade of blue, I noticed.

'It's just lovely to see everyone again,' I said.

Priya and Nettie, fresh from helping themselves to the buffet, at which there was not even the merest sniff of a spinach whirl, came over, plates brimming.

'Elderly ladies really like pavlova, don't they?' Pri observed. 'There's hardly any left.'

'Well, there isn't now.' Nettie gave Priya's plate, which bore a representative sample of all the desserts, a meaningful look. 'But it's a lovely spread. Happy birthday, again, Ruby.'

I looked around the room. Debbie was there looking relaxed and happy, along with two of the nurses from the Secure Unit, one of whom was wearing a fair-isle knit hat with a pom-pom, several sizes too small. Several of my recent counselling clients had also come along with their elderly parents, ostensibly for a tour of our facilities, and had stayed for the party and there was an episode of jiving breaking out among them. It was perfect. I squeezed Zac's hand and his smile broadened.

'Go on, you can say it. Life's not so bad now, is it?' He squeezed back. 'Even though you're a year older and have wrinkles you could lose a small donkey in.'

Just for the tiniest second I felt that snatch of panic that said *'is he trying to tell you you look old? Is he going off you? Falling for a blonde woman whose father owns a football club?'* But the panic just couldn't compete with the yelling happiness that drowned it out. Zac loved me. Zac had organised this event; buffet lunch, Bob's star turn, just for me. He'd arranged for us both to have the day off and, even though we'd spent much of the morning so far moving furniture into the larger flat – rationalising that we were merely moving in together to leave the small flat vacant for visiting doctors – it was turning out to be one of the best days of my life.

Even Miriam, now almost inexplicably Bob's manager, had brought me a box of chocolates and given me a warm cheek kiss. 'Found my perfect job,' she'd whispered, nodding towards Bob as he'd sashayed his way into the room. ''E does the words and the readin' an' stuff. I does the money. We've got *loads* of bookin's!'

'Well, I don't suppose many people would say "no" to Miriam,' Zac had whispered in my ear. 'Not without head-to-foot Kevlar and a riot shield, anyway.'

And now Bob was giving the performance of his life to a hugely receptive audience, who all whooped and cheered when he finished to a confetti-cannon and rain of glitter. The buffet was refreshed by the kitchen staff who had been lurking around in the background admiring Bob's shoes, and the conversation which had been halted by the act, restarted.

I couldn't remember when I'd ever felt so happy. My job counselling those whose family members were beginning to show cognitive decline was turning out to be something I'd been born to do, Zac was stressed but happy in his role of helping the residents through transitions. Miriam and Bob were delightful as a professional couple and even Priya had forgiven me for abandoning her to YouIn2Work's tender mercies. She'd got the office to herself now and an entire drawer system for filing the confectionary.

Life wasn't totally perfect, of course. I still needed my tablets, although the doctor was hopeful of weaning me off slowly soon. Zac's mum was stable but we both knew she could worsen at any time and, although Gareth had paid his share of the house debts off, I was still paying mine.

And yet... and yet. Upstairs, in our new flat, on a little cushion of deep red velvet, was a ring. I hadn't quite come to terms with the implications of that yet, but I knew that the mere existence of it made my chest want to burst and let my heart envelop everyone and everything.

Life didn't have to be perfect to be happy.

MORE FROM JANE LOVERING

We hope you enjoyed reading *A Midwinter Match*. If you did, please leave a review.

If you'd like to gift a copy, this book is also available as an ebook, digital audio download and audiobook CD.

Sign up to Jane Lovering's mailing list for news, competitions and updates on future books.

https://bit.ly/JaneLoveringNewsletter

The Country Escape, another funny and warm-hearted read, from Jane Lovering, is available now.

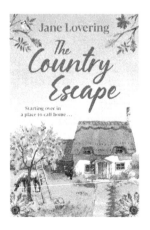

ABOUT THE AUTHOR

Jane Lovering is the bestselling and award-winning romantic comedy writer who won the RNA Novel of the Year Award in 2012 with *Please Don't Stop the Music*. She lives in Yorkshire and has a cat and a bonkers terrier, as well as five children who have now left home.

Visit Jane's website: www.janelovering.co.uk

Follow Jane on social media:

facebook.com/Jane-Lovering-Author-106404969412833
twitter.com/janelovering
bookbub.com/authors/jane-lovering

ABOUT BOLDWOOD BOOKS

Boldwood Books is a fiction publishing company seeking out the best stories from around the world.

Find out more at www.boldwoodbooks.com

Sign up to the Book and Tonic newsletter for news, offers and competitions from Boldwood Books!

http://www.bit.ly/bookandtonic

We'd love to hear from you, follow us on social media:

 facebook.com/BookandTonic

 twitter.com/BoldwoodBooks

instagram.com/BookandTonic

Made in the USA
Monee, IL
25 August 2022